Rachel Bennett currently lives on the Isle of Man (home of fast motorbikes, tailless cats, and very changeable weather). She shares her home with two kids, one angry cat, and an exceptionally patient husband.

@rakie

Author website http://rakiekeig.blogspot.com/

Also by Rachel Bennett

The Flood

Little Girls Tell Tales

Rachel Bennett

One More Chapter
a division of HarperCollins*Publishers*
The News Building
1 London Bridge Street
London SE1 9GF

www.harpercollins.co.uk

This paperback edition 2020

First published in Great Britain in ebook format
by HarperCollins*Publishers* 2020

A catalogue record for this book
is available from the British Library

ISBN: 9780008333300

Set in Birka by Palimpsest Book Production Ltd,
Falkirk Stirlingshire

Printed and bound by CPI Group (UK) Ltd, Croydon, CR0 4YY

For Jacob and Elliott

Chapter 1

August 2004

If the weather had been better that summer I wouldn't have found the body in the wetlands. We were only outside that day because, after four solid days of rain, our mum chased me and Dallin out of the house as soon as the clouds broke.

We were allowed to play in the curraghs, the sprawling acres of boggy marshland that began almost on Mum's back doorstep, so long as we kept to the main paths. Mum had told plenty of stories about how easy it was to get lost, or worse. Some of the boggy ponds were so deep, she said, that if a girl stepped into one it would swallow her forever. I was mostly convinced the stories weren't real.

My brother Dallin was twelve; two years older than me. He'd spent countless hours playing in the curraghs and reckoned the bog-land held no secrets from him. He never missed an opportunity to lord it over me, this advantage he'd gained by living full-time here with Mum, while I was stuck in Douglas with our dad.

So it was only natural we should follow him without question. Dallin went racing ahead down the main path. His was all legs and arms, like a disjointed puppet. Right behind him was Beth, who'd been in the same class as Dallin since they were at playschool. Her parents had dropped her off at Mum's house earlier that day. Beth was a quiet soul, as if she'd long ago decided Dallin would be the brash, noisy one. Her brown hair hated being confined to a ponytail and was always escaping in wisps and tufts. Beth and Dallin would never call each other best friends, but only because they never needed to voice such things. When Beth was with us, I felt superfluous.

'This way!'

Dallin ducked off the main path, vaulted a water-filled ditch, and set off into the trees on the other side, without checking to see if we were following. The trees were spindly and twisted, as if there wasn't enough substance to the ground to anchor them, and one grew above fifteen feet tall. But that was tall enough. Once we were amongst them, I could no longer see the mountains to the south, my only point of reference on that flat stretch of land.

'This is more muddy than last week,' Dallin said over his shoulder. 'But you'd expect that, right? After all that rain, it's gonna be like a proper swamp in here, we better not take a single step off the path—'

He chattered away as we walked. Dallin was always talking, always making noise, always restless. Sometimes it was exhilarating to be caught in his slipstream. Other times it was exhausting.

Today I didn't have much tolerance for him. Maybe it was

because we'd been cooped up in the house, or maybe it was the calm press of the trees, but I found I didn't want to listen. I walked slowly, putting a little distance between us. Beth glanced back once and smiled at me. One of those understanding smiles she was so good at. She was beautiful, I realised in surprise, with golden sunlight caught in wayward strands of her hair. It was the first time I'd noticed.

The path we were following ran along the top of an old dry-stone wall. A hundred years ago, this whole area had been drained for farmland, and these flat-topped walkways had stood waist-high along the boundaries of the fields. But the farmers left, the waters returned, and the trees reclaimed every inch of land. Tree roots climbed up and over the broken stone of the walls to bind them tight. I picked my way over a gnarled surface made of a dozen warring roots.

'Look, Rosalie,' Beth said, pointing. 'Wallaby.'

I hadn't believed Dallin when he'd told me there were wallabies living wild up here in the north of the island. According to him, they'd escaped from the wildlife park on the other side of the curraghs about fifty years ago, and had been living here ever since. It sounded like one of Dallin's stories, but Mum had backed him up, for once.

'They've been here longer than any of us,' she'd said with good-natured annoyance, 'so I suppose they have the right to go wherever they want. But I could do without them getting into my garden and chewing the bark off my fruit trees.'

It'd been a few years since Mum had snapped our family in two by moving out of our Douglas home and buying the farmhouse up here in the middle of nowhere. The summer holidays, when I was parcelled out to her for up to three weeks, were marked by my sullen silences and unshed tears. At age ten, I blamed her for everything wrong with my life.

Over the last two summers, I'd spotted several wallabies while we were out in the curraghs. They were always at a distance, sitting so still they could be mistaken for broken tree stumps. There was something vaguely sinister, I thought, about the way they watched us. Like sentinels of the swamp.

I followed Beth's pointing finger and saw the wallaby. It looked bigger than the ones in the wildlife park. Obviously it had spotted us, because it was staring straight at us both, keeping a cool eye on what we were doing.

'She's got a joey,' Beth whispered.

Beth's eyes were much sharper than mine. I had to squint before I made out the tiny woolly head poking from the mother's pouch. I wouldn't have seen it at all except it was restlessly shifting around.

'Neat,' I said.

Beth flashed another smile at me.

We kept walking. I glanced back a few times but the mother wallaby was quickly lost to sight. Still, I couldn't shake the feeling that others were watching us.

The track stepped down off the remains of the wall and wound off through the trees. I kept my eyes on my feet. The path was reassuringly solid, but the ground on either side was muddy and soft. My blue wellies left perfect imprints. On either side of me, standing pools of water gave off a sweet-stagnant smell. The air was heavy and damp with humidity. I looked up. Above the treetops there was nothing but the round bowl of the sky, dotted with clouds. It made me dizzy. Better to concentrate on my feet.

It was maybe five or ten minutes later when I raised my eyes and realised I was alone.

I paused to listen. Dallin would still be talking, I knew. His voice had been a constant drone throughout the summer holidays, half comfort and half annoyance. But now I couldn't hear him. The only noise was soft birdsong, water dripping from leaves, and the murmur of the wind in the trees.

Dallin and Beth must've been somewhere ahead. I'd fallen behind a little, then a little more, until they were out of sight. But soon enough they'd realise I was being slow, and they'd wait for me.

I kept walking.

It didn't occur to me that I might be lost. The wetlands weren't *that* big or sprawling. Probably they were no bigger than the plantation of pine trees near Douglas where me and Dad went out for walks. And I'd never managed to lose myself there. But maybe that was because the plantation was on the slope of a hill. The thousand or so pine trees in their regimented straight lines drew clear pathways back to safety. Even if I got turned around there, I could walk downhill until I found the road.

The curraghs were different. Everything was flat, with no landmarks. There were plenty of paths – dozens of them – but many led in circles or disappeared into bogs.

I walked for some time, thinking – if I was thinking at all – that I was bound to catch up with Beth and Dallin soon. I figured I would come around a clump of trees and there they'd be, waiting for me with a sarcastic remark. But I kept walking and I remained alone.

In the mud off to one side I spotted several elongated, parallel footprints. Wallaby tracks. They led off along an ill-defined trail that headed in what I thought was the direction of the road. I stepped off the path to follow the trail, even though it soon became little more than a line of slightly firmer ground between the stagnant mud puddles.

A few broken chunks of stone protruded from the earth here and there. The remains of a wall, marking the edge of someone's land? Or maybe part of a sheep-pen, which would lead me round in a loose circle. Perhaps part of someone's house. There were no clues. Everything had been swallowed by the trees.

At that point I began to feel frightened. Not because I was alone or possibly lost – neither were new experiences for me – but by the evidence of history around me; of time reclaiming the land. A hundred years ago there'd been people living here, but now there was nothing left, except the faint tracery of the walls they'd built. It shocked me to think that time would eventually sweep away the fragments of my own life, the crooked trees tangling over everything that made me unique and memorable.

I had the sudden urge to drop to my knees and dig down through the mud. Buried somewhere must be a few lost remnants of the people who'd gone before.

Later – weeks, months, years later – I would piece the day back together from fragments of memory, looking for signs and augurs I should've spotted. There must've been something to warn me my life was about to change. Was it significant, the way the wind dropped to an eerie calm, or how the wild geese chattered somewhere off in the distance, or how I spotted those clumps of bogbean – that beautiful, delicate white flower Mum had told me to look out for – growing in sudden abundance in an overwise unremarkable clearing?

It was the flowers that made me pause. The trail I'd been following had petered out to nothing. Ahead, the ground looked boggier, like it might not take my weight. I stopped. The bogbean flowers on their slender stems nodded in the gentle breeze. They poked up between a tangle of sticks in a muddy pond. The sticks were whitish grey, stripped of their bark. I thought of the wallabies that'd chewed Mum's fruit trees.

I studied the jutting curve of the sticks where they emerged from the water. It took me a surprisingly long time to recognise it as a ribcage.

I'd never seen one in real life, of course. But I'd seen the plastic skeleton at the St John Ambulance headquarters, where my schoolfriend Amanda went to Badgers. I'd spent a long, bored time fiddling with the artificial joints of the skeleton, nicknamed Boney M, while I waited for Amanda to finish training so her mum could give us both a lift home.

What I was confronted with now didn't look much like Boney M. The ribcage, if that's what it was, was squashed and malformed, with half the ribs bent at the wrong angle. The bones were discoloured to the same greenish grey as the lichen on the trees. An arm – a possible arm, I told myself – was loosely attached at the shoulder by tatters of greyish material.

The hands could be under the water, tucked up beneath the chest. Sleeping. Peaceful.

I brushed aside a few bogbean stems and found what might be the skull. It was partly submerged. Above the water was a smooth curve, part of an eye socket, and the edge of the jaw, complete with a few grimy teeth. The lower jaw had fallen open, or fallen away. One of the molars at the back had a filling in it, grey metal, like the ones my aunt showed when she laughed too loud.

I straightened up, suddenly dizzy. It was a person. I'd found a person.

An unpleasant tingle of surprise worked its way through my stomach. What should I do? In movies, if someone discovered a skeleton, they screamed, or cried, or threw up, or ran away. None of those reactions seemed justified right then, in that sun-dappled clearing, with the birds calling from nearby trees. This wasn't someone who had died yesterday or the day before or even a week ago. No one was looking for them. And neither was it someone alive and hurt who needed me to run and get help.

This person had been dead a long, long time, perhaps even as long as the farmland had been flooded. Nothing about the scene made me want to scream or cry. There was no blood, no guts, not even a particularly bad smell – or at least, no worse than the rotted-vegetable smell of the mud itself.

Instead of fear or disgust, I felt only sadness. Who was this person? How come they were here? Had they worked in these ancient fields, before the land was reclaimed by trees?

I took a step closer and my boot sank deep into the mud.

I jerked back in a hurry. The mud sucked at my boot as I pulled it loose. I stumbled back, breathless.

The first sting of fear hit me then. This was such a lonely place for someone to die. What if the person had been just like me, a little bit lost and a little bit abandoned, and she'd stumbled into the mud and couldn't get out?

If I got stuck, would anyone hear my shouting? How long would Dallin and Beth search for me? What if I was never found?

I eyed the mud. The divot my boot had made was already filling with scummy water. How deep did the mud go? Could it swallow me whole, as fast as sinking sand? Would I disappear forever, like Mum had warned, held close in a freezing, muddy embrace?

It was that thought that sent me stumbling away, onto a barely-delineated trail that switched back and forth and sometimes vanished altogether. I walked as quickly as I dared. My boots clomped over roots and stones. I almost blundered into another deep pocket of mud, and, after that, I forced myself to go slower. With each step I eyed the ground. Several times I stopped and prodded the mud ahead of me with a stick I'd picked up, to check the ground would definitely take my weight. I took long circular routes around even the smallest ponds.

I had no way to measure time. Later, a great many people would tell me I'd been wandering out there for almost three hours. At the time, the minutes blended together, until it felt like I'd always been walking. My legs ached and my calves were chafed red raw by the top of my wellies.

When I at last stumbled out onto a road – far from where I'd thought I was – I was so numb and exhausted that I kept walking for another half-dozen steps before I noticed I was no longer amongst the trees.

Then a woman I didn't recognise snatched me up and started shouting, 'She's here, Rosalie's here, we've found her,' like I was an Easter egg that'd been hidden too well, rather than a ten-year-old girl who was so tired she could barely stand.

Someone put a warm jacket around my shoulders. Someone else gave me a packet of biscuits – a whole packet, just put them in my hand and told me to eat, eat as many as I wanted. And then Mum was there, crying and gasping like she'd been drowned, pulling me into a crushing embrace. The biscuits were squashed between us and ended up mostly as crumbs.

'Where were you?' Mum asked into my tangled hair. 'Where did you go, pumpkin?'

I pulled away so I could see her face, and said, 'I found a dead person.'

The police were already on the scene, having been called by Mum an hour earlier, when Dallin had finally found the courage to go home and tell her he'd mislaid his little sister. I could see the bright police car blocking the road near the car park. There were eight or nine other cars, I realised, clogging the road and parked in the passing places. I would later discover that over two dozen people had turned up to look for me.

'I found a dead person,' I said again, because Mum was

staring at me like she hadn't heard. It was important everyone should know.

'Hush,' my mum said. She pressed my head back to her shoulder. 'Hush.'

The police searched the curraghs for the skeleton I'd seen. They kept going until the light faded, and then continued the next day, and the day after. They found nothing.

Three days later, I went back into the curraghs, with a search team of five people, in the hope I could lead them to the clearing with the bogbean growing up through the stripped bones. But, just as I couldn't find my way out before, now I couldn't find my way back. Every path looked the same. Nothing was familiar. It was as if the wetlands had shifted and rearranged overnight.

The search team reassured me, but I could see annoyance on their faces.

'She's had a nasty scare, being lost,' one of Mum's friends said later. 'It's enough to play tricks on anyone's mind.'

'It's no surprise she'd make up something like that,' a few people whispered when they thought I wasn't listening. 'She's always had an overactive imagination, that one.'

'She did it on purpose,' only one person said to my face – Dallin. 'She must've heard us shouting for her. We yelled like crazy. She heard us. She just wanted to stay lost.'

I knew other people thought the same. I told my story as many times as I had to, and only stopped when I realised no one believed me. Not my family, not my friends, no one.

'The police would've found something,' Mum said, at her

most diplomatic. 'They searched everywhere. They took sniffer dogs in to help. I'm sorry, pumpkin, but if there was anything to find, they would've found it.'

The only person who supported me was Beth. 'I'll help you search again,' she offered one day at the end of summer, in her soft, sincere voice. 'We'll keep looking until we find it.' And every time we went into the curraghs after that, I knew she was scrutinising the ground as we walked, both of us looking for the bones that haunted me.

In time though, everyone else quietly decided I had, at best, been mistaken. The phantom skeleton in the curraghs was forgotten.

Chapter 2

Fifteen Years Later

In the mornings, mist would collect in pockets throughout the curraghs, like fragments of stuffing caught on a thousand thorns. It was slow to disperse, waiting until the sun rose high enough to burn it away.

I liked to stand at the back door and watch the sun come up. It hit the slopes of the hills to the south first, soft and golden. The air around our house stayed chill for another hour or so, even after the sun found its way to our garden. Sometimes, I couldn't help but think the curraghs were to blame for this; that the chill seeped outwards from the wet, shaded ground.

Early morning was the only time I could bear to look out at the wetlands. In those soft, half-awake moments, when the land was still slumbering, I could look at the gnarled and twisted trees and feel a shadow of the peace they'd used to inspire. When we'd first come to live here, six years ago, to the house Mum had treasured, the trees gave me a sort of reassurance. We shared a secret, after all, them and me. I would listen to their whispering and smile.

Now, though, I couldn't stand to look at the trees for long. Their whispering voices sounded harsh. Like they knew too many of my secrets.

As the sun reached our garden, I turned away from the wetlands. The birds had woken up with a dozen competing songs in their throats. The top leaves of the trees twisted in the breeze as the branches stretched to greet the sun. But the marshy ground beneath the trees was still dark. The shadows would linger there for a while yet.

I shut the porch door and put my cup down on the table. The herbal tea I'd made half an hour earlier had cooled, half-finished. I still hadn't found a tea I liked to drink first thing in the morning. They were all either too sharp or too sweet.

I miss coffee. The thought cropped up quite often and always made me sigh.

The next step in my morning routine was to go through the house and open all the curtains. As usual, I had to force myself do it. Over the last eighteen months, I'd been careful to maintain the necessary, everyday routines to keep the house in shape, even when there seemed no point. *Especially* when there seemed no point.

Sometimes I struggled to remember when I'd had an actual schedule, imposed by factors outside my own head. When I'd had to get up and dressed and out of the house in time for work. How had I ever coped? The idea of rushing around in the early morning to meet a deadline made my chest tighten. And yet, I'd used to love how busy I was. I'd used to love my job.

Strange how quickly everything could change.

I opened the kitchen blinds to let in the morning sun. That was relatively easy. The curtains in the front room were more difficult, because allowing light into that room illuminated Beth's trinkets and ornaments, which covered almost every flat surface. I hadn't wanted the knick-knacks cluttering up the house, but Beth loved them, so we compromised. Beth had restricted them to the front room. And now, even though I couldn't bear the sight of them, I also couldn't face getting rid of a single one. Wherever Beth was now, she would've laughed to see me forever tethered to the hundreds of tacky ceramic animals.

I swished the curtains open and left the room quickly. It was too early in the day to deal with heartbreak.

Out in the hall and up the stairs. Here were more reminders of Beth, her face smiling from almost every framed picture on the wall. But there were also reminders of Mum. The wallpaper was her favourite shade of green. There were ring marks on the pale wood of the lowermost three stairs, where she'd rested her cup of tea while she'd chatted on the phone to my aunt for hours. After Mum moved out, we could've changed the wallpaper or sanded the stairs, but again Beth had talked me round. 'It's charming,' she'd said. 'Gives the place character.'

After I'd opened the curtains in the two upstairs bedrooms, I went into the study and sat down. There were no blinds in here because the dormer window was such an awkward shape, and the sun hit the room squarely at this time of day, gradually warming the dusty air. I rolled the chair into the rectangle of sunlight and closed my eyes.

The house was too big for me on my own. Together, me and Beth had filled the rooms, but now I was too aware of the echoing hardwood floors and high, cavernous ceilings. It'd turned out Beth was right – we could've used more clutter. It might've disguised the hard edges of the house that I'd never noticed.

But I knew I could never move. For a start, there was no way I could afford anywhere half as nice. The house was still in Mum's name, but after I was signed off work, she quietly stopped asking me for rent. My benefit payments covered the utilities and my daily expenses. I knew exactly how lucky I was. Not everyone in my position could live somewhere so lovely.

Lucky. My mouth twisted. Lucky me, to be living in a beautiful house in a beautiful location, where every little thing reminded me of what I'd lost.

I'd taken a week off before and after the funeral. Then my doctor had signed me off for another week. My employers had been understanding; how could they not? They'd told me to take as much time as I needed. Maybe they would've thought twice if they'd known how long I genuinely needed to recover. Like maybe forever. Eighteen months later and here I was. Still not whole.

In fact, if it wasn't for Mum I'd probably never leave the house. It was a ten-minute journey into Ramsey, where Mum lived in her conveniently pokey flat. I made the drive once a week, every Sunday afternoon, combining it with a visit to the supermarket. I stuck to the routine for the same reasons I made myself draw the curtains each morning. Because it was too easy to sink. I had to keeping kicking my legs, at least a little, if I wanted to stay above water.

It frightened me how simple it was to give up. Although my employers had told me they'd keep my job open, in case I ever came back, I'd long ago accepted I wouldn't return. I'd felt nothing but relief when I'd finally admitted it.

Since then, the house had become a sanctuary, despite the constant, unavoidable reminders of Beth wherever I looked. It was the one thing that rooted me to the world. I tidied, I sorted, I tended the garden. The garden in particular never failed to calm me. Here, the influence of my mother was strongest. Mum had planted these flowers, tended these beds, pruned these saplings. I would smile at the smallest things, such as the chicken-wire still wrapped loosely around the trunks of the fruit trees to guard against marauding wallabies.

'A garden's a promise you make to yourself,' Mum would say. 'You're promising you want to be here to see it grow.'

It made me sad Mum couldn't visit more often to see the garden growing. Every couple of months, I would take her for an outing, driving her back to the house so she could visit the garden and the curraghs. Those trips had been more frequent before Beth died, of course. Everything had declined since then.

I got out of the chair in the study and went back downstairs. Time for another cup of tea before I got dressed. I checked the doormat automatically and breathed a silent sigh of relief to see there was no post that morning.

After that I changed the bedsheets, hoovered the bedrooms, and put the bedding in to wash. That took me until lunchtime.

After lunch, when the washing machine had finished, I hung out the sheets, in time to catch the sun at its warmest. Then I worked quietly in the garden. I spent a considerable amount of time tying up the honeysuckle at the side of the house, which had exploded into a million trailing shoots, each determined to burrow its way into the gutters or drainpipes. I loved the honeysuckle, but between it and the clematis at the opposite side of the house, I was fighting a constant battle for control.

Maybe that was the attraction of the garden. Mum had been smart to encourage me to spend as much time as possible with my hands in the dirt. As if she'd known I'd someday need this to occupy my mind and my hands.

I'd just come inside to make my fifth cup of herbal tea when the doorbell rang.

I washed my hands quickly and wiped them on my jogging pants as I went to the door. It was half past four on a Thursday afternoon. I wasn't expecting any callers. But answering the door was an accepted part of life. I didn't want to become the sort of person who hid from the outside world.

As I approached the door, I saw a letter lying on the mat, and my stomach dropped like a lead weight. I recognised the plain Manila envelope with the sloped handwriting on the front. It must've come while I was in the garden, unless ... unless it'd been delivered right now, by the person outside.

Through the frosted glass of the upper half of my front door, I could see the fuzzed outline of my visitor. They rang the bell again, then cupped their hands to peer through the glass. I was sure they saw my shadow.

'Rosie?' the person called. 'Rosie, you there?'

The voice was muffled, but I recognised it.

I snatched up the envelope from the mat and dropped it facedown onto the phone table before opening the door.

'Rosie,' my brother Dallin said with a smile. 'Hi! How are you?'

I took a bit too long to answer. I blinked several times, as my brain processed this shock, on top of the unpleasant nausea provoked by the arrival of the envelope, before I remembered to smile back. 'Dalliance,' I said. If he could use childhood nicknames then so could I.

Dallin laughed and swept in to hug me. I was taken by surprise but didn't try to stop him. Over the past couple of years, I'd become used to people hugging me, whether I wanted them to or not. Plus, it gave me another moment to deal with the fact that he was back, suddenly, inexplicably.

'What on earth are you doing here?' I asked into his shoulder.

Dallin pulled away, although he kept hold of one of my hands. 'I'm so sorry,' he said. 'I should've called. I've got a million excuses why I didn't.'

I kept the smile on my face. *Yes*, I thought. *I'm sure you do.*

'Here.' Dallin took a step back. 'This is Cora.'

I'd been so fixed on Dallin I'd barely noticed the woman who hovered awkwardly nearby. She looked as if someone had stapled her feet to the floor to keep her from fleeing. As she made eye contact she flickered a smile. It looked like she'd coached herself to smile at strangers. Honestly, that made me warm to her. It looked like we both knew the difficulties of social interactions that everyone else took for granted.

'Thank you for this,' Cora said, with another flickering smile.

I frowned, but Dallin was already leaning past me to look into the house. 'Wow,' he said, 'the place is going great. I love the ... those, y'know, those flowers there.'

He was pointing to the vase of sweet peas I'd placed on the phone table. 'You should come in,' I said, standing aside, because that's what was expected of me.

Dallin stepped into the hall. 'That's brilliant, thank so much. Hey, I'm glad you kept the wallpaper, Mum always loved that colour.'

It was so familiar, the flow of thought and speech that characterised Dallin. Hearing it again, in this house, was a weird mix of jarring and comforting. The house was missing voices, I realised. The hardwood floors and high ceilings cried out for warm conversation and soft laughter. I hadn't been able to provide either recently.

I ushered Dallin into the kitchen. The woman, Cora, followed. Briefly, I wished today had been the day for tidying the downstairs rooms rather than the bedrooms. It wasn't like the place was a mess, just not as spotless as it might've been. I picked up a pile of magazines from the kitchen table then, realising there was nowhere better to stash them, put them back down.

'The kettle's just boiled,' I said. Although, now I thought about it, I would need to boil it again, with enough water for three. 'And – I don't have any coffee. Or tea. I mean, I've got herbal tea. Peppermint. Or mint. Or spearmint.'

'Tea sounds great,' Dallin said. It was likely he'd only heard half of what I said. He was making a slow circuit of the room, examining everything. He studied the fridge magnets as if they held the secrets to the universe. I was glad I'd brought him and his friend into the kitchen rather than the sitting room. I couldn't have coped with Dallin examining Beth's ceramics with that somehow mocking, supercilious smile on his face. At least there was nothing in here except those stupid magnets, most from places me and Beth had never been.

I busied myself with the kettle and tried to gather my thoughts. Dallin was here. That was unexpected, to say the least, given it was six years since he last set foot in this house. But what could I do, tell him he wasn't wanted? Shut the door in his face? Maybe I should've. But when I considered it, I almost felt Beth poking me between the shoulder blades. She never would've tolerated me acting like that towards my brother. Even if Dallin deserved it, and a million times more.

'What were those kinds of tea again?'

I jumped. I hadn't expected Cora to appear at my elbow. 'Sorry?'

'The teas.' Cora tried another smile. This one didn't look like she'd practiced it. 'Three types of mint, right?'

'Yeah. The peppermint is shop bought, but the mint and spearmint are from the garden.'

'Like, leaves?' Cora's eyes crinkled. Her blonde hair was cut into bangs which fell forward whenever she dipped her head. Her ears had five or six piercing holes each, although she wasn't currently wearing earrings.

'Leaves. Yeah.' I tucked my own hair behind my ears. I hadn't showered that morning or done anything more with my hair than pull it into a messy topknot with tangled strands hanging down on all sides. All at once I was aware of how I must look to outsiders. I'd got used to no one seeing me for days at a time. 'I'm sorry I don't have any proper tea.'

'It's okay. I can't have proper tea anyway.'

'No? Why not?'

'Because proper-tea is theft.' Cora smiled, a little wider, a little more genuine, with a shrug that acknowledged the pun but refused to apologise for it.

I laughed. 'So ... mint?'

'Sounds good. Thank you.'

I fished two extra cups from the cupboard. 'So, why are you—?'

'I can explain all that,' Dallin said. He adjusted a seat at the kitchen table before sitting down.

Immediately he looked at home. Which was fair enough, I thought, since technically this had been his home before it was mine. The thought caused a twist of discomfort deep in my stomach. If Dallin had stayed, instead of running, it might've been him living here instead of me. I might've never had those beautiful years here, with Beth.

'Cora's looking for her sister,' Dallin said.

I crinkled my brow. 'Oh?'

'Simone went missing twenty years ago,' Cora said. Her attention stayed on my hands, watching as I made the tea, as if eye contact was too difficult right then. 'She was fifteen. I was only nine. We never found out where she went.'

Dallin fidgeted in his seat. It was obvious he wanted to tell the story. 'Cora thinks—'

'I've been trying to put together what happened to her.'

Cora's voice was soft but she spoke over Dallin with ease. 'Trying to ... piece things together. I've spent a lot of time chasing down vague hints and old clues. The police were involved at the time, I guess, but not for very long. Simone ran away. Nothing more to it than that. If she didn't want to be found ...' Cora shrugged one shoulder. There was a softness to her movements as well. I got the sense she'd said these words a dozen times or more, and she'd become used to crushing the emotion so her voice didn't shake, so now there was no inflection to her words at all. 'It was only recently I started asking questions. My parents refused to talk about it.'

I stirred the mugs and scooped the leaves into the compost bucket. I wasn't exactly sure why Cora was telling me all this. But I was used to people telling me their stories. It seemed to come with the territory. I had lost someone I loved. Apparently that meant other people needed to tell me their own traumas.

'We know she went north.' Cora took one of the mugs from me with a grateful half-smile. 'The night Simone left home, she was caught on CCTV, getting onto a train. After that, she vanished. Never seen again.'

'I'm sorry.' I said it automatically, even though it always annoyed me when people apologised. *Everyone's sorry. It goes without saying.* But even so, the quiet sadness in Cora's expression made something twinge inside me. I'd spent so long pretending to be hardened, careful not to feel anything in case it set off the tsunami inside me. As harsh as it sounded, I didn't want to feel sad over Cora's story. I wanted to stay as I was. Feeling nothing.

'Tell her the rest,' Dallin said. There was a bright excitement in his eyes that he tried to hide.

'There was a possible lead,' Cora said. 'Someone thought they saw Simone getting onto a ferry at Heysham. The police checked the CCTV at the time.' She looked away to conceal the haunted look in her eyes. 'They told me it showed a girl who was about the right age, right height, wrong clothes, but that doesn't prove anything either way, does it? She could've changed her clothes easily enough. And the camera was pointed the wrong way. The police said they couldn't see her face. And, of course, they didn't bother keeping the footage on file, so I have to take their word for it.' She blew on her tea to cool it. 'Anyway, the footage wasn't enough for the police. They looked into it – at least, they said they did. But they never found her here. Or anywhere else.'

I glanced at Dallin. From the look on his face, he was expecting something from me. But I couldn't see what Cora's story had to do with me.

Cora also frowned, looking hesitant again. 'Did ... did Dallin tell you this? He told you, right?'

Dallin said, 'I sent you an email, Rose. Did you get it?'

I rolled my eyes. 'What on earth made you think *that* was the best way to get in touch with me?'

'I don't know. Everyone does everything by email.' Dallin raised his hands in weak apology. 'I figured it might be a bit much for me to call you out of the blue.'

'But turning up on my doorstep, that's fine?'

Cora set down her mug. 'I'm sorry. I had no idea ... I

thought you'd invited us here. I wouldn't have ... I'm sorry.' She picked up her bag from the chair when she'd left it.

'Wait. Cora, wait.' Dallin intercepted her before she could walk out. 'It's okay. Rosie, it's alright that we're here, yeah? I'm sorry you didn't get my message. But we've both come a long way. You need to hear what Cora's got to say.'

He looked at Cora, expectant. He was still hanging onto her hand, like he'd hung onto mine at the door. Cora had her bag on her shoulder. It was obvious she wanted to stay, for whatever reason, but she was also reluctant to intrude where she wasn't welcome. I knew how she felt.

Cora sighed. 'I think you found my sister,' she said to me.

'I—?' I frowned. 'You think she's living over here somewhere?'

'No, I—' Cora tucked a strand of blonde hair behind her ear. 'I think you found her. When you were a kid, when you were out in the marshes.'

Realisation dawned. 'Oh my God.' I looked at Dallin, aghast. 'You told her about that?'

'It was on a website.' Cora rooted in her bag for her phone. 'I can find it for you. I read about the skeleton you found. Just near here, right?'

'Um. Right.' I couldn't get my brain back in gear. 'It was in the curraghs ...' I half-turned to gesture through the kitchen window, but lost what I was trying to say. 'You read it on a *website*?'

'It's more of a forum,' Dallin said. 'There's a lot of stuff about myths and urban legends and, y'know, that sort of stuff. Big cat sightings. There's a page about your story.'

Cora held her phone out to me. The screen showed a black screen with white text that wasn't formatted properly for mobile phones. It made me immediately think, *I'd love to show this font to Beth, she'd hate it.* Beth had been a keen blogger, right up to the end, and nothing wound her up more than white text on a black background.

I almost smiled, until I remembered what I was reading.

I skimmed the text. As if reading it fast might protect me. The page consisted of several long paragraphs and a few stock photos of the curraghs – at least, I figured that's what they were, but the pictures were loading one line at a time on Cora's phone. I sped-read through a slightly glorified account of how I'd found the body. It matched the story I'd told dozens of times to dozens of people over the years, with a few embellishments that hadn't happened, and a few that I myself had forgotten. It was shocking to see it all written down in white and black.

'People ... people believe this?' I scrolled up and down the page. 'They believe me?'

'Why wouldn't they believe it?' Cora asked. A brief flicker of anguish crossed her face. 'Are you saying it's not true?'

'No, no. It's just ... no one ever believed me.' I couldn't help but laugh in disbelief. 'Fifteen years I've been telling this story. No one ever believed me. And now apparently there're people talking about it on the internet.' I scrolled to the bottom of the post and skimmed the comments. 'People believe me.'

'Don't ever read the comments, Rose-Lee,' Dallin said. He took the phone off me and gave it back to Cora. 'But sure, yeah, of course people believe you. They always did.'

I could only laugh again. Did he really think that? Wasn't he paying attention when people were quietly shaking their heads and catching each other's eyes over the top of my head? Had no one told him about the months when our dad had kept me out of school, when I was having bad dreams every night?

'The timelines fit,' Cora said then. 'Simone disappeared in June 1999, and you found the skeleton in August 2004. That's right, yeah? It could be her.'

'You think ...?'

'I think you found Simone, yes. Possibly.' Cora was trying hard to hold back the hope, I saw. How many years had she spent chasing fruitless leads and false hopes? 'There's a chance it could be her. I mean, it has to be *someone,* right?'

I examined my hands because I couldn't look at either Dallin or Cora. 'I'm sorry,' I said. 'I don't know what to tell you. It was so long ago.'

'You don't remember it at all?' Cora asked.

I couldn't bear how the woman was staring at me. 'I remember, sure. But it was fifteen years ago, and I was a kid. I don't think I can tell you anything that isn't on that website there. I'm sorry.'

Dallin started to say something else, but I turned away quickly and walked to the back door. I was overwhelmed – by Dallin coming back into my life, by Cora, by the past getting dredged up. I couldn't deal with any of it.

I opened the back door and stepped outside.

Chapter 3

The sun was going down, casting long shadows into the back garden. I followed the path to the rear wall. There was a bench, sheltered beneath the sweet pea trellis, which only caught the sun at this late stage of the day. I rarely came down here anymore. Weeds had sprung up between the flagstones. I laid my hands on the rough limestone of the wall at the back of the garden; felt the coolness of the day against my palms. The smell of the curraghs was strong but not unpleasant, just a warm green scent that slowed my heartrate and smoothed out my tangled thoughts.

How many times over the past few years had I come here to calm down? Whenever I'd woken in the early hours and been unable to get back to sleep. Whenever me and Beth argued. On the day Beth got her diagnosis, when I'd realised I couldn't cope. I had come here. Looking for something that could root me to the ground.

On those occasions, when nothing in the real world made sense, I would stand with my palms on the cool stone wall, and whisper to the ghost of the skeleton I'd found.

It'd started when I was still young, maybe three or four

months after I found the skeleton. No one else would listen to me. Beth went to a different school, so I only ever saw her outside term time, and I missed her support desperately. It felt like the only person who might possibly know what I was going through was the person who'd got lost and died out there in the wetlands. When it got too much for me, I would beg my dad to let me stay with Mum for a few days, and then I would come down to the end of her garden like this.

I'd often imagined who the person in the curraghs had been. They'd had a life, a name. In the absence of the truth, I'd invented details. I pictured a girl my own age, wild and windblown, barefoot, running through the curraghs. I'd even given her a secret name: *Bogbean*, like the tiny white flowers that had blossomed in abundance around the gravesite. Sometimes I'd whisper the name aloud, into the silence of the evening air, but I'd never told it to anyone.

Good thing too. Otherwise it'd be on that stupid website right now.

My mouth twisted. Bogbean, the lost girl in the wetlands, had always belonged just to me. For fifteen years, whenever I needed to ground myself, I would speak my fears, aloud or inside my head, to Bogbean. Sometimes I imagined I heard the whisper of her answer.

'Simone,' I murmured now. 'Is that your real name?'

There was no answer except the wind in the trees.

Everything had become so weird and so different, in the space of an evening. All of a sudden, Bogbean had a possible name, a possible life, family, friends. She was no longer a figment of my imagination.

'Who are you?' I murmured. If I half-closed my eyes, I could imagine Bogbean at my side, just beyond my peripheral vision, leaning her bare forearms on the top of the wall. But she said nothing, not even a whisper or a faint shrug. Right now, no one had any answers.

I heard the back door open as someone else came outside, but I didn't turn around. I shut my eyes and breathed the cool air.

'Hey,' Dallin said from behind me. 'You okay?'

'Sure. Why not?' I sighed, then turned to face him. I had a moment of disconnect, because I remembered him as a gangly teenager charging around this garden, leaping the flowerbeds like they were hurdles in his way. Now he looked awkward and out of place in what should've been his home. He kept his shoulders hunched, and avoided looking at the twisted trees beyond the back wall of the garden.

'I'm sorry.' Dallin lifted his hands in a shrug. 'I thought you got my email. I didn't mean to rock up here without warning. I know you don't like that sort of shit.'

'I just ... I don't understand why you're here.' I gave him a shrug of my own. 'How did Cora even find you?'

'We met on the forum. I stumbled onto it a while ago, and, y'know, obviously I was interested, because there was at least one person on there who remembered,' Dallin flapped a hand at the curraghs, still without looking in that direction, 'all this. I ended up chatting to some of the folks. That's how I met Cora.' He came to stand next to me, turning so he could lean his back against the wall, facing the house. 'I told her I knew about the curraghs legend first-hand. I mean, obviously, that wasn't something I should've done. There's a lot of crazy people on forums like that. And when Cora told me her story …' He put his hands in his pockets. 'I had to take it with a pinch of salt, you know? I was okay with messaging her and hearing her story, but I was ready to bail if it turned out she was one of the crazies.'

'What convinced you she wasn't?' It hadn't occurred to me to doubt Cora's story. But then, I always thought the best of people. Yet another thing that had consistently driven Beth nuts.

'She understands it's a longshot,' Dallin said. 'She's not coming here with a burning sense of surety that this time she'll definitely find Simone. This has been going on for a lot of years. She says she began looking seriously about three years ago, and she's not let up since.'

Why then? I wondered. What had kickstarted her search after so many years, rather than when she was much younger?

'What she's doing here is following one more possible lead,' Dallin said. 'She understands, *completely* understands this might come to nothing. And she's prepared for that.'

'So, if I went back in and told Cora I didn't see anything in the wetlands that day, that I'd made the whole thing up, she'd be okay with it?'

Dallin laughed. He leaned his head back so he could look at the dusky sky. 'C'mon, Rose-petal. We all know you didn't make it up. You invented some daft stories in your time, but you didn't have that morbid sort of imagination.'

It was a backhanded compliment at best. 'You shouldn't

have brought Cora here,' I muttered. 'All you've done is give her false hope.'

'It's not false hope. There's a chance she'll find something.'

'No, there's not.' I turned so I was facing him. 'Do you know how many times I've walked the curraghs? I've searched every inch of that place. If there was anything to find, don't you think I would've found it?'

Dallin gave me a lop-sided smile that was so familiar I had to stop myself smiling in return. 'Not necessarily. I'm not *doubting* you. I'm just saying there's an outside chance you're wrong.'

My expression hardened. 'If you won't tell her she's wasting her time, I will.'

Dallin laughed again and gestured at the house. 'Go ahead. Let me know if she listens to you, because she sure as hell didn't listen to me when I told her the exact same thing.' As I walked away towards the house, he added, 'I should probably mention, she's come prepared. *Very* prepared.'

Chapter 4

Cora's bag was a green satchel, decorated with applique owls. From inside the satchel, she produced a wodge of folded papers, which she spread out on the table.

'There aren't a lot of maps available online, would you believe that?' Cora said. 'But I got what I could and I cross-indexed it with a bunch of aerial photos, so I think we've got as accurate a picture of the land as we're going to get.'

Dallin put the kettle back on. It looked like he was starting to feel more at home. I ignored another pang of distress. Everything about this situation was distressing. When was the last time there were this many people in my kitchen? My eyes watered from trying to look at both Dallin and Cora at once.

'The main paths run through here and here,' Cora said. She drew a finger along a pale line that meandered from one corner of an A3 photo to the middle. Her nail polish was a delicate pink, chipped at the tips. 'As I understand it, there are dozens of other paths that lead off from the main trail. Plus unofficial animal tracks and such. Is that right?'

I startled, realising the question was addressed to me. 'Um. Yes.'

'And there aren't any trail maps of the marshlands? Not even unofficial ones that people or tourists maybe use to find their way?'

I dropped my gaze to the photos so I didn't have to maintain eye contact. 'No,' I said. 'If anyone's walking around the curraghs, they either know where they're going, or they stick to the main paths.'

'Does anyone ever get lost in there?' Cora seemed to have a direct way of asking questions which, honestly, was preferable to Dallin's habit of skirting around every issue. She fished a pencil out of her satchel and held it poised over the maps.

'Depends what you mean by lost.' I picked up my mug of mint tea, which I'd left sitting on the side. 'Now and again someone wanders off the trail. Last year a group of ramblers on a wildflower walk got distracted trying to follow a wallaby. It took them an hour to find their way back.'

Cora's lips twitched in a frown as she glanced at Dallin. 'So there really are wild wallabies here?'

'Told you so,' Dallin said. He stirred a hefty spoonful of demerara sugar into his tea. 'You owe me a tenner.'

'Forgive me for not believing such a weirdly specific bit of trivia.' Cora looked at me again. 'How big are the marshlands anyway? It doesn't look like much on the photos.'

'It's not, I guess.' I was trying to figure out whether our house was on the photos. It was difficult to tell from the aerial shots. 'It's not the biggest area of forest on the island, not by a very long way. But it's easy to get lost in there. It's—' My throat went dry. How to describe the curraghs to an outsider? Looking at those maps and photos, it was difficult to imagine how anyone, even a child, could lose their way in such a small patch of land.

'Are you able,' Cora asked, 'to narrow it down at all? When you found the body, do you know roughly where you were? Even as little as, "more to the north" or "more to the south"?'

I chewed my lip. 'Listen, I don't know what you're expecting from me. But I was a kid. I don't even know – I'm not certain what I saw.' I closed my eyes. For so many years I'd insisted on telling the truth, even when no one believed me. Now, with a person who for some crazy reason *did* believe me, I couldn't come up with a convincing lie.

But I had to try. Because, as I knew perfectly well, no hope was better than false hope.

'Sometimes,' I said slowly, 'you have to accept that what you think you saw isn't necessarily what you *did* see. Especially when you're a child. People searched the curraghs. I searched. No one found anything.' I lifted my chin and shook the stray wisps of hair out of my face. 'I was mistaken. There's nothing here for you to find. I'm sorry.'

A few seconds passed in silence. Then Cora said, 'Thank you.'

'For what?'

'For being honest. There's been a lot of people over the years who've been happy to spin me a story, for whatever reason.' Despite the way she held herself with hunched shoulders and restless fingers, there was steel in Cora's gaze. 'Some people will do anything for attention.'

Dallin took a tentative sip of his tea; grimaced. 'Rosie,

you've stuck to your story for fifteen solid years,' he said. 'This is a fine time to start doubting yourself.'

I glared at him. 'Please stop calling me Rosie.'

'Oh, right. You hate that.' He smirked. 'I totally forgot.'

Cora studied the maps. 'Is there *anything* you can tell us which wasn't on forum? Any details we might've missed?'

I pulled up a chair and sat down, suddenly exhausted. My heart went out to the poor woman. 'I can't help you find your sister,' I repeated. 'Even if what I saw when I was a kid ... even if I wasn't dreaming or hallucinating or—' I set my jaw. '—or making it up. Even if I really did find a human skeleton that day, there's very little possibility there's anything left of it by now. It could've sunk into the bog without a trace. The bones could've been scattered.' I watched Cora as I spoke, anxious not to cause more upset than I had to. 'I've spent a lot of time trying to find it again. I never have. Neither has anyone else. There's every chance there's nothing out there to find. I can't lead you to your sister.'

Cora nodded. She took a breath in through her nose and out through her mouth. 'I know. I understand.'

'Okay.' I thought about reaching for her hand, to give it a reassuring squeeze. But I'd never been good at spontaneous human contact. 'So?'

'I'm still going to look for her.' Cora glanced at me. That smile flickered again; somehow soft and steely at the same time. 'Nothing can stop me.'

In that moment, I completely believed her. 'I'm sorry I can't help,' I said. 'I just don't remember. I don't know if I was near the south end of the curraghs or the north end.'

Cora produced a plastic ruler from her bag and started measuring distances on the photos, comparing them to an Ordnance Survey map. 'I'll search every inch of that place if I have to,' she said. 'I'm not leaving until I'm certain whether or not my sister was here.'

'Really?'

Cora pushed her hands across the maps to smooth them flat. 'I'm going to search this swamp from one end to the other, one square metre at a time, until I've covered the whole damn lot. I'll start along the north edge here, work west to east, east to west, moving south with each sweep.'

I leaned over the maps, letting myself see them properly for the first time. Someone – presumably Cora – had drawn a grid over the top of the maps and the photos. Each small square was numbered. The ones at the very perimeter of the curraghs were shaded pale yellow, as was a section in the north-west corner.

'We can probably discount those areas,' Cora said, following my gaze along the yellow squares. 'You were found coming out of the trees on the eastern side of the road, so you can't have been in this north-west section, otherwise you would've had to cross the road. And, from what you've said, it sounds like you weren't on the edge of the swamp. You would've noticed, right, if there were fields instead of trees in front of you?'

I nodded. 'There were trees all around. When I found the skeleton, I stood up and looked around. Like, I don't know, like maybe someone was there who could've helped.' That's what you do when you're a kid, even if you know for one hundred per cent certain that no one's there except you. 'I looked around, and there were trees on all sides. No farmland.'

Cora nodded, pleased. 'And, how far can you see when you're in the thick of it? Ten feet, twenty feet? More? Less?'

'It depends where you are. If there's lots of undergrowth you might not see more than five or ten feet in front of you. If the trees are thin, you can see quite some distance. Fifty, a hundred feet. It depends.'

Cora nodded again. She leaned over the pictures and started making pencil marks on one of the photos.

I was forced to re-evaluate the woman. I'd jumped to the assumption that she'd come here with nothing more than false hopes and unreal expectations. But it looked like she'd done her homework. She'd researched maps and photos, several of which were new to me, despite my living here for most of my adult life. Cora was as prepared as anyone was likely to get.

Watching her, hunched over the maps, I couldn't suppress a twinge of excitement. If anyone could do this, it might be her.

I tried to smother my hope. 'When I found it, there was nothing left but bones,' I said. 'It will have broken down a lot more since then. We could walk right over it and see nothing. Plus,' I sighed, 'I mean, really I might've been mistaken. It could've been a sheep skeleton for all I know. Or it could've been hundreds of years old, someone who was buried on the land and the grave forgotten about, then the tree roots shoved it to the surface. You have to consider these things.'

'There were fillings in the back teeth,' Cora said. 'That's what you saw, right?'

I made a face. 'Oh my God, how much of my life is on that stupid website? Is there anything the whole world doesn't know? How'd they even get details like that?' I'd forgotten about the fillings myself until right then.

'You're not going to talk anyone out of this search,' Dallin said. He'd remained standing, leaning against the counter with his arms folded. 'Believe me, plenty of people have tried. But we're here, and we're not leaving until we've finished the search. Right, Cora?'

Cora pressed her lips together and nodded. 'Right.'

The pair of them were staying at the campsite at Ballaugh, a few miles down the road. I came out to the doorstep to say goodnight.

Cora gave me an awkward smile. 'Thank you,' she said. 'For helping us. I know you think you can't do anything, but thank you for at least hearing me out and not dismissing us straight away.'

'Don't worry,' Dallin said. 'Rosie's been called a crackpot for years by folks around here. If anyone's likely to believe you completely, it's her.'

Cora winced at his crass words; tried to cover it with another hesitant smile. 'We'll let you know how we get on, yeah?'

'Sure.' They were going out into the curraghs early the next day, to start the search. She'd hinted I was welcome to join them. 'Drop round any time you need a cup of tea,' I said. 'I'm almost always here.'

'Certainly will.' Cora grinned again then got into the driver's seat of the car.

Again, I couldn't help but admire her determination. There was a lot to admire about Cora. I almost wished we were meeting under different circumstances.

I hunched my shoulders. I could practically feel the weight of Beth's gaze pressing down on me from the house. I looked away from Cora quickly.

Dallin remained behind for a moment. He reached to hug me and I instinctively stiffened as he put his arms around my shoulders.

'It's good to see you, sis,' he said.

'Yeah, well.' I turned my face away so I was staring over his shoulder at the garden. 'Have you been to see Mum yet?'

'Not yet, no.'

Something in his tone made me pull away from him. 'I usually visit on Sundays, but I could go with you tomorrow if that's better?'

'I'll have a think, sure.'

There it was again, that dismissive tone. 'Dal, you *have* told her you're here, right? She knows you're back on the island?'

'I figured it might be a nice surprise.' Dallin gave a weak, apologetic grin.

I looked away. 'I don't know why I expected anything different.'

'That's hardly fair.'

'Don't tell me what's fair and what isn't.' I kept my voice and my expression neutral so Cora wouldn't notice anything wrong. 'You're quick enough to run and help when a girl you barely know needs it but you wouldn't come home when your actual family needed you.'

Dallin started to say something else, but I turned away and went back into the house. I closed the door and twisted the key in the lock.

I stayed there in the hallway with my arms wrapped tight around myself, until I heard the noise of the car fade as it turned left at the end of the road. And then, at last, the house was silent again.

If I tried hard enough, I could almost pretend none of the evening had really happened. That no one had invaded my self-contained world and threatened to upend it.

My eyes fell on the Manila envelope on the phone table. Before I could stop myself, I snatched it up. There was no stamp, because it'd been hand-delivered, like all the others. The flap was held closed with a strip of Sellotape.

I opened the envelope and took out the folded papers inside. Even though I'd known exactly what they would be, still my stomach twisted with fresh nausea. My eyes skimmed the printed sheets which, as always, had been highlighted in yellow for my convenience.

Near the bottom, I saw one highlighted word, and it was enough for me to want to fling the sheets away from me.

Death, it said.

You never wanted to leave. You just never really wanted to stay.

Things were difficult for us both. Difficult parents, difficult family, difficult life. You were thirteen when you told me you'd realised something important: you didn't have to stick around to endure the fights and the arguments and the occasional stinging slap from our ma. All the negative stuff that would echo through the house and leave us with ringing ears and red marks on our legs. You could walk out at any time.

'The world is waiting for us,' you used to tell me.

But I was never scared you genuinely would abandon me.

Not until you met him.

Chapter 5

The next morning I wanted nothing more than to stay in bed. I could've kept the curtains closed, the door locked, the lights off. I wanted to stay like that until the sour feeling in my stomach went away. Until I felt strong enough to restart my everyday routine.

But maybe the shadow of Beth was still at my side, because something made me wake before dawn and get out of bed. I made tea and toast without observing my usual ritual of watching the sun rise over the curraghs. Today I hurried around the house to open the curtains even before I'd finished my tea.

I had somewhere I wanted to be. It was something that hadn't happened for over a year.

You can help them, Beth would've said. Yes, that was definitely it. Beth would've laughed and made a game of it. Chased me out of bed. Held the door and told me off for dawdling. Smiled like she always had, from the day I'd got lost in the wetlands right up until the day she died. She'd always smiled like we were both still children. Still capable of taking on anything the world could throw at us.

You can help them.

Wrapped up in my warm coat and bobble hat, I paused on the front doorstep to breathe the chill morning air. It wasn't just Beth who was urging me on. There was a second shadow on my other side, just outside my field of vision. *Bogbean.*

For them, I could do this.

Besides, I wanted to not think about the letter that'd arrived yesterday. I didn't want to be tempted to take it out from inside the photo album where I'd hidden it the night before.

I got into my car and started the engine. It always hated to start, especially on cold mornings. The problem was I never drove enough to keep the engine in good condition. I usually only took it out once a week, on Sundays, to visit Mum. The rest of the time it just sat there. Several times over the winter months I'd tried the ignition only to find the battery had gone dead. If it hadn't been for Mum, I probably wouldn't have bothered to call out the garage to get it fixed.

Today the car started after two attempts, which was fairly good, on average. I drove out to the main road and around to the car park in the curraghs without seeing another car on the road. The drive took almost ten minutes, even though the car park wasn't geographically that far away from our house, because the road curved half a mile out of the way then back again. Plus the road was shockingly bad. I stayed in first gear most of the way, slowing to a crawl over a few particularly bad potholes. I hoped Dallin had thought to warn Cora.

When I reached the curraghs, I found Cora and Dallin already there. Cora was sheltering under the open boot of the car as she packed a backpack. Dallin was standing a short distance away, smoking a cigarette. It must've been a recently acquired habit. He'd never used to smoke.

You haven't seen him in years, I reminded myself. *He could be a completely different person by now, with a hundred bad habits you don't know about.*

As I pulled up behind Cora's car, Cora looked up in surprise. Her face was tight with concern. But a smile lit her face as she recognised me.

I got out of the car and pulled my jacket a little tighter against the chill. Dallin nodded to me but stayed distant while he finished his cigarette.

'Morning,' I said.

'This is a lovely surprise,' Cora said. 'Everything okay?'

Now I was closer, I could see the gauntness of her face. She looked like she hadn't slept. I drew a breath then asked, 'I wondered if you could use an extra set of eyes today?'

'Oh, wow, yes, definitely. Are you sure? I don't think the weather's going to get much better than it is right now.'

'I'd like to help.' It was the truth. I'd sat up for half the night thinking about her story. I still didn't think we'd find anything, but I wanted to help her look.

'That's really kind. Thank you.'

Her smile made warmth rise to my face. I made a pretence of looking at the road we'd come in on. 'Did you get here okay?' I asked. 'I forgot to warn you about the road.'

'Yeah, that was a bit of an adventure. It was like *Wages of Fear* finding this place.' She adjusted her bobble hat, tucking loose strands of blonde hair out of the way. 'I thought this was a fairly popular spot. For walkers and stuff? Why don't they maintain the road?'

Dallin laughed. 'This is completely average for the roads over here. I've seen potholes you could lose a Smart car in. Are we ready?'

In all honesty, I wasn't sure if I *was* ready. The morning had a weird sense of unreality hanging over it. I tried not to think too hard about what we were doing here or what we hoped to find. If I avoided that, I could pretend this was a normal outing. No big deal.

Except that's a lie too. When was the last time you went on an outing with anyone?

'I've got the maps here,' Cora said. She'd spread them out in the boot. 'We're going to try to cover sections A12 through A27, then back along B28 through B11 this morning. Once we get back to the road—'

'What's that in English?' Dallin asked.

'We're going to start at the top of the map, roughly in the middle where the road cuts through and work our way across, left to right, then back again. English enough for you?'

Cora held out one of the maps so I could see. The hand-drawn squares were marked with letters and numbers. A1 was in the top left; Q39 at the bottom right. I saw at once the route she'd described, running from the road eastward through the curraghs until it came almost to the field boundary, then doubling back on itself.

'Once we get back to the road,' Cora said, 'we'll assess how much we've done and figure out whether we have to pick up the pace or not.' She looped a dark green scarf around her neck and tucked the ends down the front of her waterproof jacket. 'Weather forecast is changeable, but we hopefully won't get rained on until later this afternoon. Be aware it might get warmer. Hope everyone wore layers.'

Dallin rolled his eyes. 'She wouldn't let me out of the tent this morning until I proved I was wearing at least three layers,' he said. 'She's like a mother-hen.'

'I'm sure your mother would kick me in the shins if she thought I was letting you catch a cold out here,' Cora replied. I saw Dallin wince.

I picked up my own backpack from my car. I'd been worried the others wouldn't think to bring snacks and water, but now I saw I'd been concerned for nothing. Cora was better prepared than I was. As well as the maps, she had two bottles of water, a large bar of chocolate, a small first aid kid, and a torch shoved into her bag. She adjusted the water bottles so they wouldn't dig into her back, then swung the bag onto her shoulder.

'Which way first?' I asked.

The car park was little more than a slightly wider bend in the road. If more than a few cars arrived at the same time, the road could get completely blocked. On all sides the trees hemmed us in. Off to the left, a faded noticeboard showed a map of the main route through the curraghs, as well as a few diagrams of the local wildlife. Beyond it, the path cut through the trees towards a five-bar gate, which led to the main track.

I'd assumed we would be starting from the main track, but Cora paced off up the road in the direction we'd come.

'Are you really planning to go cross-country right from the

off?' I asked. I snuck another look at the map before Cora tucked it into a pocket of her backpack. 'I don't know if there are any real paths at that end of the curraghs. At least, not any that'll go right the way through and back again.'

'We'll have to go cross-country at some point,' Cora said. 'Might as well get used to it.'

I fell into step beside her. I wasn't sure it was such a great idea to stray off the main trails on the first day. The going would be tough, if not impossible in places. It might be enough to discourage Cora from her search before it'd even begun.

I glanced down. Cora wore decent wellies, with waterproof trousers tucked into them. None of her gear looked new. Either she did a lot of hiking, or she'd borrowed good clothes from someone who knew what they were doing. Either way it was reassuring. She'd done her homework and she'd come prepared.

Out of interest, I glanced back at Dallin. He wore a bright blue waterproof jacket that still had the sheen of newness, but also jeans and scuffed trainers. He'd have to take care where he trod, or he would spend the day with wet feet. I wondered if no one had bothered to tell him to dress appropriately ... or if he'd deliberately not listened.

I shrugged off the question. Dallin had grown up playing in the wetlands. If he didn't know to wear wellies, it wasn't any of my business.

At least he's wearing layers. I started to smile, then stopped as I remembered his offhand comment. Dallin had made it sound like him and Cora were sharing a tent. Was that true?

I watched them both as we walked, looking for clues as to whether they were something more than friends. I told myself I was just curious.

No one spoke as we marched off towards our starting point. It occurred to me Cora hadn't asked if I had anything else to do that day – like going to work or seeing friends. Maybe Dallin had already briefed her on my situation.

I glanced again at Dallin. It stung a little, to think of him talking to people about me, telling them my private life. How much had he said? Did Cora know about my mum and dad? Did she know about Beth?

And then I wondered who else he'd spoken to. Perhaps everyone in his life knew about his sister who lived, broken and alone, in her house in the curraghs.

I shoved my hands into my pockets. For the last year, I'd felt safe and forgotten. No one came to visit anymore. The few friends I'd had – Beth's friends – had phoned and texted and emailed, with less and less frequency as time went on, until at last, no one checked in with me anymore. I'd ignored my social media accounts for so long they'd probably been deactivated.

I still received those letters, of course, in their plain hand-written envelopes. Nothing could stop them arriving.

Possibly it was being out here in the curraghs which had so quickly soured my mood. Me and Beth had walked those pathways so often. It felt weird being there without her. I hadn't properly taken that into consideration before leaving my house that morning.

Cora was consulting her smartwatch. She slowed, stopped,

took two more paces then a shuffling half-step. 'That's us,' she said. 'Right here.'

We'd all but reached the edge of the curraghs. From here, along the rest of the length of the road, there were only sparser trees and hedges. Cora double-checked her watch, which showed a bare-bones map and GPS coordinates, then turned to look at the trees at the side of the road. They appeared no different to any other section of the curraghs. The most obvious difference was there was no path of any sort leading into the wetlands. There was also a ditch separating the road from the trees.

'So, how're we finding our way, exactly?' Dallin asked.

'We're trailblazing.' Cora half-smiled at him. 'Shall I lead the way, or do you want to?'

Dallin muttered something under his breath. There were shadows under his eyes, like maybe he'd been drinking the night before. Not that I blamed him. In a way I was almost jealous. It'd been a long time since I'd last had alcohol.

How sad do you have be, to be jealous of someone with a hangover? This thought, at last, did bring a smile to my face.

Cora jumped over the ditch and pushed aside a couple of branches. The twisted, shallow-rooted trees that grew in the curraghs were springy and resistant, and didn't much like being shoved out of the way. Cora stepped through them with difficulty.

I looked at Dallin, but he seemed happy to bring up the rear.

I took a short run-up and leapt across the ditch, but lost my balance on the other bank. I would've fallen backwards into the brackish water if Cora hadn't shot out a hand to grab me.

'Thanks,' I said, a little breathless, as I regained my footing. 'It's been a while since I did anything strenuous.'

In fact, just that small bit of exercise made me realise how out of shape I'd become. I knew I'd put on weight over the eighteen months, due in part to my medication, but it hadn't really affected me. Staying indoors so much, I wasn't bothered when my lightweight summer clothes no longer fit. Loose fitting T-shirts and jogging pants had always been my preferred outfits anyway. Without Beth to encourage me to cook meals from scratch, I'd fallen into the bad habit of easily prepared processed food and ready meals; without Beth to drag me out for long walks in the countryside, I'd lost the inclination to go outside.

Now, all of a sudden, I felt self-conscious as I followed Cora through the half-gap in the trees.

There was no path, not even an ill-defined trail left by animals. We were immediately stepping over mud pockets and sunken tree roots. At least the trees were less tightly clumped together here. Weak morning sunlight slanted in through the thin leaves. A few metres to our right, a barbed wire fence marked the edge of someone's field. Beyond it, tall grass swayed in the soft breeze.

'We're too near the edge of the curraghs,' Dallin said. He'd hopped over the ditch without any issues. 'We need to search further into the middle.'

'We need to search all of it,' Cora said. 'If we start in the middle we might miss out whole sections by accident.' She kept one eye on her GPS as she walked. In her other hand she also carried her compass. 'Has this area changed much in fifteen years?' she asked me. 'I mean in terms of size. Has it spread out, or have people built in on the edges, anything like that?'

'I don't think so,' I said. 'The only building that might've expanded into it would be the Wildlife Park.' I pointed south, in the vague direction of the park. 'But I'm not sure if anyone would be allowed to expand outwards into the curraghs. This is all protected land.'

'Protected by who?' Cora asked. 'We're not going to get arrested for going off-piste like this, are we?'

Dallin laughed. 'National Heritage have got better things to do than prosecute ramblers. If anyone complains, we'll say we got lost. Happens all the time, apparently.'

Cora set the pace, moving steadily between the trees, keeping to the scant dry patches of land, but never letting herself get drawn off the arrow-straight path she'd mapped. We followed her. I fell into a rhythm, glad we weren't walking too fast. I worried now about exhausting myself before the day was half done. How had I not noticed my stamina was so low?

But, even with my internal concerns, it felt good to be out of the house. The curraghs were peaceful that morning. The early birds had flitted off to find breakfast, and the only noise came from the trees quietly whispering as they brushed together.

It was so peaceful in fact that I completely forgot I was supposed to be checking the ground for signs of the missing skeleton. It was Cora who reminded me. She cast her gaze back and forth with each step, searching the mud on either side, delaying each step forward until she was totally sure there was nothing there to find. I felt a pang of guilt. Neither me nor Dallin were paying as much attention as her. Perhaps subconsciously I agreed with Dallin – we were too close to the edge of the curraghs, and therefore there was no real point in looking out for anything.

After fifteen or twenty minutes, the trees thinned out further and the ground became a lot boggier. I spotted where a drainage ditch at the side of the field had burst into the curraghs. The water had an oily, polluted sheen to it.

'I knew things were going too smoothly,' Cora said. She stepped gingerly onto a tussock of grass, testing to make sure it wouldn't spill her into the bog. 'I think we can get across like this.'

'I thought you'd figured it all out from your maps,' Dallin said. 'How come a patch of bog can sneak up on you?'

'Maps and photos are all well and good,' Cora said, 'but no plan survives boots on the ground.' She hopped to the next tussock. The movement sent ripples through the muddy water. 'There'll always be surprises. Not that I'm happy about it, of course. I don't like guesswork. Don't like not being sure. In an ideal world, a superior plan will always beat any surprise the world might throw at you. But, what can you do? I don't—'

The next clump of grass was too small to bear her weight, and tipped her off balance. Cora made an ungainly leap for the safety of solid ground. She fell only a little short. One foot went down into the mud, almost to the top of her welly, but she was able to grab a branch and haul herself free. Her booted foot plopped free with a sucking noise and a belch of bad air. Still hanging onto the tree, Cora kicked some of the mud off her boots, flapping her free hand in a vain attempt to disperse the silage smell. She glanced at her GPS.

'It's okay,' she said. 'We're still on track.'

'Balls to this,' Dallin said. 'I'm going around.'

'Quitter.' Cora grinned.

It took me considerably longer to get across, but with Cora calling encouragement, I made it, via a more circuitous route. I got a high-five and a smile from Cora, which made the whole endeavour worthwhile.

'Great. We're still on course,' Cora said. 'Well, two thirds of us are, anyway.' She tilted her head. Some distance away, Dallin was trying with little success to find a dry path. It was possible to track his progress by the steady stream of swearing coming from amongst the trees.

'I'm glad we're not relying on him for directions,' Cora said. 'He's more ... out of his element than I expected.'

'It's a long time since he's been home,' I said, then corrected myself. 'Since he's been *here*. And, I know he lived with all this on his doorstep, but he never ... he never felt comfortable out here, in the curraghs. He stuck to the main paths. Never went off exploring like this.'

'He's missing out.' Cora consulted her GPS, and pulled her hat down more securely over her ears. 'This place is something else. What about you?'

'Oh. I lived with our dad. When our parents split up.' I shrugged. 'Well, you know what it's like, when things go bad between people. Me and Dallin were caught in the middle. He ended up living with Mum; I lived with Dad.'

'That must've been difficult.'

'You get used to things.' It hadn't seemed too strange at the time. Lots of kids at school had unconventional home-lives. 'But it meant me and Dallin were never really close. We went to different schools, had different friends, only saw each other at weekends and holidays. What about you?' I asked then. 'Were you and Simone close?'

'No.' Cora laughed at my obvious surprise. 'Not all the time. We could fight like two cats in a bin liner when the mood took us.'

'So why—?' I bit my tongue.

Cora smiled sadly, like this wasn't the first time the question had come up. 'A lot of the time, I wasn't as good a sister as I could've been,' she said. 'It took me a while to realise that. And longer before I knew I had to make up for it. Searching for Simone now is pretty much the only thing I can do for her.'

I peered through the trees. We could still hear Dallin but couldn't see him. 'Should we wait for Dallin?' I asked.

'He'll catch up,' Cora said. 'C'mon. We don't want to lose time.'

Chapter 6

Dallin did indeed catch up. But he remained sullen and uncommunicative. I couldn't help notice his trainers and the cuffs of his jeans were covered with mud.

There was an odd mood to the search party as the morning wore on. We couldn't forget why we were there. But the very fact gave us a purpose.

'It's weird,' Cora admitted. 'I've been planning this for so long. *We've* been planning this.' She glanced back at Dallin, who was still bringing up the rear. There was a look on her face that I hoped I'd misinterpreted. 'It's hard to believe we're finally here. This feels like ... I don't want to jinx it. But you feel it, right? This feels like something. Like this could be the real thing.'

I didn't know what to tell her. 'You've been searching for about three years, right?'

'I ought to say I've been looking since Simone disappeared, but that's not really true. I've always been asking questions. Three years ago I started properly searching.'

'Why then?'

'My mother got ill. Pneumonia. For a while we thought

– we thought we were going to lose her.' Cora brushed her fingers against a tree as she passed, letting her touch rest a moment on the bark. 'She was delirious for a bit, in hospital. She kept thinking I was Simone. It made me realise ... none of us ever got closure. When Simone vanished, she ripped a big hole in our family. I hadn't properly understood what it'd done to us. So that's why I started looking.'

I raised my eyes briefly to the tangled tree branches above us. 'And it led you here.'

'Eventually. There's been a hell of a lot of false starts.' Cora pushed aside a springy branch that attempted to bop her face. 'There were a few times when it felt like we were getting close. Last year I was convinced I'd traced her to a remote part of Scotland. I trekked all the way up there and spent a very long weekend in the weirdest bed and breakfast ever. Ask me about it after a couple of drinks sometime.'

'How do you find those leads?'

'Oh, y'know. Everywhere. Newspapers, websites, gossip, urban legends. I know where to look, and I've got friends online who'll notify me if something new pops up. Like they did with your story about the curraghs.' She favoured me with a smile. 'It appeared on the forum about six months ago. I'm a regular on that board so I noticed it pretty quickly. As soon as I did, I thought, *this could be it*.'

I paused to catch my breath. The steady pace helped me avoid getting winded. Even so, my calf muscles ached from the unaccustomed exercise. Cora kept walking.

'So, did you have to get time off work to come here?' I asked as I started moving again.

'Sort of,' Cora said. She'd unfolded the map from her pocket and held it flat in front of her with the compass laid on top as she walked. 'I work for a charity. They know my situation and they give me a lot of leeway.'

'That's good of them.' I wondered whether she looked forward to a time when she could return to work without this search weighing on her mind. I thought about my own job.

'They employ a lot of people who – who're like me,' Cora said. 'Not my exact circumstances, obviously, but similar difficulties. Believe me, a lot of them are far higher maintenance than I am.'

'What about Dallin?' He was far enough behind me that I didn't think he'd overhear. 'Did he have trouble getting time off from work?'

'Not as far as I know. He hasn't mentioned anything.'

'You guys must be good friends. Not everyone would drop everything to help a person out. Especially if it involved travelling across the country and wading around a marsh.' I was fishing for information. I couldn't help it.

Cora smiled. 'We only met for the first time a few weeks ago. There was no way I would've asked him to do this. I was already booked on the ferry and ready to go. Then he announced he was coming with me. He said I could use his help when we got here, to find my way around and know who to talk to, stuff like that. Plus I think he wanted to see you.'

I stopped myself from making a nasty comment. There'd been more than enough opportunities for Dallin to come home. 'What about your family?' I asked instead. 'Didn't any of them want to come with you?'

'I haven't told them I'm here.'

'You haven't?'

Cora kept walking. It was difficult to be sure what she was thinking, since her eyes were alternating between watching the ground and checking her map and compass. 'Simone kinda broke our family when she left,' she said. 'There were a whole bunch of arguments and fallings out, and half of us still aren't talking to the other half.' She brushed another tree trunk with her fingertips. 'You know what families are like. Anyway, the upshot is, I don't have a lot of people I can fall back on in times of need. The last time I told my parents I was going on one of these expeditions, it caused a huge argument. Mum thinks I'm wasting my time. Dad thinks I'm deliberately dredging up the past to cause fights. So, I've stopped telling them where I'm going.'

'I would've thought they'd be keen to find out what happened to Simone.'

Another faint smile. 'I would've thought so too.'

I wondered about Dallin. Possibly he was here because he'd genuinely wanted to help Cora. Helping out a friend, I could understand that. Helping a friend he'd only met a short while ago, on what was probably a wild goose chase that would take him away from home for a whole week? That didn't sound like something Dallin would do on a whim.

They're definitely more than just friends, I thought.

'What about you?' Cora asked, changing the subject. 'What're your family like?'

'I don't have very many people. My dad died when I was twenty.' I skipped over what exactly had happened to him. I also skipped over Beth. I couldn't face raising either subject right then. 'So it's just my dear brother Dallin, and our mum.'

Cora looked surprised. 'His mum lives over here?'

'In Ramsey. She's got one of those new-build flats. It's quite nice, but I know she misses her garden. She used to own the farmhouse where I live. Still does, technically.'

Cora's brows knitted together. 'Dallin didn't say anything about her. He made it sound like you were the only family he's got.'

I glanced over my shoulder, to where Dallin was plodding along some distance behind us, with his sullen gaze firmly on the ground. 'Why would he say that?' I wondered aloud.

'We've only known each other a short while,' Cora suggested. 'He's under no obligation to overshare with me.'

'Hmm.' I didn't particularly want to speculate. It upset me that Dallin hadn't mentioned Mum. Had they fallen out? On the rare occasions when Dallin's name came up, Mum always sounded wistful, as she said how she wished he would get in contact more often.

I recalled my conversation with Dallin on the doorstep last night. It'd sounded like he didn't intend to tell our mother he was on the island at all. The callous nature of that made something hot bubble inside my chest.

When was the last time you felt angry about anything? The thought surprised me. But it was true. There'd been plenty of anger – impotent, directionless, hopeless anger – throughout Beth's illness, but in recent months a kind of dull funk had settled over my life. I didn't feel angry or inconsolable anymore. In fact, I pretty much felt nothing. The tablets my doctor had prescribed probably contributed, smoothing out my emotions so I no longer had to deal with the horrific lows and occasional, sickening highs that'd plagued my life after Beth died.

So, I could look at this sudden bubble of anger towards Dallin with a strangely clinical detachment. The anger was brief and unformed and not even particularly strong – it faded almost as soon as it appeared. But it was something I hadn't felt for a long time, and that was interesting.

A little further on, we reached the east edge of the curraghs. Cora made us walk ten paces south, then turn west to walk back to the road.

'We just walked this section,' Dallin complained. 'There's nothing here but mud.'

'That's how the plan goes,' Cora said. 'We cover each square metre. So far we've done this bit.' She showed him on the map. 'Now we're doing this bit. If you want to make things smoother, walk next to one of us, not right at the back. That way we'll cut down on the chances of missing something. Or, even better, go back in time three weeks to when we were discussing this exact point and put forward your arguments then.'

Dallin shifted the straps of his backpack. 'Seems like we're wasting a lot of time going over the same ground, that's all.'

'If it bothers you that much, I will happily put the maps into your hands.' Cora presented the map to Dallin with a flourish, then hastily snatched it back. 'Actually, no, that's a lie, these are my maps and I love them. If it bothers you that much, you can go buy your own map and plot your own course.'

I looked out over the fields. There were clumps of bog myrtle growing here, and the air was perfumed with its distinctive smell. It made me think of Beth, who'd often brought home sprigs of the pungent leaves, insisting it would keep midges away in the evenings when she sat out in the garden.

Usually, I would've avoided dwelling on the memory. There were so many things that reminded me of Beth. Everything I did or said would contain some echo of another time. I'd learned not to focus too long on each memory as it surfaced, because they all had sharp edges, even the happy ones. Especially the happy ones.

But now, for a moment, I breathed deeply and remembered the times Beth had come home with pockets full of wild mushrooms or foraged leaves or pignuts, those knobbly ground-nuts which she would leave scattered on the draining board, still half-coated in mud.

Beth had loved the curraghs, and they'd been good to her in return. Now, she was gone, but the land remained the same. This bog had been here long before me and Beth ever ventured into it, hand in hand, and it would be here long after all trace of us vanished from the earth. It was a permanent yet ever-changing place.

Behind me, Cora and Dallin had come to some kind of peace. We set off walking back towards the road.

I found myself at the back with Dallin. He was still in a huff, his hands shoved deep into the pockets of his jacket.

'You agree with me, right?' he said to me.

'About what?'

'We're wasting time searching up here.' Dallin gave a curt nod towards the fields which were visible through the thin trees to our right. 'You weren't anywhere near here when you found the body. Otherwise you would've said you could see the fields. So why're we wasting our time?'

I thought about it before I answered. 'I said I couldn't remember seeing the fields,' I admitted. 'But I also said I'd been everywhere in the curraghs since that day. And I can honestly say I've never been here, in this exact spot. It never occurred to me to search at the edges. So maybe Cora's right – maybe she has to search everywhere, including the places that don't seem likely. If she skips bits, she'll always wonder if Simone's remains were lying in one of these out-of-the-way spots where she didn't think to look.' I shrugged. 'She needs to be sure. That involves checking everywhere.'

Dallin grunted. 'Still seems daft to me.'

'You know what seems daft? The fact you're here at all. It would've been much easier for you to just point Cora in the general direction of the Island and leave her to it. But you came all the way out here, in person. Why?'

'I wanted to help.' He tried and failed to sound sincere. 'She's a vulnerable person. I wanted to give her all the help I could. And I didn't know if you would talk to her if I wasn't there to smooth things over. If she'd turned up on your doorstep out of the blue, you might've turned her away.'

'So why not call and explain the situation to me?'

'I emailed.'

'No, you didn't. Last night I checked my emails from the

last two months, plus the junk folder. You didn't email me. And anyway, how much effort would it take for you to pick up the phone? It's not like you don't know the number; it's the same as when you lived at home.'

Dallin pushed a hand through his hair. 'You're mad at me.'

'Yes.' It was easy to admit. 'I've every reason to be mad.'

'Listen, if I'd known it was such a big deal for you to get prior warning I was coming here, then—'

'That's not why, and you know it.' I slowed my pace. I didn't want Cora to overhear this argument. 'I can't believe how much of a hypocrite you are. Talking about how Cora needs you and you can't possibly let her down. What about me? What about Beth?'

As I spoke, I realised this was the first time I'd said Beth's name aloud in months. It rang in my ears. I wanted to snatch it back, like it was something private, not to be shared.

Dallin kept walking. He kept his eyes fixed on the ground. 'I'm sorry about what happened to Beth,' he muttered.

'So am I.' A bubble of hurt expanded in my chest. For a moment I was filled by it, unable to breathe. Gradually it subsided. But that moment reminded me of all the moments before it, when the slightest word could trigger something. The hurt was always there. I'd come to understand it would never fully go away.

'I'm sorry I lost contact with you,' Dallin said. 'With both of you. I thought—' The words seemed to tangle in this throat. 'I thought you were fine, y'know? You were living your lives and I didn't want to intrude.'

'She was really upset you wouldn't come to the wedding,'

I said. Each word felt like broken glass. I spoke carefully so I wouldn't cut myself.

'I was out of the country. I wanted to come, believe me.'

I didn't believe him. 'You didn't even reply to the invitation.'

'I was travelling. By the time I got her email, it was too late. I'm sorry.'

'What about the other messages? She tried to contact you after that, a bunch of times, after she got sick. Why the hell didn't you reply?'

Dallin let out a long breath. 'Honestly? I didn't realise how ill she was. If she'd come right out and told me, of course I would've come home.'

'She didn't want to spell it out in an email. You should've known that.'

'Listen, in hindsight, you are completely right. I should've come home. But at the time? I thought – I don't know. The way she danced around the issue. All those half-hints. I thought it was one of her games.'

I almost choked in disbelief. 'A *game*?'

'I know how terrible that sounds. But that's what she was like as a kid. She would say something crazy and see which friends would come running. That's all I thought it was.'

'How could you think that? Why would she lie about something so awful?'

'I have no idea why she would do anything. Let's be honest, I barely even knew her by then.' Dallin kicked a tree stump in annoyance. 'I didn't know either of you, apparently.'

I stopped walking and faced him directly. 'Is *that* why you acted like a spoiled baby? Because you had a stupid childhood crush on your best friend and it turned out she wanted to be with me instead?'

Dallin met my gaze briefly. 'You never loved her like I did.'

The anger that'd been absent from my life for so long rose up in me. I swung my arm and punched him in the jaw. It happened so fast I couldn't believe I'd done it. One second I was standing there, the next, Dallin was reeling backwards. He put his foot down in a marshy puddle and almost overbalanced. If he hadn't caught hold of a tree branch for support he would've fallen.

'She was my wife,' I said. My voice rose along with my anger. 'Don't you dare talk about her that way.'

I shoved past him.

Cora was staring at me with shock on her face. I walked straight past her too.

'I'm sorry,' I said. 'I can't do this.'

It wasn't possible to run in the thick bogland, but I hurried as fast as I could in the direction of the road.

Chapter 7

I had every intention of going straight home. I planned to lock the front door and refuse to answer my phone for at least a week, until Dallin had definitely left the island again.

But my pace slowed as I made my way back to the road. My anger burned as hot as ever, but it was hard to maintain, out there in the peacefulness of the curraghs.

Dallin had always been wrong about Beth. He'd never understood her. He saw the cool distance in her eyes and mistook it for aloofness. But I knew better. I'd seen the warmth and gentleness in Beth's nature. The occasional small smile meant a thousand times more than the fake showiness that most people projected. When Beth smiled at me, she'd meant it.

The simple fact was Dallin had let us all down. Beth had needed him as a friend; I'd needed him as a brother; Mum had needed him as a son. His absence at Beth's funeral had been a gaping wound that refused to close.

I understood how hard it would've been for him, especially coming just a few years after Dad died. It was awful for everyone. *No one* wanted to be there.

And it hurt all the more to know that he *could* come home, when he wanted to. When someone like Cora wanted him to.

I kept walking. Without Cora's compass and GPS to keep me in a straight line, I drifted off course, heading south to skirt around a muddy ditch. I found my way onto a faint trail, and followed it as it wound its slow way through the marshland.

By the time I reached the road, my anger had subsided into a heavy sort of sadness that weighed down on my stomach. The argument with Dallin had dredged up a whole load of feelings I didn't want to deal with.

The path I'd found led me out onto the road some distance from the car park. That was the trouble with the curraghs. Even if you thought you were going in the right direction, you could so easily get turned around.

I went to my car, opened the passenger side door, and sat down to kick the mud off my boots. Despite my best efforts, I'd carried half the bog out with me.

'Good morning,' a cheery voice called from the other side of the road.

I looked up in surprise. I'd been so caught up in my thoughts I hadn't spotted my neighbour, Eloise, approaching from up the road.

'You're out and about early,' Eloise said. She was a tiny woman, less than five feet tall, with such dainty features I often wondered if she was some kind of wood-elf. Definitely there seemed something ethereal about her, not least the fact that she had to be at least forty but barely looked twenty. Her wispy hair was tied in a complicated, messy knot on top of her head. When I tried that, it looked like I was wearing a bird's nest as a hat; on her it looked delightful.

'It's a beautiful morning,' I said, which was as good an explanation as any for why I was outdoors.

Eloise's dog, a golden retriever called Butterscotch, came lolloping back up the road. He almost ran straight past Eloise but veered towards her when she called him. I could never figure out if the dog was losing his eyesight or if he was just exceptionally daft.

'Lots of people here today,' Eloise said with a nod towards Cora's car. 'Not sure what these folks are up to. I saw them setting off. Just struck straight out cross-country.'

Which meant she'd almost certainly seen me with them. I sighed. 'Yes,' I admitted.

'Don't know what they were thinking,' Eloise said. 'There's plenty of paths if they want to go for a walk. If I'd got down here fast enough I would've told them not to go off through the woods like that. Someone should tell them this is a nature reserve. The plants have a hard enough time without people trampling them.'

I pulled off my boots and reached into the back seat in search of the slip-on shoes I wore for driving. 'They're looking for something,' I said.

'Oh dear. They didn't lose their car keys, did they? Because it's unlikely they'll find them again, not out there.'

I looked off at the trees. 'Do you remember when I was a kid, and I found a skeleton out there?'

'Oh, heavens. Yes, I remember you telling me. Or was it Opal who told me? One or the other. Anyway, I thought everyone had forgotten that by now.'

'Apparently not.' I put my muddy boots in the passenger footwell, on top of the plastic bags I used for shopping. 'Someone's come over from England because they heard the story and want to know if it's true.'

Eloise scrunched up her face. 'They're not expecting to find anything, are they?'

'I told them there's probably nothing to find. But they're insistent they want to search the curraghs themselves.'

Eloise's eyes went wide. 'They plan to trample around the entire wetlands like that? Don't they realise the damage it'll do?'

I hadn't really thought about that. I was always careful not to deliberately crush any plants when I was out walking, but would the others be as considerate? I thought of Dallin, stamping his annoyance through the curraghs.

Butterscotch was wandering around the car with interest. When he bumped into me, he *whuffed* in surprise and delight at finding an unexpected friend. I absently scratched the top of his head.

'Someone needs to tell them.' Eloise twisted her fingers together in distress. 'They probably don't even realise the harm they're causing. People just don't think. They barge into places like this, dropping litter and snapping off saplings and scaring the birds. They don't *think*.'

I couldn't imagine Cora being inconsiderate enough to drop litter. But Eloise wouldn't know that. 'You're right,' I said instead. 'I'll have a word when they come back.'

'Are you sure? Perhaps I should go in after them.'

Butterscotch abruptly spun around twice and went galloping

off up the road in pursuit of something. After ten feet he either lost sight of it or forgot what he was doing. He jogged to a halt then sat down, his head cocked, his tail sweeping the ground.

'I'll wait for them,' I said. 'They should be out soon. They probably don't realise they might damage stuff.'

Eloise sniffed. 'People are so inconsiderate.'

She whistled to Butterscotch, who snapped out of his daydream to come bounding back towards her. Together they set off down the road.

I fished my flask out of my backpack. I wished it contained something stronger than herbal tea.

Ten minutes later, while I was still debating whether or not to drive off and leave them, Cora emerged from the trees. I must not have been paying attention, because it was like the woman simply appeared, stepping without warning from amongst the branches. Cora paused on the road as if momentarily disorientated. When she spotted me she looked relieved.

She came down the road to my car. 'I didn't realise how close we were to the road,' Cora said. 'One minute we were in the trees, the next I was on tarmac. Surreal. I can see how someone could wander around without finding the road.'

I nodded at her compass. 'Bet you're glad you brought that.'

'Are you okay?' she asked. 'I'm sorry, I should've gone with you. I didn't want to leave you on your own, but—'

'It's okay.' I understood; Cora's search took priority over everything, especially people she'd just met. 'I'm sorry you saw us arguing. Where's Dallin?'

'He's behind,' Cora said. 'Stopped for a wild wee. Boys sure do love weeing in the outdoors.'

'I might head home.' I studied the ground at my feet. 'I'm sorry. This is weird and difficult for me. I mean, I know it must be weird for you too. I just don't know if I can cope with it. But I didn't want to storm off without an explanation.'

'It's okay,' Cora said at once. 'I understand. It was good of you to come at all.' She glanced behind her but there was still no sign of Dallin. 'I'm sorry, I didn't realise there was any bad feeling between you two.'

Bad feeling. That was an interesting way of putting it. 'It's fine,' I said. 'You didn't know.'

'Dallin never said anything. He made it sound like everything was peachy. The way he told it, he'd spoken to you about us coming here, and you were completely on board.'

I'd already given myself enough of a headache that afternoon over Dallin. 'Did he say anything after I left?'

'A little. He said it was just family stuff.'

'That pretty much covers it,' I admitted.

Cora hesitated, then said, 'He didn't tell me about your wife. I'm so sorry to hear what happened to her.'

It was unexpected, and it punched a hole in the protective layer I kept wrapped around me. For an instant, I couldn't breathe. The whole world was airless. I closed my eyes until the feeling passed and my chest unlocked. 'Thank you,' I said quietly.

'If I'd known, we never would've come here. Well, I mean, I still would've come here to the wetlands, but I wouldn't have pestered you about it. You've got enough on your plate without dealing with this too.'

I hadn't thought about it in those terms. But I saw now that, if Dallin had been honest with Cora about my situation, she would've stopped him turning up unannounced on my doorstep. It made me feel a little better to know it was Dallin who was insensitive, not Cora.

'Honestly, it's okay,' I said. 'I'm just sorry I can't help you.'

'You've helped us loads already.'

I wasn't sure how true that was, but I appreciated her saying it. 'How did you get on after I left? I take it you didn't have any luck.'

'We found some bones,' Cora said. She unfolded her map and made an annotation in pencil to show where they'd searched so far that day. 'Had a moment of excitement, but they were rabbit bones. I think. It certainly wasn't a person.' Cora shook her head. 'I didn't take into account how many animals must die and decompose out there. Half the bog is probably composted animal remains. Also, do you have poison ivy here?'

I frowned. 'Not as far as I'm aware.'

'In that case, your brother is being unnecessarily dramatic. He fell over into some leaves.'

'Hey, something I should've mentioned before we set off,' I said, 'but this place is a nature reserve.'

'Yes, we know.'

'So you should be careful where you put your feet. One of my neighbours just stopped to ask why we're trampling around. She's very worried about the rare flowers.'

Cora tilted her head. 'Did you tell her why we're here?'

'I mentioned it, yes.'

'What did she say?'

'Just that we should be careful of the flowers. And the nesting birds.'

Cora tapped her pencil against her teeth. 'Does she remember the day you found the body?'

'She only moved here a few years ago. All she's heard is the story from everyone else.'

'Who would've told her?'

I shrugged. 'Everyone in this area knows about it, even if they weren't here at the time. I used to tell anyone who asked. I even had a few people from magazines phoning up, asking if I wanted to sell my story. My mum told them all to go jump in the sea.'

Cora still looked thoughtful. 'So, is there anyone who might remember the event first-hand? Anyone who joined in the search?'

'Nicole and Patrick. They live at the farm down the road. They were there that day.' It was Nicole who'd given me the packet of biscuits and told me to eat as many as I wanted. 'Do you want to talk to them too?'

Cora nodded. 'If possible, yes.'

'I can ask. I don't know what good it'll do you. They didn't see the skeleton or anything. All they saw was a hysterical little girl.'

'Yeah, but how long have they lived at the farm?'

'Decades. Nicole's family has owned the land for generations. Why?'

'Because,' Cora said, 'that means they were living here when Simone went missing.'

I frowned. 'So?'

'If Simone did come here, someone might remember her. And if someone left her body in the curraghs—' Her voice tightened around the words. She cleared her throat. 'They might've been spotted. The locals around here could know more than they realise.'

I'd never thought to ask myself how the body ended up in the wetlands. It could've been an accident – some horrible, unpredictable accident that killed the girl and left her to lie forgotten forever – but if it wasn't ... if someone had taken her there deliberately ...

In fifteen years, I'd never fully wondered whether the girl in the curraghs might've been murdered.

'If the locals knew anything,' I said carefully, 'don't you think they would've said something by now?'

'No one ever bothered to question them, because no one connected Simone's disappearance to the body you found. So maybe we just need to jog the right person's memory.'

'It's a longshot.'

'Of course it is,' Cora said. There was no anger behind her words; it was a simple statement of fact. 'Everything we're doing is a longshot.'

'Okay. I'll phone around and see if anyone remembers anything.'

'Thank you. What about your mum?'

'What about her?'

'I don't know anything about her. This is a whole aspect

that Dallin didn't see fit to share with me. She was living here when you found the remains, right? And for a while previous to that?'

'That's right. She moved here five or six years earlier.' I wasn't sure I liked where this was going.

'So, she might know something,' Cora said. She was staring off into the trees as if seeing something no one else could. 'She might've seen my sister, even if she doesn't remember.'

On days when Ma and Da fought, the house would shake like it was under bombardment. Me and you would barricade ourselves in our room. You would pull the duvet off the bed and make a protective nest for us both.

'Tune it out, Cora,' you'd say.

We'd lie with our heads close together, both watching the ceiling tremble with the force of slammed doors downstairs. We knew to keep quiet. The wrath of the storm would blow past if we kept our heads down long enough.

'We're stronger than them,' you'd say.

But sometimes we weren't fast enough to outrun the storm.

You were out of the house when a particularly bad one hit. Weren't answering your phone, so I couldn't even warn you. You walked into the middle of it, and our ma rounded on you like you were the root cause of everything.

Two nights later, you said, 'It's you and me against the world.'

During the calm, it was different. You lost your tolerance for me. I was a hinderance, an annoyance; your tag-along shadow always getting under your feet. Tempers flared between us – minor squalls in comparison to our parents', not enough to rattle the house. I don't know why I infuriated you so much.

More than once, I found myself wishing for another storm between our parents, just so you would shut the bedroom door, drag down the blanket, and talk to me like a person. Like a fellow survivor. Even though the storms left me shaken and sick, still I craved those rare moments of closeness with you.

'They can't keep me here forever,' you'd say.

And I'd wonder what it would take to make you stay.

Chapter 8

I couldn't face going into the curraghs again that afternoon. Just the morning had exhausted me. I'd always assumed I was in fairly good shape, but eighteen months of nothing more strenuous than walking up and down the stairs had apparently depleted whatever reserves I'd had. I was used to taking my time. When was the last time I'd had to run to anyone's schedule but my own?

The argument with Dallin definitely hadn't helped. I'd waited until I saw him emerging from the trees before I got in my car and drove off. Just to make sure he hadn't got himself lost or fallen into a bog. It was weird how I hadn't thought about him for so long – not to wonder where he was or if he was okay or anything – and now he'd unexpectedly come back into my life, I'd fallen into my old fretful routine. Like somehow I was responsible for him.

It was something I'd picked up from our dad. Whenever Dad talked about Dallin, it was always in terms of concern. 'I worry about that boy,' he would say. 'Cooped up in that house.' Dad never quite got over Dallin's insistence on living with Mum. Maybe I didn't either.

I stopped myself looking in the rear-view mirror more than once as I drove away.

Back home, I automatically checked the doormat, but no more letters had arrived. Thank God. Sometimes they arrived in scutches – four or five in the space of a week. Other times, a full month could pass without a single one of those awful, accusatory envelopes. If they'd been regular, I perhaps could've braced for the anger and guilt each one caused.

I made a cup of tea and drank it at the kitchen table. The kitchen was still the most neutral room in the house despite the invasion of people yesterday. I turned my chair so I was facing the room instead of the windows. The magnets on the fridge door were bright spots of colour. Places we'd never gone; never even intended to go, not really. I'd never quite understood why Beth insisted on collecting them. But maybe I saw it now. They were aspirations, dreams. Never intended to be real.

I spent the afternoon cleaning the kitchen. It was out of my routine – usually I did the kitchen on Mondays – but everything was out of routine anyway. It would take me weeks to find my equilibrium again.

Cora wanted to speak to Mum. But, of course, she didn't need me for that. Dallin could make the introductions. Presumably once he'd actually told our mother he was here on the island.

I scrubbed harder at a non-existent stain on the worktop. *Dallin.* Why hadn't he called her? His own mother. What on earth was his problem? Why was he never here except when we didn't want him to be?

Had they argued? Mum hadn't said anything. She told me everything. Didn't she?

I blew a strand of hair away from my face. Tomorrow was Saturday. I was due to visit Mum on Sunday morning as usual. If Dallin hadn't told her by then, I would have to. That would be a fun conversation.

Perhaps I should call her now. Give her fair warning her son might possibly be in contact with her.

But talking to people was something else I'd fallen out of the habit of. I hadn't used the telephone in weeks. The last person I spoke to, thinking about it, was probably the scammer who called me last month asking if I wanted to change my service provider.

No, I didn't want to tell Mum over the phone. Honestly, I wasn't sure I wanted to tell her at all. Quite apart from anything else, it was Dallin's job. I felt another flash of anger. Why should I do anything for him? After the way he'd treated me and Beth ... after what he'd said this morning ...

The house phone rang with a sharp jangle that made me jump. I stood in the kitchen, listening to the noise as it echoed through the house. Then, even though I knew it had to be Dallin, I went to answer.

As it turned out, it was Cora. Her voice was much nicer to hear than my brother's.

'I just wanted to check you're okay,' she said. 'Dallin gave me your number. I hope that's alright.'

I sat down on the third step of the stairs. The phone cable was just long enough. 'Sure, of course. Why wouldn't it be?'

'Well, I guess because you were upset earlier. And that's pretty much my fault.'

'What? No, no, of course it's not.' I laughed. 'It's just me and Dallin. Nothing to do with you.'

'Still, it wouldn't have happened if I hadn't been here.' There was background noise behind her; wind, possibly trees. She was still out in the curraghs. 'I'm heading to The Raven tonight to see if anyone remembers anything. From what Dallin says, people in the pubs here are more than happy to chat.'

'Sure.' I didn't hold out hope that anyone would remember anything useful.

'Do you—' Cora's voice was hesitant, shy. 'Do you want to come with me tonight? I'd like to buy you a drink. For your help.'

I closed my eyes. Leaned my head against the cool plaster of the wall at my side. Briefly, I pictured the warmth of the pub, the noise of people talking and laughing. Beth and I had enjoyed a few evenings at The Raven, although it wasn't our favourite haunt. It was slightly too far to walk there. But it was as close to a local as we'd had. I wondered, if I strolled in tonight, whether the same old faces would be there to greet me. People who'd known me since childhood.

I imagined sitting at one of the cramped tables with Cora, our elbows so close they would touch every time we lifted our drinks.

'I'm not sure,' I said carefully.

'It's okay,' she said at once. 'It's been a busy day. I understand if you're not feeling up to it.'

In the background, I heard Dallin's voice, asking a question. Cora covered the mouthpiece briefly while she answered him.

'Is Dallin going with you?' I asked.

'No. He's staying at the campsite. I'll be fine on my own.'

I had no doubt of that. I'd just wanted to check if he'd be at the pub. After what he'd said that morning, I was quite sure I didn't want to talk to him.

'What time are you going?' I asked.

Chapter 9

It felt as though every head in the room should've turned towards me as I pushed open the door. Thunder should've crashed or a choir should've sung. Something at least should've happened to mark what was, for me, a momentous occasion.

But no. No one even looked up from their drinks.

The Raven was a cosy pub, recently renovated to give it that modern, homogenous feel in keeping with the other pubs in the brewery's chain. Grey walls and dark wood. Some of the original features remained untouched, such as the open fire in the lounge bar and the little alcoves that were barely big enough to squash a table and two chairs into.

I paused at the threshold. The room was filled with light and noise, even though there were only a handful of people inside. I expected a wave of memories to flow over me. But I was too anxious, my nerves wound too tight, for me to focus on anything except how loud it was.

Cora spotted me before I spotted her. She gave me a wave from the bar. I went over to her gratefully.

'So glad you made it,' she said.

She'd obviously just arrived as well, as the barman was

pouring her a drink. I tugged off my hat and shoved it into the pocket of my jacket. It was warm in there after the cold of outside. I felt the heat of the fire on my face and hands. Even though my scalp started to prickle, I was reluctant to take off my jacket. I'd thrown on a T-shirt and jeans before leaving the house, and it suddenly occurred to me I might be wrongly dressed. I glanced covertly at Cora. She was wearing the same muddy trousers and jumper from that morning. Obviously she hadn't worried about getting changed.

'What're you drinking?' she asked.

I shook my head. I'd driven, since I didn't drink, but my brain stalled at the simple question. I didn't want anything with caffeine, or too much sugar, or large amounts of artificial sweeteners. That severely limited my choices. I settled on a slimline tonic.

While Cora ordered my drink, I sneaked a look at the people around us. Maybe a few had noticed me, but most minded their own business – or pretended to. I caught a couple of ill-concealed side-eyes from two women at a table. A man at the other end of the bar regarded me and Cora, flicked his eyes up and down us both, then dismissed us in favour of the television above the bar. I felt the familiar urge to hunch my shoulders and make myself unobtrusive.

'Anyone useful here?' Cora asked. She too was people-watching, although much better than me. She used the same cool, appraising glance as the man at the end of the bar, making it look like she was mostly uninterested.

I forced myself to lift my head. 'Those two women at the table near the back door,' I said. 'Kendra and Felice. They both went to school with Dallin. And over there, that fella with the dog, he's always here.' I gestured as subtly as I could at a man in a battered leather jacket at the other side of the room. He had a broadsheet newspaper spread out in front of him, covering the small table, one corner weighed down by a pint of lager. Beneath the table, a black-and-white terrier snoozed, its ears occasionally twitching if someone walked too close.

'Who is he?' Cora asked. She sipped the pint the barman had delivered.

'Lenny. He's a handyman, I suppose. One of those people who do odd jobs for everyone. I think he's a landscape gardener, officially, but he's the unofficial person everyone calls if they need something done.' I picked up my glass of tonic. 'He did some building work for Mum, before she had to move out.'

'So, he knows all the local gossip?'

'If there's anything to know, he's the person to ask.'

'Perfect. Let's go say hi.'

I was glad not to have to speak to the two women, Kendra and Felice, instead. I remembered Kendra vaguely, because she'd been at some of the same parties as me and Dallin over the years. Felice, I knew, had been good friends with Beth, once upon a time. Both Kendra and Felice – and Lenny, now I thought about it – had been at Beth's funeral. I couldn't remember speaking to any of them at the time. I certainly hadn't spoken to them since. So I had no idea how they felt about me. At best I could expect sympathy, maybe pity. At worst ...

Well, I knew how some people felt. I had the letters to prove it.

As soon as Lenny saw us approaching, he straightened up in his seat. His smile crinkled his whole face. Years of working in the sun had weathered his skin. Only the deep creases of his laughter lines were still pale.

I introduced Cora and asked if we could sit down. Lenny scooted his stool over so there was room for us at the tiny table. I kept hold of my drink rather than put it on his newspaper.

'And how're you keeping?' Lenny asked me. 'Haven't seen you out for a good while. Everything alright?'

'Fine. Thank you.' I reddened under his scrutiny.

'And your mam? I've not seen her in town for a few weeks. She keeping okay?'

One reason why Lenny knew everyone was because he made such efforts to keep tabs on us all. He'd turned up unannounced several times at my house, 'just on the off-chance you needed something doing'. He was like the caretaker of the whole neighbourhood.

I fielded some small talk until I could direct the conversation back to Cora. 'I was telling Cora about the time I got lost in the curraghs,' I told Lenny.

'Oh, aye. That was a right time. Your mam phoned me as soon as she realised you were gone. I got there first, but of course none of us knew where you'd gone.' Lenny took a sip of his pint. His eyes crinkled at Cora. 'She gave us a right scare. I was right at the front looking for her. Took me an hour before I found out she'd come back to the road. And then the next day she had us out again, looking for that skellington.'

Cora leaned forwards. 'You went searching with the police?'

'Well ... it wasn't *with* the police, exactly.' Lenny scratched his stubbled chin. 'Me and me brother went out the next morning on our own. Figured if anyone had a chance of finding the skellington you'd mentioned, it'd be folks that know the land. So we set off in there to have a skeet before anyone else showed up. Of course, once the police turned up we had to pretend like we'd only just arrived. Didn't want them thinking we were doing them out of a job.'

I hadn't heard this before. I glanced at Cora. She'd narrowed her eyes in thought. 'I take it you didn't find anything,' she said.

'Not a thing. That's not to say there wasn't something to find. Just that we didn't happen to see it.'

'And your brother, he didn't see anything either?'

'Neither of us did. I'd ask him for you, but he's been dead ten years so he's not likely to say much.' Lenny laughed.

It always shocked me how people could joke about relatives who'd died. I could barely bring myself to say Beth's name aloud. Would there ever come a time when I could make a carefree remark about her, and laugh?

Cora was smiling, encouraging Lenny. 'How come the two of you went looking on your own?' she asked. 'Shouldn't you have waited for the police?'

'Perhaps.' Lenny gave a broad-shouldered shrug. 'We were just being helpful. We figured it couldn't hurt.'

'You must live pretty close to the wetlands, if you were the first ones there.'

I missed Lenny's reply, because I happened to look across the room and saw Dallin.

He was sitting at the table near the back door with Felice and Kendra. I blinked. Where the hell had he come from? Judging by the way he was leaning forwards, elbows comfortably on the table, he'd been there a while, chatting away with the two women. He laughed at something Kendra said.

As if feeling my eyes on him, he looked up and met my gaze. His expression didn't change. There was no bruise on his face where I'd hit him earlier. I didn't know if I was glad about that or not.

He smiled, but it was clear he was smiling at something Kendra had said. His gaze slipped away from me. It felt like a dismissal.

Cora was asking Lenny something else. I leaned in to interrupt. 'When did Dallin get here?' I asked.

Cora looked surprised. 'He came with me. I told you we were heading to the pub.'

'You said he wasn't coming.'

Cora's brow creased. 'He wasn't planning to, but he changed his mind. I'm sure I told you that. Didn't I?'

I said nothing, because I couldn't now be certain what Cora had said on the phone. But I definitely would've thought twice about coming to the pub if I'd known Dallin would be here.

Lenny tilted his head to peer at Dallin. 'Oh. That one's back, is he?' He didn't sound impressed. 'Hope he's not planning on causing any more trouble.'

'Why?' Cora asked. 'What trouble did he cause?'

The question was addressed to both of us, but I could only shrug. Dallin had upset a lot of people when he took off.

'It's probably not my place to say,' Lenny said, in a way that suggested he was quite happy to do so, 'but if he's back, I hope he's brought his chequebook. There're one or two folk who might come looking for the money he owes.'

That was news to me. But somehow it didn't surprise me. Dallin had never been careful with money. Once he was old enough to leave school and start working, he would always have new clothes, or the latest games console, or whatever. As soon as money went into his pocket it went straight back out again. By the end of the week, he'd be trying to sponge off his friends.

'Like who?' Cora asked. She had a way of smiling when she asked a question that stopped it feeling pushy.

'He knows who he owes,' Lenny said. His mouth pursed into a sour line as he watched Dallin. 'I'm sure he hasn't forgotten. To be safe, you might want to remind him. Just in case.'

Dallin got up and took his empty glass to the bar. I stood up as well. 'Back in a minute,' I mumbled to Cora.

I crossed the room to Dallin, who was leaning against the bar in a casual attempt to catch the barman's attention. He spotted me approaching and his face took on a cautious expression.

'What're you doing here?' I asked.

'It's a free country, isn't it?' he replied.

I looked Dallin up and down. His eyes were slightly

unfocused. How long had he been in the pub? Cora said he'd arrived with her, but I wasn't sure I believed that.

'I suppose you're expecting an apology,' he added.

His grudging tone immediately annoyed me. 'Dallin,' I sighed. 'It doesn't matter what I expect. If you don't care what you've done wrong, it's not up to me to educate you. So, no, I don't expect an apology. I'm just shocked you don't think you *should* apologise. Don't you realise what you did to us?'

'I'm sorry I wasn't there for Beth—'

'That's not what I'm talking about. When you left, you broke Mum's heart.'

Dallin pulled a face. 'I did not. I call her all the time. She's fine.'

'Is that genuinely what you think?'

'Are you telling me she isn't fine?'

'Of course she's not.' My voice was rising. A woman at the bar looked up. 'She's needed all our help these last few years. She should've had me *and* you.' *And Beth, and Dad.* But I couldn't say that aloud without tears choking me. 'You left us to cope without you.'

'No, see—' Dallin gave a loose shrug that made him look more drunk than he probably was. 'See, I *couldn't* stay. I couldn't deal with it. I'm not strong.'

'You idiot,' I said with feeling. 'There was no call for you to be strong. You just had to be here.' I considered storming off at that point, but instead held back for a second, and said, 'I'm going to see Mum tomorrow morning. You're coming with me. Alright?'

Dallin pulled a face, which I ignored. I turned on my heel

and walked out. It didn't occur to me to go back to Cora. My whole focus was on getting out of the building.

I made it as far as the smoking area out front before Cora caught up with me.

'Rosalie,' she called. I stopped. 'You okay?'

'I need to go home,' I said. 'Sorry.'

To her credit, she didn't ask questions, just nodded her understanding. 'Will you text me when you get home?' she asked. 'Let me know you got there?'

'I don't have your number.'

Cora produced one of her many pens, but for once she didn't have a piece of paper to scribble on. With a smile, she took my hand and wrote her number on my skin. I was too surprised to resist.

She squeezed my hand then let go. 'Text me,' she said. 'Okay?'

Chapter 10

As soon as I got home I searched for a scrap of paper to write down Cora's number. I could still feel the warmth of her hand as she'd held mine.

I reached for the notepad on the phone table, before remembering the pad belonged to Beth. There were only a dozen blank sheets left, and once they were used up I would have to throw it out, and that would be another bit of Beth gone forever. I dithered for a moment, then scrawled Cora's number on the back of a phone bill instead.

The most difficult part of texting Cora was finding my mobile and, once found, locating a charger. Offhand I couldn't remember the last time I'd used my mobile. It was weird to recall how I'd once been plugged into it constantly, unable to leave it in the house when I went out. If I left the house without my phone, I'd go back for it. If it ran out of charge, I'd get sick with worry. Funny how things change.

I hesitated over what to send her, and opted for, *Sorry I had to leave. Hope you didn't have a wasted evening.*

Cora texted me straight back. Also funny, how my heart

I guess he remembered how I'd always been unable to settle when we were kids; constantly getting up to use the bathroom or get a drink of water. Except during thunderstorms, when perversely I'd always slept better than him. Dallin had a real phobia of lightning.

'I'm a lot better,' I said. And then, because I wanted to match his snippy tone, 'The tablets I'm on now help, of course.'

Dallin's gaze went back to the window. I subtly tried to see whether I'd left a mark on his face when I'd hit him yesterday. I still couldn't believe I'd done that. It'd been an awful thing to do, and I knew I should apologise. I also knew I wasn't going to.

'Honestly, I'm already missing my creature comforts,' Cora said, either oblivious to Dallin's mood or deliberately talking over it. 'I always say how much I like camping, until I actually go camping, at which point I remember what a ball-ache it is. My blow-up mattress got a puncture.'

I smiled. 'Oh no.'

'Bloody thing was brand new. Straight out of the box and it pops the first time I sit my arse on it.'

'What were you doing on it?' I couldn't stop myself from asking.

'Sleeping. Nothing else,' Cora said. 'Chance would be a fine thing.'

I shot a glance at Dallin, who'd scrunched down further in his seat. Yesterday he'd looked hungover. Today he looked like someone had kept him awake all night, then stolen his breakfast.

On the other hand, he was here, coming with us to see his

mother, even if he didn't look happy about it. I'd half expected him to change his mind.

'How did you get on at the pub after I left?' I asked.

'Okay, I guess,' Cora said. 'I want to know more about Lenny.'

'Lenny? Why?'

'Because he went into the wetlands the day after you went missing. He said it was to help the police, but what if it wasn't? What if he *knew* you'd found something, and he wanted to make sure it was better hidden?'

That sounded extremely unlikely. I couldn't imagine anyone doing such a thing. Especially Lenny.

'He's a nosy old bugger,' Dallin put in. 'That's why he led the search party for Rosie. He can't bear the thought of something happening that he's not a part of.'

'You sound like you don't like him,' I said.

'He's a busybody. Always poking his nose in. He was forever turning up on Mum's doorstep like some creepy stalker. No, I don't like him.'

'I always quite liked him,' I said, to stir the pot.

'That's his trick. He gets you on his side, and he offers to help you out with whatever, and he's all smiles until he reckons you owe him something.'

I remembered what Lenny said yesterday about Dallin's debts. I wanted to ask Dallin about the money he apparently owed, but maybe not in front of Cora.

'We talked to a few other people as well,' Cora said. 'Kendra and ... who was the other?'

'Felice,' Dallin supplied. 'Haven't seen them in years.'

'They didn't know anything about Simone though,' Cora added to me.

'Well, they wouldn't, would they?' Dallin said. 'Both too young.'

'They're the same age as you, Dallin,' I said. 'Who knows? They might remember something.' Stirring the pot again. Cora caught my eye with a smile.

Dallin glowered. 'Sure, they remember what a pain you were. That skeleton was all you'd talk about for months. Every weekend you'd remind us. They all laughed about it.'

I ducked my head to hide my expression. Beth had been part of that social group too. Had she laughed about me behind my back as well?

'Felice asked how you were getting on,' Dallin added. His tone was uninterested. 'Why didn't you keep in touch?'

'She was Beth's friend. Not mine.'

'More than just her friend, the way I heard it,' he said with a laugh.

I wished I'd hit him a bit harder when I'd had the chance.

Cora drove us to the outskirts of Ramsey, then through the housing estate to the flats where Mum lived. The buildings had that identikit, too-clean look. It would take a few years for the sheen to wear off.

Once we'd parked in a visitor space, Cora shut off the engine and asked, 'So, what's your mum like, Rosalie? How does she react to visitors? Is she cool with people just showing up, or ...?'

I glanced at Dallin, but he seemed completely disinclined to take the lead. 'Honestly, I'm not sure,' I said. 'Her friends visit all the time.' Did Dallin flinch? 'Those are people she's known for years, though. I've never tried springing two visitors on her at once. Did you call her, Dallin?'

Dallin shook his head. 'She wasn't answering the phone.'

That was an obvious lie. Mum always answered her phone.

'So, what do you think?' Cora asked.

I sighed. 'Let me and Dallin go in first. We'll see how she's feeling today.'

Really I should've sent Dallin in alone, to explain himself. It wasn't my job to cover for him. But I understood how that might upset our mother.

The flat where Mum lived was tucked away in one of the many side streets of Ramsey. When she'd first come out of the hospital, we'd looked at a dozen places that might suit her. The problem was, she'd never like anywhere as much as she loved her little house next to the curraghs. There'd been a lot of tears, those first few weeks. But the simple fact was Mum couldn't go back to her old house. I wished there'd been a way to adapt the house to her new needs. But, in the end, we found this little ground floor flat, without any stairs, with a wet-room, and with a little patch of garden out front.

Most of her plants were in tubs now, placed on top of sturdy tables to bring them to a manageable height, but it was still a riot of colour. Mum's gardening abilities were as strong as ever.

I glanced back at Dallin, who was following me at a distance. His expression was carefully neutral as he looked at the exterior of our mother's home. It struck me that he hadn't seen it before. The last time he'd been on the island, as far as I knew, was when Mum was in hospital. When it'd looked like she might not leave the hospital. He'd come home then, and stayed for a full two weeks, long enough to hear the doctors start voicing cautious optimism. I'd assumed he would stay for longer, to help get Mum home, but of course I was wrong. He'd left, like always. The task of finding Mum new accommodation fell to me. Never mind that I was grieving too.

I should've felt bitter. But there'd been no room to dwell on it during that long, awful summer. Mum had bought this flat with her savings. I'd spent two harsh months clearing out Dad's house so it could go up for sale. Then I moved into Mum's farmhouse, paying a token rent, with the understanding I would keep the place maintained. Because Mum was certain she would get better. And when she did, she wanted the option of moving back home.

'This is only temporary,' she'd said on more than one occasion.

And there was one other change that summer. The advocate who dealt with the financial side of selling my dad's house sounded vaguely familiar the first time I spoke to her on the phone. The penny dropped when she said she knew my mum from years ago. Really, I should've recognised Beth's voice. Later, she would tease me about that.

'I knew it was you straight away,' she would say. 'You're distinctive, Rosalie.'

At the front door of Mum's flat, I paused, blinking away memories. For five years, me and Beth had made these visits together. Even now, I still felt like I could've turned my head and glimpsed her shadow at my side.

I knocked on the door, then pushed it open. 'Hello,' I called. 'It's me.'

Without waiting for an answer, I went in. Dallin followed as far as the hallway.

Mum was in her chair by the window, which would've looked out over a field, except the neighbours had let their hedge get rangy and straggly over the spring, and it now all but obscured the view. Still, Mum liked to sit here, because it let her watch the birds at the feeders.

She looked up with a smile. 'Hello, pumpkin,' she said. 'How's tricks?'

It was sometimes hard for me to remember that she was only in her fifties. The accident had broken part of her spirit as well as a substantial part of her body, and left her looking far older than she should've. Her hair had faded like paper left too long in the sun. There were crinkles around her eyes that deepened whenever she was under the weather. She'd long since abandoned the loose, flowing dresses that I remembered so clearly from childhood, instead falling into the comfortable habit of jogging pants and baggy jumpers. She hadn't entirely ditched her unique sense of style, though. The jumper she wore today was red with little black dots, like the cross-section of a watermelon. Her earrings and necklace were strings of brightly coloured wooden beads. With a jolt, I recognised the jewellery as a set me and Beth had bought for her, a few years ago.

She wheeled herself forward to greet me. I caught hold of her hand. 'I'm fine, fine,' I said, laughing, because just being in the same room as her automatically made me feel better.

'Now, I've got a surprise for you. I wanted to make sure you were sitting comfortably. Don't fall out of your chair, okay?'

Mum let out a hoot of laughter. 'Wait, wait. Let me adequately prepare myself.' She picked up her glasses from the side table, then adjusted her position in her chair and drew a dramatic breath. 'Alright, yes, I believe I am now prepared. What surprise do you have for me?'

I stepped aside, to reveal Dallin hovering in the doorway, hands in pockets.

'Hi Mum,' he said.

If I'd hoped for an emotional reunion, I knew at once I wouldn't get one. Mum blinked at her son a few times, then took off her glasses with a sigh. 'I suppose I should've asked whether it was a nice surprise,' she said.

Dallin came into the room. Silence stretched between the three of us.

I wasn't sure what I'd been expecting. From Dallin's evasive answers yesterday, I'd guessed he wasn't keen on visiting our mother, but I'd assumed it was because of some Dallin-esque issue; the same thing that made him run rather than cope. It hadn't occurred to me maybe she didn't want to see him either.

For a moment I just stood there like a lump. 'I'll put the kettle on,' I said at last.

The kitchen wasn't even a separate room, just an adjacent space jutting off from the sitting area, with a lowered breakfast bar dividing the two. All the cabinets and counters were below waist height so Mum could use them. I stood with my back to the other room while I filled the kettle and put it on to boil, but it wasn't like I could avoid hearing Dallin and

Mum. Or rather, not hearing them. It was a full minute before Dallin broke the silence.

'How are you, Mum?' he asked.

'Well.' She folded her glasses in her lap, then folded her hands on top of them. 'I suppose I've been better, but I've also been worse, which makes this about average, I would think.'

Dallin moved the spare chair so he could sit near her. 'I'm sorry I didn't call before I arrived,' he said. 'I emailed Rosie but I don't think she got my message.'

I bit my tongue to stop myself correcting him again.

'Hmm. That explains your absence for the last week or so,' Mum said. 'Now, what's your excuse for the rest of the five years you've been gone without a word?'

I smiled to myself. Mum was never one to dance around an issue.

'I guess I don't have an excuse,' Dallin said. I could hear him smiling as well, that charming smile he always tried to use. 'I'm just—'

I missed what he said next, because the kettle was coming to the boil. I dropped a teabag into Mum's cup, then realised I hadn't asked Dallin whether he wanted tea or coffee. Well, he was getting tea. Decaffeinated tea, at that. As I opened the fridge to retrieve the milk, I sneaked a glance at Dallin. He looked uncomfortable and contrite in equal measures.

'I kept your letters,' Mum was saying. 'The postcards you sent when you were off on your travels. They're in a box somewhere.'

'That's good, I'm glad they arrived. You know what it's like, sometimes, when you're on the road, you never know whether the post will get where it's supposed to go.'

On the road. I rolled my eyes as I stirred milk into the tea. Dallin's much-vaulted year of travelling had got him as far as Barcelona, where he worked in a tourist bar for nine months, house-sat someone's pet turtle, and drank a lot of bad sangria. I knew this because Beth had followed his exploits on social media. We'd done plenty of eye-rolling then as well.

'It was nice to be kept up to date,' Mum said. 'Although I notice you never put a return address on your postcards.'

'I should've. Sorry.'

Even if she *had* sent him letters, there would've been another excuse why he didn't reply to them. I knew that as well, because he'd never responded to Beth's messages on Facebook.

I brought the tea over. Mum gave me a smile as I set hers down on the table next to her. Her face was strained. She kept her hands pressed tightly together in her lap.

'So, sweetie,' she said to Dallin, 'I assume there's some reason why you've come home. It's not my birthday, or yours, or Rosalie's. And I really hope you haven't burned through all your money already. So, what other reason do you have?'

Even I thought that was a bit harsh. But I'd been caught out by the mention of money. Had Mum been sending cash to Dallin? It reminded me of what Lenny had said last night.

'I'm helping out a friend,' he said. 'It was, kinda, a last-minute decision for me to come with her.'

'Hmm. Which friend is this?'

'Her name's Cora. You haven't met her, but I was hoping you could say hi. She's got a favour to ask you.'

'Is that the friend who's loitering in the hall, pretending I can't see her?'

I failed to stifle a laugh. 'Cora, you're not really in the hall, are you?' I called.

There was a pause, then Cora stuck her head around the doorframe. Embarrassment reddened her face. 'I'm sorry,' she said. 'Dallin left the door open.'

'Yes, I wondered about that,' Mum said. 'Well, come in, honey. Don't hover in the doorway.'

Cora came into the room. She tucked her hair behind her ears self-consciously. 'I'm Cora. Hi. Sorry. This is a lot more awkward than I was hoping.'

'We weren't sure how you'd feel about us all coming in at once,' Dallin said.

'I can see your point,' Mum said. 'I would've liked a chance to fetch some extra chairs from the other room. Now you'll have to stand.'

I blew on my tea. 'You don't have spare chairs. I used to bring a garden chair if I wanted to sit down.'

'It's a cunning ploy to stop people outstaying their welcome.' Mum held out a hand. 'Lovely to meet you, Cora. I'm Opal. Excuse me for not getting up.'

Cora smiled as best she could. I knew people tended to get flustered by my mum. Half the time they looked aghast when she joked about her wheelchair. 'Lovely to meet you too.'

Cora was awkward and hesitant, standing there in the

middle of Mum's sparse room, but I could see the resolution behind her eyes. She'd steeled her nerves before coming into the room. I recognised it from the first time we'd met.

'Cora's looking for her sister,' Dallin said.

I moved a couple of magazines so I could pull up the sewing seat for Cora. We did the awkward thing where she insisted on me sitting down instead and I had to pretend I was happier standing. Once she was seated, I went back into the kitchen. It was getting crowded in the small front room.

'My sister came here about twenty years ago,' Cora said. 'At least, we think she did. I'm trying to find out if anyone remembers her.'

'Well. I don't know,' Mum said. 'Twenty years? I would've moved to the farmhouse about then. Where Rosalie's living now. You two were just kids,' she said to me and Dallin.

'Simone would've been fifteen,' Cora said, reaching into her pocket. 'I've got a photo.'

The photograph was tucked securely into a pouch of her wallet. I wondered why she hadn't shown it to me. Even if there was zero chance I would've recognised Simone, wasn't it instinctive to show everyone the picture?

Mum had to put her glasses back on. She scrutinised the photo carefully before passing it back. 'She looks a lot like you, doesn't she?' Mum said.

'Do you think?' Cora glanced at the photo as well, as if she'd never been aware of any family resemblance.

I looked over her shoulder. The girl in the picture was slim and blonde, with a carefree smile. The camera had captured her sitting on a woollen blanket on the grass somewhere. I would've known at a glance Simone and Cora were related. Perhaps if Cora had been less burdened down with worry right now, they would've looked even more alike.

'Do you recognise her?' Cora asked hopefully.

'I'm sorry, love, I don't.' Mum shook her head with a sad smile. 'Do you have a more recent photo?'

'She disappeared a few months after this was taken. That's why I'm here, to figure out what happened to her.'

Mum raised her eyebrows in surprise. 'Twenty years is a long time to look for someone. Have you considered she might not want to be found?'

'Mum,' Dallin said, his expression pained.

'I don't mean to be insensitive,' Mum insisted. 'But if someone's been gone for that long and they've not been in contact ...'

'I'm not expecting to find her,' Cora said. 'I just want to know what happened.'

Mum's face crinkled. She reached out and patted Cora's knew. 'I'm sorry. Genuinely I'm sorry. I know what it's like to lose someone you care about. You never quite get over it.'

I turned away and pretended to be looking at something out of the window.

'She looks a little like – oh, who am I thinking of?' Mum tutted to herself. 'Can I see the photo again? My memory's so bad these days. You'd think it'd be easier to remember the important stuff, now I don't have so much everyday nonsense to remember. Let me see.' She raised her head then. 'Rosalie, did you ever meet Nicola and Patrick's niece? She's a bit older than you, lives in Birkenhead these days?'

I shook my head without even trying to recall a face. I was dimly aware of other people's families, but if there was someone important I needed to remember, Beth would remind me. And, now she was gone, there seemed less point keeping tabs on random people.

'We think Simone came here in June 1999,' Cora said. 'I know it was a long time ago, but do you remember seeing her around? She might've been travelling through this part of the island, or catching a lift off someone ...'

The thin edge of desperation in her voice was painful. What were the chances of someone remembering a random teenage girl wandering along a country road twenty years ago? Chances were, I wouldn't remember something like that from a month ago. We sometimes felt like we were a long way from the busier towns, but we weren't really that isolated. A person could drive up from Douglas in half an hour. So we often saw strangers, walking their dogs or strolling along the footpaths. Unless Simone had spoken directly to anyone for a length of time, it was unlikely they'd remember her.

Mum shook her head again. It was obvious she wanted to help, and equally obvious she couldn't. 'Have you asked around the neighbourhood?' she asked. 'Not here, obviously, but around the back road. There's a good few of us who've lived there for more than twenty years.' She pursed her lips. 'However. If you'll accept some advice, I don't think you're going to have much luck.'

'We know that.' It was Dallin who spoke. He held his cup of tea cradled in both hands, although it must've been almost too hot to hold. 'I told her, if there was any interesting gossip, we would've heard it long ago. You can't keep anything off the Manx grapevine.'

Mum raised her eyebrows. 'Still, it's very noble of you to help Cora look for her sister. How long have you two been together?'

Dallin coughed into his tea.

'We're just friends,' Cora said smoothly. 'We met online.'

'Oh, really? A lot of people are doing that these days.' Mum looked from Cora to me. 'What about my Rosalie? Are you more than just friends with her?'

'Mum,' Dallin said, like a teenager. His cheeks were red.

'It's a fair question.' Mum leaned towards Cora and added in a stage whisper, 'Our Rosalie has been on her own for a bit long now. It's probably time she found someone to look after her.'

I sighed. 'Mother—'

'Beth wouldn't have wanted you to be on your own forever.'

I thought Mum was wrong about that. I was never the sort to need constant company and constant reassurance. Beth had been the same. She always disparaged people who couldn't possibly go to the cinema or a museum on their own. 'How can you go through life like that?' she would ask. 'Why can't people be alone?'

If our situations were reversed – if it'd been me who'd died – I wouldn't have wanted Beth to be lonely, obviously, but I also couldn't picture her diving into a new relationship just for the sake of being with someone. It wasn't who she was. I assumed she'd felt the same about me. The question had never come up between us, not when she got sick, not when it became clear I would have to spend the rest of my life without her, not ever.

I'd never thought about finding someone else. I didn't miss company or closeness. The only thing I missed was Beth.

But no one seemed to understand that. So I put on a difficult smile. 'I'm just helping Cora,' I said. 'Sorry.'

'Hmm.' Mum didn't look nearly convinced. 'Well, even if your sister did come here, she certainly didn't stay. We hardly ever get new people moving to this area.'

I chewed my thumbnail. 'Mum, do you remember the skeleton I found, when I was a kid?'

'Oh my goodness, yes. Everyone remembers that.' Mum scrunched up her face as if the thought caused her physical pain. 'We were so scared when you went missing. I know it was only a few hours, but it felt a lot longer to us, I can tell you. How would I ever face your poor father if I'd managed to lose his only daughter?'

'But you remember me telling you about the skeleton, right?'

Mum pursed her lips. Over the past few years she'd gained some extra wrinkles, and they made her face more expressive, exaggerating everything she did. 'I remember you telling everyone, of course. But, you have to understand, I also remember you telling plenty of other stories. Do you remember the invisible cat that would follow you to school? Or the mice who stole things from your bedside table?'

Heat rose to my cheeks. I recalled those stories well enough.

'Remember the ghost lights you saw up on the hill?' Dallin asked. 'You told everyone a flying saucer had landed.'

'Children have the most amazing imaginations,' Mum said gently. 'They can tell a story so many times it becomes real in their heads.'

I remembered arguing with Dad about the invisible cat that followed me to school. I recalled how three of my earrings went missing, and I'd been convinced they were somehow stolen by mice. I remember fretting about aliens landing on the hill behind our house.

But those were daft stories. Even at the time, I'd known there was no truth behind them. There was never any intention for anyone to take them seriously.

I had to turn back to the window to hide my expression, because it hurt me that Mum and Dallin would lump the discovery of the skeleton in with those obviously fake things. Had anyone fully believed me?

'I'm going to get some fresh air,' I said. 'Back in a minute.'

I emptied my tea into the sink and headed for the door before anyone could object.

You were scowling. You didn't want to be there. I told you I didn't either, and you said, 'So what?'

The whole family had gathered – Ma and Da and Da's brother with his gaggle of toddlers and his frazzled wife. We sat on mismatched blankets on the scrubby grass of the park, feigning excitement about the decadence of cheese sandwiches and scotch eggs in the open air. The toddlers chased a football. Jason dozed on the blanket next to us, his arm over his face. I turned my face to the sun in the vain hope of a tan.

'Smile, will ya?' said Ma. She held up the camera. 'It's not a bloody funeral.'

You smirked for the camera. I tried to copy you, but my face was softer and rounder, so when I saw the picture later, it looked like I was actually enjoying myself.

'At a funeral there'd be better catering,' you said.

Mum scowled at you. 'Don't start, Simone. Not today.'

More family trickled into the park. Mum's niece, who looked too old to be anyone's niece, and her yappy Pomeranian. A couple more cousins we'd only see once in a blue moon. That one guy who always came along but no one was quite certain how he's related to us. The Pomeranian and the kids were equally spooked by each other.

A collective groan went round when a woman appeared, heading in our direction, with him *in tow.*

'I thought she wasn't coming,' Ma said under her breath.

'I tried to put her off,' said Da. Then, to all of us, he added, 'Remember, unless I say different, we treat him like family. Understand?'

It wasn't framed as a request. You smiled and said, too quiet for him to hear, 'We know how to treat family, right enough.'

'Florrie seems happy,' Ma said with cautious optimism. 'Maybe this one won't be so bad.'

No one except me was paying attention to you, so you tilted your head towards the sun and closed your eyes, with a smile that suggested you knew something we didn't.

Chapter 11

Outside, a wind had picked up, enough to pluck at my clothes and fluff my hair over my eyes. I shoved my hands into my pockets.

Breathe, I told myself.

'Rosalie, wait up!' Cora stepped out of Mum's flat behind me and pulled the door shut.

I waited, glad Dallin hadn't followed. I hoped he'd use this time to talk through whatever problem stood between him and Mum.

'Are you okay?' Cora asked.

'Just wanted some fresh air,' I said. 'I get a little ... hemmed in, when there are so many people in a small room. It can feel a bit overwhelming. But you should stay. Talk with Mum.'

'She told me to check on you. I think she wanted some time with Dallin. And, to be honest, I think she's told us everything she knows. She doesn't remember Simone.'

'I thought she probably wouldn't. Sorry.'

'I know. It's just ... you can't help getting your hopes up, can you?' The wind blew strands of hair across her face. 'I keep expecting to get a sudden breakthrough, where someone will turn around and tell me, yes, I remember your sister. It's hard not to hope for too much. I've been chasing weird rumours and old stories for so long, almost anything can sound like a solid tip-off. I have to stop myself jumping on the slightest thing that sounds promising.'

She unlocked the car. I got in the passenger seat, moving aside a paperback that'd been left lying on the seat. 'I'm sorry it wasn't more helpful,' I said.

'It's okay. I'd just like to get this search over and done with, y'know? It's infuriating when it feels like I'm running in quicksand. I don't like being,' Cora made a circling gesture at her own face, 'like this. Obsessive. I know that's how I act. It's upsetting. I just want some closure so I can go back to my normal life.'

I nodded. I would've liked a normal life again. I just needed to figure out what *normal* looked like.

'What happened to your mum?' Cora asked.

'A car accident. Quite a while ago now.' I decided that was probably as much as I wanted to say.

Cora nodded. 'Why doesn't Dallin talk about her?'

'I have no idea why Dallin does anything.' I picked up the book that'd been on the passenger seat. 'Is this yours?'

Her eyes drifted to the book. 'It's about the curraghs.' Cora put a finger on the cover. 'I found it on Amazon before we came here. It's mostly a catalogue of the fascinating different types of orchid you may or may not see, but it's got some of the history as well. Probably nothing we can use, but I like to know as much as I can.' Another smile. 'You never know when something will be useful.'

I buttoned up my coat. The car engine was off, the heater not running, and it was cold in there. I began to regret storming out of Mum's flat. 'Why did Simone run away?' I asked. It was something I'd been wondering.

'I don't know the exact reason. Everything. Nothing. Some people are like that, aren't they? I was upset when she left, but I wasn't surprised. She was never the sort of person to keep her roots. Still, it hurt when she upped and left without a word. I thought she'd at least say goodbye.'

'She didn't tell anyone where she was going?'

'No. She didn't have a lot of close friends anyway. She was difficult to know.' Cora smiled at a memory. 'When we were little, I thought we were like this,' she held up two fingers, crossed as if for luck. 'I think that's just how I remember it. I was nine when she left. How much can an immature nine-year-old and an over-mature fifteen-year-old have in common? I worry our friendship was all in my head.'

'What about the rest of your family?'

She pursed her lips. 'Ours is a big, sprawling family, y'know? The type where you've got five hundred cousins and half-cousins and no one's ever completely sure how you're related to each other because no one except me bothers to sit down with a pen and paper and map it all out.'

I nodded, although in honesty I didn't know what that was like. My family had consisted of me, Mum, Dad, and Dallin. A tree with few branches. If I'd ever troubled to draw it out in full, it would've made a depressing tree, petering out as it went down. Me and Dallin were the last of a slender line. I knew for a fact I would never have children, so if anyone wanted to carry on our lineage it'd have to be Dallin.

'And everyone was always falling out with one another,' Cora said. She took the book and flicked through it at random. 'We'd argue over the most pointless stuff, like whose fault it was that so-and-so argued with such-and-such on Christmas day twenty years ago. At any given time there's at least ten per cent of my family who aren't talking to a different ten per cent.' She lifted her gaze with a frown. 'I wonder if I brought it with me … I *did* draw out a family tree one time. It's in one of my notebooks.' She laughed. 'Family trees are like maps. I understand maps.'

'Cora …' I thought about what I wanted to say. 'What'll happen if you don't find Simone here? What then?'

'I'll keep looking.' There was no hesitation. 'I know it's difficult, and I know it's only going to get harder as more years go by and fewer people remember, but if I keep looking, I know I'll find her. She left traces behind when she vanished. I just have to track them.'

Her conviction was unnerving. 'How can you be so sure?'

'Because I always get where I'm going.' Cora smiled at me. 'Even if I hadn't found your story on Dallin's webpage, I would've come across it eventually.'

I blinked. '*Dallin's* webpage?'

'Yeah, the one with the skeleton in the marshlands story. I showed you the page, right?'

'Why do you say it's his?'

It was Cora's turn to blink. 'Because he wrote it. He told you that, right?' From my expression she must've guessed the answer. 'Oh my God. I always assumed he'd worked with you to put the story online ... he didn't tell you at all?'

Mutely, I shook my head. 'I didn't know it existed until the other day.'

'Fucking hell. I'm sorry. That must've been—' Cora shook her head in wonder. 'Wow, that's a shocker. I can't believe Dallin hadn't told you. What the hell must you have thought when we pitched up on your doorstep? I thought you'd been fully briefed about all this.'

I shook my head again. Inside, my stomach was twisting itself up in knots. Why hadn't Dallin told me the webpage was his work? Except, thinking about it, I already knew the answer. He knew I'd be upset he'd exposed my secrets to the online world. Far easier for him to pretend it was the work of some random person who'd heard my story and typed it up for all the world to see.

'I did wonder who'd written it,' I said, keeping my voice level. There were details on the webpage I didn't recall telling anyone – except maybe Dallin, when we were kids.

Cora's gaze turned to the window. 'Families,' she said, making the word sound like a curse. 'Most of mine lost patience with me a long time ago. As far as they're concerned, Simone is gone, and there's no point constantly chasing her shadow. One time my mum asked me, "Why do you even want her back?" I couldn't for the life of me think how to answer that.'

'What was Simone like?'

'Bitchy.' Cora glanced at the window, as if Simone's ghost might've unexpectedly come within earshot. 'I mean, what teenage girl isn't? But Simone took it to extremes. All the normal stuff – drinking, smoking, hanging out with incredibly unsuitable men, you know how it goes. She stole our dad's car once and crashed it into a roundabout. It was insane.' Cora sighed. 'Her and Da were always arguing. She made Ma cry at least twice a week.' She hesitated, then added, 'Not that we didn't love her, of course. I idolised her for a while. And then, after she disappeared, I blamed myself. I thought I'd put the idea into her head.'

'Why? What did you say to her?'

The front door of Mum's house opened and Dallin came out.

Cora started the engine. 'I told her to follow her heart,' she said, with a mirthless smile.

Chapter 12

Cora offered to drive me back to my house, and I surprised everyone – myself included – by inviting her to stay for lunch.

'Are you sure?' Cora asked. 'We can pick up some sandwiches if it's easier ...?'

'It's fine, I've got plenty of food. I can't guarantee it'll be better that the sandwiches from the Co-op though.' I smiled at her, although already my stomach was knotting itself and I was wondering if I could back out gracefully from my invitation without looking impolite. Also, I wasn't one hundred per cent certain I *did* have plenty of food.

'Alright, you're on.' Cora checked the time on the dashboard clock. 'It's still early. I'll do another hour or so of walking and then break for lunch, does that sound okay to you, Rosalie?'

'Sounds fine.' I twisted my hands in my lap. 'That'll give me time to fix something for lunch.'

'Am I invited too?' Dallin asked. It was the first thing he'd said to either of us since getting in the car.

I couldn't think of a reasonable way to say no, so I had to say yes.

'We don't need anything fancy,' Cora said. She reached over to touch my arm. It was a gentle, almost unconscious gesture, but I felt heat rush to my face. I stared out of the window because I was scared if I looked at her she'd see something in my expression I'd rather keep hidden.

Cora drove back to my house without needing directions. It didn't surprise me she was already finding her way around. I suspected she'd checked out the local routes on one of her trusty maps.

I unlocked my front door, while Cora did a seven-point-turn in the narrow lane outside my house. She waved before she drove off. It made me smile. Dallin kept his gaze fixed forward.

It was hard to figure out what Dallin's problem was. I hadn't asked him to come home. He'd made it clear from his years of silence that he wasn't interested in my life. Was he upset that me and Mum hadn't welcomed him back with open arms? What had he expected?

Dallin was the sort who assumed everyone's lives were on hold when he wasn't there. It must've been a shock to realise we hadn't been waiting anxiously for him to show his face.

Suck it up, Buttercup, Beth would've said to him.

There was a letter on the doormat. A plain Manila envelope with my name written in blocky handwriting on the front. No postage, because it'd been delivered by hand.

I felt all the confidence drain out of me. Two in one week? Why now?

I picked up the envelope like it was a twitchy snake. Right at that moment, I couldn't face opening it, or dealing with what it contained. I tucked it on the hall table underneath a pile of other post. Just its presence made a lead weight settle into my stomach.

They can't hurt you unless you let them, Beth would've said.

I went into the kitchen and dumped my bag on the table. Usually when I came back from visiting Mum, I would have groceries to unload. Again I felt the sting of my upset routine. In a way I was glad I'd offered to make lunch. Otherwise I would've had no idea what to do with myself. Tidy? Clean? I had no frame of reference for my current state of mind. Without something to occupy my hands, I would've sat at the kitchen table with a cup of tea, staring at nothing until night fell.

I rummaged in the fridge. A new edge of panic pushed its way into my stomach. What on earth possessed me to invite two people to my house for food? I hadn't cooked for anyone other than myself in over a year. And even before that, I wasn't exactly a regular hostess. Beth did the majority of the cooking. I had two or three fall-back dishes, which I would make two or three times a month.

I went to look in the pantry instead. It was a large cupboard, really, at the back of the kitchen, but Beth had said she'd always wanted a pantry, so that's what it became.

There wasn't a lot of inspiration in the cupboard, but there were potatoes. I checked the clock. An hour was long enough to make decent baked potatoes. Since I hadn't remembered to check whether Cora was vegetarian, they were also a safe option. I could make a load of toppings, grated cheese and tuna mayo and that sweetcorn-pepper relish that tasted way posher than it actually was.

With a plan in place, I cleaned the potatoes then popped them in the oven.

It was a simple action, but it kick-started my routine. When I washed my hands, I thought I could clean the sink while I was there, then wipe down the counters. From there it was a natural progression to sweeping and mopping. An hour later I turned the oven down. The potatoes were cooked; they just needed to stay hot. I pulled stuff out of the fridge to prepare the toppings on my nice clean counters.

An hour and ten minutes after I'd returned home, I had lunch ready for three people, and a beautiful clean kitchen. Rather than lose momentum, I went out into the garden to choose flowers for the table. I could get some of the early lettuce leaves to make a rough salad as well.

I'd just cut half a dozen dahlias of various colours when I heard the phone ringing inside the house.

I hurried back in, leaving the dahlias on the kitchen table. The phone must've rung a dozen times before I got into the hall, but whoever was calling didn't ring off. That meant it was probably Mum. She knew I wasn't always speedy.

'Hello?'

'Rosalie? That you?'

It took me a moment to recognise Cora's voice. She sounded distant and faint. 'Hi, it's me, yes.' I looked at the clock on the wall. 'Are you on the way here? Lunch is nearly ready.'

'No ... Rosalie, something's happened. Can you come pick us up?'

My scalp prickled. 'What happened? Are you okay?'

'I'm fine. We're fine. It's a problem with the car.'

I should've felt better at that, but the obvious distress in Cora's voice said otherwise. 'Why? What's wrong?'

Cora let out a breath. I heard her swear quietly. 'Someone's slashed our tyres.'

Chapter 13

By the time I got to the car park in the curraghs, Cora had finished swearing, but only just. She looked like she was working herself up to start again. As I got out of my car, she stalked back and forth, muttering under her breath.

Dallin was standing at the rear of the car with a cigarette in his hand. He nudged the back tyre with his foot.

'Someone's done a right number on these,' he said to me. He sounded more surprised than angry.

'We came back to the car and found it like this,' Cora said. 'We were only out for an hour or so.'

I crouched so I could see the damage. The front and rear passenger-side tyres had been cut open with deep slashes. The tears were ragged, as if whoever did it had been in a hurry, or hadn't used something sharp enough.

'Who the hell would do that?' Cora asked the air. '*Both* tyres, man. I've had this car for four years and no one's so much as scratched it. I thought this island was supposed to be safe?' She glared into the trees as if the culprit might be hiding just out of sight. For all we knew, they could've been.

I touched a finger to the torn rubber. The tyre was thicker

than I'd expected. Someone had properly sawn into them. I changed my guess – this would've taken more than just a few moments, and it needed something sharp and jagged, like a small saw. Not the sort of thing a person would carry around with them for no reason.

'It was probably kids,' Dallin said. He bounced his toe off the rear tyre again. 'Vandals.'

'Out here?' Cora demanded. 'How many roving gangs of teenagers do you get in the sticks? And why us? Why not one of the other random cars that get parked up here during the day? And *two* tyres.' She picked up a stone and flung it at a tree. 'Two!'

I stood up and looked at the other tyre. The cut there was deeper and less ragged, as if the first had been a practice. The car had been parked with the passenger side facing the road. The tyres on the other side were intact.

'At least they didn't do all four,' I said.

Cora picked up another stone and hurled it at the trees. 'They did two on purpose,' she said. 'They knew we'd have a spare tyre, so doing just one wouldn't stop us, so they did two. That's the fastest amount of damage they could inflict and be certain we couldn't drive away.'

'C'mon, Cora,' Dallin said. 'No one was thinking that hard about this. It's just – I don't know—'

'It was targeted, and it was calculated.' Cora stalked away, then came back, still simmering. 'Someone did this on purpose and they knew exactly what they were doing.'

I stood back from the car, trying to see a way the damage could've been accidental. Someone driving too close ...

swerving to avoid one of the dozens of potholes in the road ... a jagged edge of wheel trim or something similar ...

I couldn't make the mental image line up with reality. But still, I didn't want to believe someone had done this on purpose. It was too upsetting to contemplate.

'Who do you think it was?' Dallin asked. To my surprise, he was looking at me. 'This is only our second day. This afternoon we've been parked for hardly any time. No one knows we're here.'

'Except your mum,' Cora said.

Dallin scoffed. 'My invalided mother did not drive out here and cut up our tyres.'

'No, but she might've told people we were here.' Cora lifted her shoulders in an angry shrug. 'I don't know.'

She looked at me as well. I could only mirror her shrug. 'She might've phoned her friends to tell them about us,' I admitted. 'She's got a pretty solid network of people.'

Dallin grunted in agreement. 'The whole north of the island probably knows what we're up to by now.'

Cora was swearing under her breath again, but at least she'd stopped flinging stones. It made me edgy to see her react like that. I wasn't a big fan of confrontation.

'We need to call the garage,' I said.

'Already tried that.' Dallin dropped the end of his cigarette and ground it under his toe. 'The garage in Ramsey doesn't have a tow-truck today. They said they could fit new tyres, if we can get to them. I told them what we thought of that idea. They suggested we call a garage in Douglas instead. Or try Green Flag.'

I glanced along the narrow road. It might be possible to get a tow truck to the car park, but it would've been an effort. 'Okay,' I said, 'what if we take off the damaged tyres and put them in my car, then I'll drive to Ramsey and get them replaced. Would that work?'

Cora shook her head. 'I couldn't ask you to do that.'

'I'm not sure what other use I can be. I've got a working car; you don't. How else are you going to get the tyres replaced?'

Cora pulled at her bottom lip in thought. It was only then I spotted her mobile phone in her hand. 'The police are on the way,' she said. 'I called them first. They told us not to touch anything till they get here.'

'So ... we should leave the tyres like that?'

'I guess. Once they've, I don't know, taken photos and everything, then we can probably get them fixed. I don't know how long that'll take.'

I had a sudden thought. 'I'll need to nip home anyway and empty my boot,' I said. 'Otherwise I won't have room to fit two tyres.'

Cora nodded. She was looking at the trees again. 'Okay. Dallin, can you wait with the car?'

'What?' Dallin looked like he wasn't paying attention. 'Why?'

'Someone needs to be here when the police arrive. Can you do that?'

'What about you?'

'I'm going to keep searching.'

It took me a moment to understand. 'You're going back into the curraghs?'

'How long will it take the police to get here?' Cora asked. 'And when they do, how many of us need to tell them what happened? I can keep searching the wetlands. I'll do another small section and be back in an hour.'

'On your own?' Dallin said.

'Why not?' Cora had that same determined expression on her face. Her gaze was on the trees, and I could tell she was itching to be out there, searching, rather than standing around doing nothing.

Still, I felt it necessary to ask, 'Are you sure we shouldn't all wait? If someone deliberately damaged the car – I mean, what if they come back?'

'I'll be here,' Dallin said. 'You're not the only one who can swing a punch, Rosie.'

My cheeks went red.

'I can't lose any more time,' Cora said. 'I need to keep looking.'

'What if I go with you?' I asked. I didn't want to admit it, but I was worried about her, out there on her own. Especially if there was someone around who was crazy enough to cut her tyres.

But Cora shook her head. 'I'll do the next leg, you can empty the boot of your car, and Dallin will field the police. We'll meet back in an hour, okay?'

It sounded like she didn't want to argue further. 'Alright,' I agreed, reluctantly. 'I can bring food too.' I was thinking of the baked potatoes, going wrinkly in the oven where I'd left them. At least I'd had the presence of mind to turn it off before I ran out of the house.

Dallin had taken out his phone and was snapping photographs of the tyres. His frown deepened. 'What should I tell the police?' he asked. 'About why we're out here? Do I tell them about Simone?'

'If you want,' Cora said. She shouldered her backpack and picked up the maps. 'They might think we're barmy. Or there's an outside chance they might believe us and offer to help.'

'So long as we don't get into trouble for tramping around off the main paths.' Dallin leaned in to take a closer photo of the rear tyre. 'I might say we're looking for wallabies. Save some hassle.'

His words reminded me of Eloise. I remembered her gripping her hands as she said, *what about the wildflowers?*

Cora gave me a reassuring smile. 'See you in an hour.'

'Don't get lost,' I said, then wished I hadn't.

I didn't want to be left there with Dallin, not after our arguments, so I hurried to my car. When I glanced back, Cora was already pacing off the distance along the road, working out where next to go into the curraghs, and Dallin was looking at the photos he'd taken on his phone. *Probably putting them straight on social media.* It occurred to me I hadn't had an opportunity to confront him about his stupid website.

One more thing for us to argue about later.

I drove back slowly along the rutted road, my thoughts swirling.

It was difficult to believe anyone would deliberately damage a stranger's car. But, obviously, these things happened. There were always stories in *The Courier* about random, nasty acts of vandalism. Not all of them were in the towns. There'd been incidents in the plantations, out along the footpaths, and even at the ancient monuments like Cashtal yn Ard in Maughold. I never failed to wonder at a person who would walk a mile uphill just to deface something.

What was more upsetting, random violence or someone deliberately targeting Cora's car?

I thought again of Eloise. She'd been unhappy, definitely, but unhappy enough to damage two tyres? It seemed unlikely. I couldn't think of anyone who would do something like that.

At the end of the road I turned right onto the slightly smoother but no less narrow track. If the hedgerows hadn't been in the way, I could've seen my house, but there was no direct route, unless I drove through two fields. The road looped round so I had to pretty much double-back on myself.

As I followed the road, I saw Nicole and Patrick's farmhouse. It was a beautiful building, raised up from the surrounding land to dominate the gardens. At one time, the half-dozen fields behind the house had also belonged to Nicole's family, but they'd been sold over the years to neighbouring farms. Nicole sometimes regretted it, she said, but only because if she'd sold the land now it would've been worth five times what her father got for it. Otherwise, she was happy with what she had – the house and its gardens.

I spotted Nicole out in the front garden, bent to weed a flower-bed. On impulse, I pulled into the layby in front of their house.

Nicole looked up and waved. 'Hello, neighbour,' she called. 'What brings you out this way?'

I came as far as the garden gate and rested my arms on it.

Nicole was right to be proud of her garden. Many times, I'd made an excuse to walk past the house, just so I could breathe it all in. My own garden looked shabby and ill-tended in comparison. I tried my best to plan my planting, but whatever I planted struggled to thrive, whilst things left behind by Mum grew and spread and crowded out my own attempts. The only bit I could control was the vegetable patch.

In contrast, Nicole must've planned her planting from the very start, yet made it look spontaneous and effortless. There was always something new to see. One set of flowers would leap up like fireworks and, as soon as they died down, another would sprout to take their place. I had extreme garden envy.

Nicole came to the gate with a smile on her face. She was a tall, willowy woman with delicate, slender fingers. Pianist fingers, Mum called them. There was a little crescent of dirt under each nail. Nicole pushed up the brim of her gardening hat, which had gone floppy from being washed too many times.

'I hear you've got visitors,' Nicole said. 'Young Dallin's found his way home at last, has he?'

'Just for a visit, that's right. How did you know?'

Nicole waved an airy hand. 'Oh, the jungle-drums. As soon as there's the slightest bit of skeet we'll be on the phone to pass it along.'

So Dallin had guessed correctly; Mum had wasted no time telling everyone the news. 'He's come over with a friend,' I said. 'They're camping at Ballaugh.'

'I could never understand sleeping in a tent. I like my own bed, me.' Nicole laughed. 'Hardy lot, are they?'

It hadn't occurred to me to wonder why Cora hadn't booked a hotel instead of the campsite. It wasn't like there was a shortage of places to stay. 'They wanted to be close to the curraghs, I guess.'

'Oh, aye? Fans of the wallabies, are they?'

'No, they're here because—' I faltered. It wasn't a secret, was it? 'I don't suppose you remember, all those years ago, when I was ten and got lost in the curraghs?'

Nicole blinked, then laughed again. 'Now *that* was a lot of years ago. I remember it well enough – your mum called us in a frightful panic, saying how you'd got yourself lost. She didn't know what to do with herself. I told her it was the sort of things kids do all the time. Dallin disappeared from home a bunch of times and always came back as soon as his stomach got empty. But Opal was terrified something had happened to you. Me and Patrick came out to look, but almost as soon as we got there, out you popped from the trees.' She shook her head, still smiling. 'I don't know whether Opal wanted to keel over from relief or smack your legs for scaring her. Did you ever decide what possessed you to run off like that?'

'I got lost.' Even now, it annoyed me that no one really believed my story. 'I didn't want it to happen. I just lost my bearings. And I found a skeleton.' I said the last bit quickly.

Nicole gave a tolerant smile. 'I remember you saying, yes.'

'It really happened.'

The smile faded a little. 'I know,' she said, although it didn't sound like she meant it. 'It was all a long time ago now though.'

'That's why Dallin's brought his friend Cora here,' I said.

'She believes me. She thinks the skeleton is all that's left of her sister.'

Nicole's smile disappeared altogether now. 'Rosie—'

'I know it was a long time ago. But Cora's sister went missing twenty years ago, and they think maybe she ended up here.'

'Oh, Rosie,' Nicole said. I'd always hated being called Rosie. 'If there'd been anything to find, don't you think the police would've found it? And if your friend has someone who went missing all that time ago, don't you think the police would've investigated that too? They would've put out a nation-wide hunt. I know we're slightly removed from the adjacent isle, but someone would've connected the dots ...'

'Everyone thought she'd run away,' I said. I felt like I was channelling some of Cora's stubbornness. 'They looked for her, but not very hard. No one thought to search for her here.'

It all would've been so much easier if the police had found the skeleton, I realised with sudden clarity. They would've done DNA testing and linked it to Simone. Cora wouldn't have had to go through all these years of not knowing.

Nicole shook her head gently. 'And this – Cora, is it? – she's basing this all on the story you told her? About the skeleton you found? Don't you think – I'm not trying to be horrid here, Rosie, but don't you think it's a tad irresponsible of you, to let the poor girl go on believing this story?'

'I didn't—'

'I'm not saying you did, not for a moment. But this Cora is obviously grieving for her sister, and that can do funny things to a person. It might be she's not thinking straight.

Perhaps it won't do her any harm to go looking in the curraghs. But perhaps it will.' Nicole shaded her eyes from the sun. 'I'm surprised Dallin's let her come all the way here. You'd think he would've set her straight.'

'Dallin's the one who told her about the curraghs in the first place.'

'Really? That's odd. He always tried to talk you down. I wonder when he changed his tune.'

It wasn't something I'd thought about. I made a mental note to properly peruse his website when I got home. It'd seemed genuine enough to me, but what if it was secretly mocking me and my story? That sounded far more like Dallin.

'Can I bring Cora round sometime?' I asked. 'She'd like to talk to everyone who lived here twenty years ago, in case they remember her sister coming through.'

Nicole sighed. Her gaze slipped sideways so she was examining an ox-eyed daisy that had sprouted its pushy flowers across the path. 'You can come round, of course,' she said. 'Patrick's out right now, but he'll be home later, after tea. I don't know what you hope we can tell you, though. What was the girl's name?'

'Simone.' I gave her a vague description, based on the photo Cora had shown to Mum. 'She would've been fifteen when she came here.' *If* she came here.

Nicole pushed up her hat. 'Doesn't ring a bell,' she said. 'I don't think I've ever known a Simone in my life. Except my half-brother Simon, but that's a different story entirely. I doubt we can help her. Sorry.'

Which was pretty much what I figured. Except—

A noise distracted me. A police car, approaching from the south, had overshot the junction and reversed with a crunch of gears. Moments later, the car came up the road, driving more cautiously now. I waved them down.

The officer slowed and wound down her window. 'Are you looking for the car with slashed tyres?' I asked. 'They're near the curraghs car park. Take the next left then the first left after that. Go slowly, the road's terrible.' I didn't want to be indirectly responsible for a police car ripping out its undercarriage.

'Much obliged,' the officer said. As she pulled away, I stepped back onto the verge. Her colleague in the passenger seat waved to me. I lifted a hand in response.

'They've made good time,' I said. 'Barely twenty minutes from Douglas.' It was an automatic observation. If someone's driven all the way down from Douglas, you remark on how long it took them. It was as much second nature to us as commenting on the weather.

'What did you say?' Nicole asked. 'A car's had its tyres slashed?'

There was no point trying to hide the truth. Within no time, everyone would know there was a police car here, and soon afterwards, everyone would know why. That too was second nature for us.

I filled Nicole in on the basic details. Behind her surprise, she showed a certain amount of well-concealed glee at being the first to know. I could practically see her fingers itching to dial phone numbers.

'That's just terrible,' she said. 'Who would do a thing like that? And is this Dallin's friend? The one that's come all this way? That's just dreadful.'

Cora probably wouldn't thank me for telling the whole world her misfortunes. But experience had taught me that it helped to give people something. Nicole would pass the gossip to her network of friends, and she would also mention why Cora was here. Maybe that would be enough to nudge someone's memory.

If there was anything to remember.

You were always sneaky, secretive. You hid everything from everyone, so often it became a habit. I learned to read your moods, as clearly as we read the sea-changes in our parents' tempers, and knew when I could talk and when I couldn't. I wanted to be just like you but I didn't know how. I started to gather my own secrets, hoarding them close to my chest.

When you started sneaking out to see him, *I knew at once. Or I felt like I did. I knew something was wrong, at least. Your moods rose and fell in new and frightening patterns. You went from happy to sullen and back again in the space of an hour. Our parents speculated when they thought I wasn't listening.*

'What d'you reckon it is this time?' Ma asked. 'School or boys?'

'Buggered if I know,' Da said. I could hear him in the kitchen. 'Could be anything. Those girls she hangs around with are a right bunch of sour-faced bitches. You should hear the way they talk about each other.'

But it wasn't your friends. Not this time.

I put myself in your way one night when you tried to

sneak out. You told me it was none of my business where you were going.

'I could make it my business,' I said, raising my chin like you did when you argued. 'I could tell Ma.'

'Don't you dare.' You reached for me and I flinched. But you smiled as you ruffled my hair. 'You wouldn't do that, now would you? It's me and you against the world, Cor. Don't forget that.'

Chapter 14

When I got home, I parked in the driveway and opened the boot. In all honesty, there wasn't much in there, but I hadn't wanted anyone to dump tyres on top of my stuff. On top of Beth's stuff.

I took the two bags of clothes out of the boot. The bags were white and red, the lettering asking for clothing collections in aid of the Red Cross. I'd filled them several months ago. No, that wasn't true – I'd *started* filling them several months ago. Then I'd taken the clothes out and re-ironed them, because what if the charity shop threw them away rather than spend time getting the creases out? I could just about accept giving them away for resale. I couldn't bear the thought of them getting binned.

So, I'd ironed and folded the clothes and started stacking the bags. It took me at least a month to fill them. Probably more. I kept putting it off. And then, once they were finally full of neat, ironed, saleable clothes, I'd tied them up and put them in the hall. I left them there for another couple of months. At last I moved them into the boot of my car. That was about six weeks ago.

None of this was deliberate. I understood perfectly that I had to get rid of Beth's stuff. The clothes in the bag weren't even her favourites – it was a literal mixed bag of her everyday, normal clothing. Generic. Boring, even. I'd taken them out of the drawers by the window. I hadn't felt strong enough to tackle the big wardrobe, where she kept her best and favourite dresses. And yet, even this, the clearing out of two bags of not-special clothing, was still defeating me. It would've been incredibly simple to drive into Ramsey and drop it off at the charity shop.

I tried to ignore the twinge of relief I felt as I moved the bags back into the hallway of my house, one step further from being lost forever.

Apart from the two bags, there was nothing much else in the boot. I shoved the carjack back into the alcove at the side, where it refused to stay, then I slammed the boot shut.

Consciously or not, I drove slowly back to the curraghs, in no hurry to talk to the police, if they were still there. I'd had enough of talking to police officers to last me a lifetime. For a week after Mum's accident, it'd seemed like every officer on the island wanted to talk to me.

As I came down the bumpy road to the car park, I encountered the police car coming in the opposite direction. I pulled into a passing place and waved as they went past.

Arriving at the car park, I found Cora had returned, in just as foul a mood as before. She'd got the carjack out of her boot and was lying down on the road, trying to figure out where exactly to place it. She must've come back early, because I hadn't been gone an hour.

'Where's Dallin?' I asked as I came over.

'Went with the police,' Cora said. 'They wanted him to give a statement. He phoned me to let me know he was going, so I figured I should come back and wait with the car. Keep an eye on it, y'know?'

That explained the scowl on her face. She was annoyed at curtailing her search that afternoon. 'How did it go with the police?' I asked.

'Pretty much how you'd expect.' Cora tucked the jack under the car. Jiggled it around to make sure it wouldn't damage anything when she lifted. 'They took photographs and looked for fingerprints but didn't find anything.'

I hadn't thought about fingerprints. Now I was looking, I could see a powdery residue covering both tyres. 'They had a fingerprint kit with them?'

'Officer Bony-butt was a forensics ... person. You know what I mean. They had the kit with them yesterday for something or other, and it was still in the car.'

From the glimpse I'd got of the two police officers, I guessed she was referring to the passenger, who had indeed been bonier than the driver. 'Fortunate.'

'Not really, given they couldn't get a single print off either tyre.' Cora expanded the jack so it was tight against the undercarriage of the car. 'But at least it means we don't have to leave the car like this until a tow truck can get here tomorrow. The police said it's fine for us to take the tyres off.' She sat back on her heels. 'You know how to change a tyre?'

'In principle, sure. In practice? Not so much.'

'Pity. I've got this far, but once the car goes up off the ground, that's a bit spicy for me.' Cora shrugged. 'Well, I'm sure it's not that awful. People do this every day, don't they?'

It took less time but more effort than we expected. Also a certain amount of swearing. We got the rear tyre off and replaced it with the spare from the boot. Then we tackled the front tyre. Once that was done, we dumped the two wrecked tyres in the boot of my car.

'I don't think you even needed my help,' I said. My arms tingled from the effort of lifting the tyres. 'You've obviously done this before.'

'My uncle ran a garage for a while.' Cora wiped her hands on the back of her jeans. 'I say my uncle, but he was just this guy who was dating my aunt for a while. And I don't think he *ran* the garage, he just owned a share in the business and liked the idea of wearing overalls and tinkering with cars. When I was very young I got it into my head that I wanted to be a mechanic, so I would hang out there sometimes during the school holidays. A very appropriate place for an eight-year-old, don't you think? Anyway, there was this huge family spat – not about me, about the way my "uncle" was treating my aunt – and we all stopped talking to one another, so that was pretty much the end of it. He wound up selling the business and moving away.' She scratched her ear. 'But I still remember the basics of looking after a car. Which is fortunate, otherwise I never would've kept Priscilla running for this long.'

'Your car's name is Priscilla?'

'Queen of Desserts, because she's too slow and heavy to

get up hills. If there's a hill, you have to take a run up, or unload some passengers.' Cora laid an affectionate hand on the bonnet. 'She's a grand old lady, though. Can't believe someone would cut her tyres.'

I was still struggling with the idea myself. 'What did the police say?'

'Ah, they never commit to anything, do they? They asked a few questions about whether I had any ill-wishers who might've done this. Jilted lovers, angry ex-husbands, that sort of thing.'

'I take it you don't.'

'Hey, don't say it like that. I might have jilted some lovers in my time.'

I laughed. It was weird, how quickly a mood could change. An hour ago, Cora had looked ready to do a murder, but now she was smiling and joking as she looked at her car. Priscilla – if that really was its name – was still raised up on the jack with its front wheel missing.

'It'll be alright like that for a wee bit,' Cora said, following my gaze. 'Are you still okay to drive into town and get the tyres replaced? If they can do that, we can get the new one put on straight away and drive home.'

'Home?' For a moment, I thought she meant England.

Cora laughed. 'To the campsite. Our home under canvas.'

I smiled. 'How come you opted to camp instead of a hotel?'

'Force of habit, mostly. I like campsites. They don't care if you trample in at midnight with mud on your shoes. Plus, y'know, it's cheap. I have to keep the costs of these excursions down as much as I can.' Her lips twisted. 'However. If I'd known how much complaining your blessed brother was planning to do, I might've gone for a hotel after all.'

'Dallin doesn't like sleeping on the ground, right?' It wasn't a surprise. Dallin liked his home comforts, like Nicole.

'To be fair, not many people do. It's an acquired taste. And, honestly, I don't think he's really done it before. A few nights roughing it in a pop-up tent at festivals, perhaps, which is barely the same thing.' Cora brushed strands of hair back from her face. Her fingers left grimy marks at her temples. 'He hasn't *said* anything. But you can tell he's not enjoying the experience.' She laughed then. 'And, of course, there's the issue of the tents.'

'What issue?'

Cora tilted her head. 'When Dallin decided to accompany me, I don't think he envisioned us bringing two tents. I think he was expecting it just to be him and me. Snuggled up in a two-person tent.'

My cheeks reddened. 'And you ... weren't on board with that?'

'What do you think?'

I avoided her gaze, instead studying my hands. There was grime under my nails as well. 'I've no idea,' I mumbled.

Cora laughed. 'I've got many character flaws, but sharing accommodation with random people I've met on the internet isn't one of them. Besides, no offence to your brother, but he's not exactly my type.'

'What—?' I bit my tongue before I could ask. That was what living on my own had done to me – I'd lost the knack of interacting normally with people.

'Anyway.' Cora shut the boot of my car and gave it a bounce to make sure the lock had engaged. 'Are you sure you're okay to get these tyres replaced?'

'It shouldn't be too difficult.' I hesitated. 'Are you coming with me, or ...?'

Cora looked torn. 'I hate dumping it on you. But I really ought to stay with my car. In case – well, in case anyone tries to damage it again. I don't feel happy leaving it like this out on the road.'

It was a fair enough concern. 'I can sort out the tyres,' I said. 'It shouldn't be too much of a trial. Touch wood.' There wasn't anything wooden nearby to touch, so I put my fingers against my forehead. Another little joke that always reminded me of Beth. Was there anything in the world that didn't?

Cora waved me off as I drove away up the road for what felt like the fifteenth time that weekend.

Chapter 15

Ramsey was busier than usual. Or possibly this was how the place always looked on a Saturday afternoon. I couldn't remember the last time I'd broken from my routine and come here anytime other than a Sunday.

I drove through the one-way system to reach the garage on the quayside. It wasn't my usual garage – once a year I would drive into Douglas to get the car serviced by the same mechanic I'd been going to since I first learned to drive – but I'd driven past it a hundred times and, according to the signage out front, it was open on weekends and could change tyres while you waited.

What took the most time was explaining to the young mechanic in the blue overalls what'd happened. Two slashed tyres from the same car obviously wasn't a common problem. He hefted the first tyre with a lot less effort than it'd taken me and Cora, and said he'd have them replaced in forty minutes.

I used the time to go to Shoprite for my shopping. I picked up a few extra bits I thought Cora might like. Our plans for lunch were scuppered, but maybe I could invite her for dinner instead. I turned the idea over in my mind. It held the usual edge of anxiety – inviting people? To my house? To the shared space where for a brief, wonderful time it'd just been me and Beth? I tried to look at those anxieties objectively. Could I get past them?

For the moment, I kept it purely hypothetical. Nothing could hurt me if it was only hypothetical. Even so, it didn't terrify me like it would've done a week ago.

Besides, analysing those feelings meant I wasn't constantly thinking about who might've slashed Cora's tyres. And why.

I grabbed a jar of coffee and some teabags. The idea of having stimulants in my house sat worse with me than the idea of having people there. For over a year, I'd taken care not to stock anything in my kitchen that might alter my mood. No coffee, no caffeinated drinks, definitely no alcohol. I wasn't certain about tea but I'd cut it out anyway. By now, it probably wasn't a risk. The tablets I'd been prescribed since shortly after Beth died had stabilised me enough that I probably didn't need to worry about anything unbalancing me. But still. I'd spent so long in thrall to my moods. I didn't want anything to disrupt them. A cup of tea certainly wasn't worth the risk of a relapse.

But, if I was going to have guests in my house, I would need normal drinks, not just herbal tea and leaves from my garden. I put the coffee in my trolley. If no one drank it, I would donate it to the local bookshop to help caffeinate their monthly book group.

I also grabbed a packet of pink wafer biscuits. They used to be Dallin's favourite. I was still angry at him for more reasons than could be catalogued, but not angry enough to withhold biscuits.

By the time I got back out to my car, I felt less anxious. I was still way out of my routine, but, if I didn't focus on it, I could keep going. Only once did I remember I should still be upset about Cora's tyres. I caught myself and thought about something else. Was that selfish? I knew how quickly I could slide into panic and distress. Sometimes, I had to think of my own sanity first.

Back at the garage, the mechanics loaded the tyres into the boot of my car. 'Hell of a thing,' one of them – a different, older guy, who nonetheless looked enough like the first mechanic that I had to wonder if they were related. 'Two tyres, cut up like that? Did someone do that deliberately?'

'I've no idea.' I kept my eyes averted. 'It was my friend's car. She just asked me to bring them here.'

'Well, I hope she's planning to pay you back.' The man grinned.

I hadn't thought whether Cora would reimburse me. She hadn't said anything, but obviously she would, wouldn't she? I didn't want to be a hundred and twenty pounds out of pocket. I made sure to keep the receipt.

I dropped the bags of shopping off at my house. While I was there, I put tinfoil over the baked potatoes and toppings, stuffed them in the fridge for later, then put the cut flowers from the garden into water. I switched on the kettle and rummaged in the cupboard until I found the thermos flask we used to use for picnics. Cora would appreciate a hot drink.

As I poured coffee into the flask, my eyes fell on the wash

basket next to the door. I hadn't started the washing machine that morning like I usually did. Alternate Saturdays were towels and the throws from the sofa.

Leading on from that thought was the fact I hadn't tidied the front room like usual.

Tension knotted inside me.

I made myself pick up the flask of coffee and leave. If I started on any of the necessary jobs, I would stay there all day, finding one thing then another to occupy my time.

When I got back to the curraghs, there was no sign of Cora. The likelihood was she'd got bored of waiting. I should've texted her to let her know how long I would be.

I took out my phone and dialled Cora's number. The call failed to connect, which didn't greatly surprise me. Reception was spotty out there.

I walked around Cora's car, which was still propped up on the jack. The doors were locked. The passenger doors at least. When I tried the boot, on impulse, it popped right open. Cora must've forgotten to lock it after we got the spare tyre out. Probably she'd been too angry and worked up to think about it.

At the back of the boot, I found the tyre iron, tucked away out of obvious sight.

For a few minutes I stood waiting. The trees murmured in the breeze. Clouds had rolled in to cover the sun. Although the day had started out nice it looked suspiciously like it planned to rain at any moment.

I went back to my car and, with a certain amount of difficulty, manhandled one of the new tyres out of the boot. Once it was on the ground I could roll it to Cora's car. The process only took a couple of minutes but left me winded. I paused to rest against the car.

It'd taken both me and Cora to change the other tyre. But that had involved taking the old one off first. Putting the new one on had been less strenuous.

I waited another few minutes in case Cora showed up. Then I took off my jacket and got to work.

It turned out that me on my own was a lot less than fifty per cent as efficient as Cora. I struggled just to lift the tyre into place. And once it was there, I struggled more to hold it steady.

This is a terrible idea. You'll never manage. And even if you do, it'll be wrong, and Cora will have to take it off and do it properly.

But I persevered. I put the nuts on one at a time, like Cora had shown me, then tightened them with the tyre iron. The metal was cold against my palms.

It bothered me that Cora wasn't here. Her backpack was gone as well, so she'd probably gone to search another segment of the curraghs. But the sensible thing for her to do – the thing we'd agreed on – was to wait right here for me to get back with the tyres. It irked me that she'd wandered off instead.

Unless she didn't wander off.

The thought came into my head then refused to budge.

Someone damaged her car. Then you left her here. On her own.

I tried to scoff at the idea. If there was someone lurking around in the curraghs intending harm, Cora was way more qualified to deal with them than me. If anything, I would've gotten in the way, or made things worse. I shouldn't be anxious. Cora could take care of herself. Flakes of rust from the tyre iron dug into my fingers. I wished I'd worn my gloves.

Although I put in as much effort as I could, I was certain the nuts weren't tight enough. But they were the best I could do. When Cora returned she could check. We would probably have to drive – slowly, carefully – to the garage on in Ramsey and get them to tighten the nuts with their electric doodah.

I straightened up and went to lean nonchalantly against the front of the car. It appealed to me, the idea of Cora stepping out of the forest to find me here, with the newly repaired car. I stood there for about five minutes. My fingers drummed a beat against the cool metal of the car bonnet. At last, I gave up on being nonchalant, and instead fished out my phone. Cora still didn't answer when I called. I sent her a quick text. Just to let her know I was here.

I tried not to worry about why she wasn't replying.

I went back around to the back of her car and opened the boot again. If I climbed up to kneel in the boot, and leaned through to the passenger compartment, I could just reach the door release of the rear door. The soft clunk as it sprung open gave me a nice sense of satisfaction. I had changed a tyre by myself, I had interacted with a bunch of strangers at the garage, and now I had successfully unlocked a door. It might not have seemed like much. But for me, who for the last year had stuck so tightly to a routine that it threatened to choke me, it was most definitely progress.

The real reason I'd gone to the effort of opening the door

was because I'd spotted Cora's book about the curraghs lying on the seat. It intrigued me because, although I had a vague knowledge of most books about the island, I didn't know this one. That wasn't bragging. There were a finite number of books about the island. The popular ones tended to pop up frequently on the shelves of the bookshops and libraries over here. But this one, on the backseat of Cora's car, I'd never seen before.

The cover was distinctive, showing view over the hills from Ramsey looking south, with a tangle of gorse bushes in the foreground. Its title was *Tramping an Island*, which made me smile. When I cracked it open, it was clear it was an American book – or at least pitched to an American audience – which explained why I hadn't seen it before. I sat down on the back seat and flicked through the book.

I found a chapter detailing the curraghs. The accompanying photos were pleasingly familiar. There was always a particular delight in opening a random book and finding pictures I recognised. I got a little thrill as I found one picture taken from the fields behind my house. At the very edge of the picture was my own house in the 1920s. What little I could see of it seemed the same – the sweep of the roof, the big windows, the stepped slope of the garden. The only major difference was a tree in the southeast corner of the garden. It looked like a big oak, although it was difficult to tell from the grainy photograph. The tree must've been chopped down before I was born. I wracked my brains but couldn't think where exactly it would've stood. Even the stump must've been removed.

A rap at the window made me almost jump out of my skin. I dropped the book into my lap and looked up to see Cora smiling in at me.

'Making yourself at home?' she asked when I opened the door.

'You left the door open,' I said. I got out of the car, embarrassed to be caught looking at her property. 'Where'd you go?'

'I went to search some of the area nearest the main track. It has to be done at some point, and I figured I'd be close enough to hear if anyone came back to the car.' Cora pursed her lips. 'I wandered a bit further than I meant to.'

'It's okay. I've been here.'

'So I see.' Cora looked at the tyre. 'Who put this one on?'

My cheeks flushed. 'Me. So, I mean, you might want to check it won't fall off halfway down the road.'

Cora squeezed my shoulder. 'It looks great. Thank you.'

The flush in my face deepened. 'I've got the receipt for you. It's in my pocket ...' I fumbled looking for it.

Cora was looking at her phone. She swore. 'I've run out of battery. I told Dallin I'd keep in touch. He's probably been calling for an hour.'

'I can call him.' I was grateful for the distraction, for the chance to pull out my own phone. 'What's his number?'

Cora reeled it off without having to think, which surprised me. Maybe she didn't regard him as anything more than a travelling companion, but she'd taken the time to memorise his number. Hardly anyone did that anymore.

Maybe it was simple jealousy that niggled me. I missed being so close to someone that I knew their number by heart.

I dialled the number but, instead of speaking, passed it to Cora when it started to ring.

Cora pressed my phone to her ear, her lip caught anxiously between her teeth. I wondered what she was worried about.

'Hey! Dallin, it's Cora. Where are you?' Cora asked. She turned, perhaps unconsciously, so her back was to me. 'Are you still—?'

She listened for several moments. I could hear Dallin's voice, distorted and tinny through the phone speaker, but couldn't make out what he was saying. He sounded irritated.

Cora said, 'Yes, okay, okay, yes,' a few times, then said goodbye and ended the call.

'How is he?' I asked.

'Not greatly pleased.' Cora kept my phone in her hands as if it was a comfort object. 'He says he's texted me a bunch of times. I don't think he guessed my phone was dead.'

'Is he mad?'

'At me?' Cora smiled. 'No, of course not. He's just not a massive fan of the police. It sounds like he's been giving them grief.'

That surprised me. Since when did Dallin dislike the police? 'Is he in trouble?'

'He said he's fine.' Cora waved it away. 'I'm sure he knows not to do anything too stupid.'

Belatedly she gave my phone back. 'Will the police give him a lift back to the campsite?' I asked, although I knew the answer.

'Doesn't sound like it. I better go pick him up. He wouldn't be stuck there if it wasn't for me.' Cora went to the driver's side door.

'Are you sure you want to drive to Douglas?' I asked her. 'I'm not a hundred per cent sure I put that tyre on correctly. We can go in my car, if you rather.'

'I couldn't ask you to do that.'

'It's no bother. I should probably make sure Dallin's okay.' If he got himself arrested for being rude to an officer, Mum would never forgive me.

'Ah, Rosalie.' Cora's face scrunched into a smile. 'What would I do without you?'

Chapter 16

We compromised a little. She drove very carefully to the campsite and left the car next to her tent. I followed in my car. At every pothole I expected the wheel to pop off Cora's car and go bouncing down the road. But we got there safely, and Cora transferred to the passenger seat of my car.

'That was slightly hairy,' she laughed. 'Still, I'm glad we didn't have to wait until Monday for a tow-truck. Good job, us.'

I took the opportunity to sneak a look at her tent. It was small, standard, unremarkable, showing a few signs of wear around the edges. Dallin's, next to hers, was bright blue and very new-looking. I drove out of the campsite and back to the main road.

'Whereabouts is the police station?' Cora asked. 'Is it difficult to get there?'

'Nowhere's difficult to get to. Unless the roads are closed.' I turned right, towards Ramsey. 'Not that I've ever had to pick someone up from the police station.' I was doing a whole lot of new stuff that week.

'Never?' Cora laughed. 'When I was a teenager, me and my

friends were always in trouble. If one of us had to get picked up, we had a system where someone would pretend to be our mother or big sister or whatever. It worked surprisingly often. Hey, have we got time to stop for coffee?'

I smiled. 'There's a flask by your feet. I thought you might need a hot drink.'

Cora's face broke into a grin. 'Ha. I knew you'd have our back.' She patted my arm affectionately.

The physical contact made warmth spread up through my chest.

Cora took off her woolly hat and shook out her hair with her fingertips. 'Should we save some for Dallin?'

'There's enough for both of you,' I said. 'If he deserves coffee.'

Cora laughed. She rummaged in the bag I'd left in the passenger footwell until she found the flask. She poured a small amount into the cup and blew on it. After she'd taken a couple of sips, she held it out to me.

'You want some?' she asked.

I shook my head. 'I don't drink coffee.'

'Aw. You made coffee for us even though you don't drink it yourself?'

The soft teasing note in her voice made me smile. 'I can't have stimulants. Well, I mean, I can, but I don't like to. It screws up my moods.'

Mostly I threw that out again to see how she reacted. Some people clammed up as soon as I mentioned my wonky brain chemistry. Like they were scared to acknowledge it, in case I told them a bunch of details they didn't want to hear, or because my illness might somehow attach itself to them too. I'd encountered that reaction so often when Beth was sick. People would look away or change the subject or start apologising. It had annoyed the hell out of Beth, and I guess it annoyed me too.

'Oh, sure,' Cora said. 'I have that too. The doctor put me on something different and it messed up my mood swings so badly. I was literally crying over the slightest thing. One time, this guy on the bus leaned over to ask me the time, and his breath smelled so bad I burst into tears. In my defence, his breath was really bad. Like he'd been eating cat food for breakfast. And I told him so, which didn't make me look any less crazy.'

'I think you were justified.'

'I think so too.' Cora smiled.

Once past Ramsey, the road to Douglas twisted its way up over the hills. It was the most famous part of the TT course, the bit that was always featured on TV, showing motorbikes zipping over the hilly terrain at ridiculous speeds. Because it formed part of the racecourse, there were no metal barriers or crash protectors at the side of the road. If a bike or a car was unlucky enough to swerve off the road, there was nothing except an occasional gorse bush to prevent them rolling all the way to the bottom of the valleys. Driving the mountain road always made me edgy. I would never attempt it in bad weather, especially not in fog or high winds. But I wouldn't drive the coast road to Douglas, which bumbled its way gently south from Ramsey, past half a dozen smaller towns until it finally found its way to Douglas. Just the thought of that road made me feel sick.

Today we got stuck behind a Tesco van, but that didn't bother me. It gave me an excuse to drive at a sedate pace.

'It's weird,' Cora said as we crossed the tram tracks at the Bungalow. 'I keep wondering if Simone came along this road. I keep thinking, did she see that building? Or those trees?' She shook her head. 'Like there'd be any way for me to tell.'

'How did the search go this afternoon?' It'd slipped my mind to ask.

'Same. No sign of her.' Cora sighed. Her gaze was on the hills outside the window, but it didn't look like she was seeing anything. 'I know I shouldn't expect anything. All I'm doing here is crossing off a possibility. But still ... every time I go into that marsh, I keep expecting some flash of recognition, like somehow I would recognise the place where Simone wound up. That sounds mad, doesn't it?'

'Yes,' I said, because it did.

'I know. I don't even believe in that stuff, psychic resonance or whatever, you know, our actions leaving echoes on places. I *know* there's nothing out there that'll jog something loose in my brain. Even if Simone did end up here ... there'll be no trace of her. And even if there *is*, I'm not going to sense those traces. But I still find myself trying, y'know?'

I thought of the way she'd gone through the curraghs ahead of me yesterday, touching the trees as if they would give up their secrets through the bark. Maybe that was exactly what she'd been hoping for.

And didn't I do the same thing, in my own way? How many times had I run my fingers over the ornaments in the front room? There was nothing to sense from them; no resonance of times past; no echo of Beth's life. But still I pretended I could feel something from those objects. Beth had cupped them in her hands. Shouldn't they still contain a tiny fragment of her warmth?

I tried to bury the thought. Already I was finding it difficult to let go of things. A few weeks ago I'd broken a mug and cried for half an hour at the thought of putting it in the bin. It hadn't been one of Beth's favourites, but it was an object she'd used, touched, held. And now it was broken. For a moment, I'd considered keeping the shards. Sweeping them into a plastic container to keep below the sink forever.

I knew those thoughts were dangerous. Maybe not individually – what harm would it do, to keep one single broken cup? – but because if I couldn't throw one broken thing away, I wouldn't get rid of the next, or the next. Eventually I'd end up in a house full of useless objects, none of which I could ever dispose of, because I no longer knew the difference between rubbish and treasure. I could feel the compulsion itching inside me. It wouldn't take much to put me on a downwards slope.

'I've not spoken to my parents since Christmas,' Cora said then, as if she'd been following an internal conversation without me. 'We had a massive fight. About Simone, of course. Dad had smashed one of the picture frames of me and Simone when we were kids. Not on purpose, obviously, but he also hadn't gone out of his way to fix it. I accused him of – well, I said a lot of stuff I regret. But I don't understand why they don't want me looking for Simone. It's like they don't want me to find her.'

She paused to pour more coffee into the lid-mug.

'When I was a teenager, I would ask them a million questions about Simone,' Cora said. 'Half the time they'd just refuse to talk about her. Can you believe that? Their eldest daughter, and they were happy to pretend she'd never existed. Sometimes, Ma would say she'd heard from Simone – she was in Canada, she was travelling through Asia, always places which were too far away for me to run away and check for myself.' She sighed. 'Later, I got Ma to admit those stories were made up to keep me quiet. Not that *that* worked, of course.'

'Where did they think she'd gone?'

'I don't think it mattered to them. Mum saw it as an inevitable fact. Bound to have happened, sooner or later.' Cora cracked open her window to let in a little air. The wind whistled through the gap. 'Simone was a restless soul, my dad always said. And, of course, there was a guy involved.' Her mouth twisted. 'She was always hanging out with inappropriate men. Guys that were way too old for her. The night before she vanished, I heard her arguing with our dad about her latest boyfriend. Da was angry. Like, weirdly angry.'

'I can imagine why.'

'No, see, he never really interfered with Simone's relationships. Even when he disapproved, he would never say anything to her face. He reckoned she would push back twice as hard against anyone who told her not to do something.'

'So, why was this time different?'

Cora sighed. 'It was my aunt's boyfriend. Simone was seeing him as well.'

'When she was *fifteen?*'

'Before that as well, I think. He'd been dating our aunt for a year or so. I don't know when he took up with Simone.'

I couldn't keep the disgust off my face. 'No wonder your dad was angry.'

'Maybe. Da knew Simone was seeing someone, but not who it was. Anyway, by that point, the guy had dumped my poor aunt and done a runner, so he wasn't even on the scene. I don't know for sure why Da was so angry that night.'

'Did you ask him?'

Cora's brow pinched. 'When Simone disappeared, we didn't realise she was missing straight away. We thought she'd gone to stay with friends. That happened a lot. Then, when we finally realised she wasn't coming home, there was a lot of shouting in the house. Mum wanted to know who Simone's boyfriend was, because, y'know, she figured that was the first person we should speak to. Da didn't know who it was. Said Simone never told him. He also completely denied arguing with her about it before she vanished. But I know what I heard.'

'And you've never confronted him again?'

'Sure I have.' Cora gave me a wicked smile. 'I bring it up every damn time Simone gets mentioned. He only slipped up once, when I said we should track down the guy and shake some answers out of him, and Da said, "He doesn't know anything, I guarantee it."'

She lowered her voice almost to a growl as she said it, and

I heard a hint of what her dad must sound like. It was enough to make me flinch. He didn't sound like the sort of person who liked to be asked the same question twice.

'I've Googled the guy as well,' Cora said, 'but no luck. We reckon he must be using a different surname or something. Anyway, I figured one of three things had happened. Either Simone ran off with him, or he abducted her, or – and I think this is most likely – she got sick of us at home and decided to leave. She always talked about running away.'

'Really?'

'Oh, you know, in that generalised way everyone does when they're kids. We all thought about running away, right?'

I thought about Dallin, who'd left it until his twenties before he'd run. 'Sure,' I said.

'I ran off just once,' Cora said. 'When I was twelve. I had it in my head that Simone was still around, y'know? Keeping an eye on me. I thought I spotted her a few times outside my school. So, I invented this whole story in my head, about how she'd left home because of our parents, but now she was eighteen she was coming back for me, to take me to live with her.' She gave a brittle laugh. 'I slipped out of the house and waited at the bus station with my bag all packed and ready. I figured that would be the easiest place for her to pick me up. But, of course, she never appeared. I snuck back into my house before anyone even realised I was missing.' She sighed. 'Pretty daft, right?'

'We're all daft when we're kids,' I said, which was the most diplomatic thing I could think of.

'You know what the stupidest thing was? Once I figured out

Simone wasn't coming to get me, I could've still got onto a bus. I considered it for maybe half an hour. But in the end, I went home. I always thought I was just as strong-willed as Simone.' Cora shrugged. 'Turned out I was wrong. What about you?'

'Sorry?'

'Did you do the whole running-away-from-home bit when you were a kid?'

'No, I ...' I cleared my throat. 'I never really got round to the teenage rebellion thing. I was a late developer, I guess. And then our dad died when I was twenty, so ...'

Cora looked aghast. 'God. I'm so sorry. I had no idea.'

I suspected it was one more thing Dallin had neglected to mention. 'It's fine,' I said. Then, because I knew she would ask, 'He died in a car accident.'

'That's awful.' Cora frowned. 'You said your mum—'

'That's right. Same accident. Mum was driving.'

'I don't know what to say,' Cora said. 'And then to lose your wife as well ...'

If anyone else had said it, it might've sounded like they were fishing for information. But Cora's tone was soft, subdued, as if she understood the level of heartbreak.

Because of that I said, 'It's okay. I don't mind talking about it.'

Cora gave me a faint smile. 'What happened to her?'

'Cancer.' Instinctively, I let my expression go slack as I said it. It was a trick I'd learned, to take away the power of that hideous, evocative word. It meant my voice sounded like it belonged to someone else. 'In her ovaries. We only discovered it because—'

But I stalled there. Turned out some truths were more painful than others.

I cleared my throat again. 'She had no symptoms or anything. By the time they found it, there was nothing anyone could do. She was gone in eight weeks.'

There. The simple, bare-bones facts. Each time I said them aloud, they seemed a little less real, like those eight weeks had happened to someone else.

Cora nodded. I was concentrating on the road, so could only see her in my peripheral vision. It meant I didn't have to puzzle out her expression. 'When my gran got really bad,' Cora said, 'we agreed she should go into a hospice. She never forgave us for that, literally. Said it was our fault she'd ended up in a soulless institution. It was a really nice place, but to hear her talk, it was the fifth circle of hell, and we were the bastards who'd put her there.' She shook the hair out of her eyes. 'Mum said she was just angry. Angry at the whole unfair universe. The only people she could take it out on was her family.' She sighed. 'Either way, she refused to speak to any of us again. Two weeks later she was dead, and none of us got a chance to take back what was said.'

I could understand that. 'Beth was in the hospice for five days,' I said. 'But she didn't want to stay there. She was adamant she wanted to die at home.'

I thought about Beth, sitting on the bench at the bottom of the garden, looking out over the curraghs, on that very last day. We'd sat out there all evening. It'd suited Beth's sense of symmetry and rightness, I think, to wait until the sun had gone down before she closed her eyes for the last time.

I'd stayed outside till morning. I hadn't wanted to let go of her hands, even after they went cold.

Cora reached over and touched my arm, very lightly, very briefly, then folded her hands back in her lap. We didn't say anything else until we got into Douglas. I liked her quite a lot for that.

Chapter 17

Douglas Police Headquarters was just off the main road, a hundred yards down from the huge grandstand that marked the start of the TT course. I turned off onto the lane that ran between a football field and the gravelled area where the temporary marquees were erected for the motorbikes every June and August. The crocodile of cars that'd been following me since Creg-Ny-Baa were probably happy to see me turn off the main road. I wasn't necessarily a slow driver, but I did seem to be slower than most people.

Dallin looked exactly the sort of person who'd be found skulking outside a police station on a dull Saturday afternoon. His hands were shoved deep in his pockets and there was a scowl on his face that would've frightened a bulldog.

'When they offered to give me a lift here,' he said as he opened the rear passenger door of my car, 'I didn't realise it was a proper one-way ticket. They couldn't even give me a bus timetable. Best they could offer was telling me there's a stop at the end of the road and there'll probably be a bus sometime this afternoon, if you're lucky.' He flung himself into the seat. 'Thanks for coming to get me.'

'You're welcome,' Cora said. She twisted in her seat to smile at him. 'Rosalie brought you coffee.'

Dallin snatched the proffered flask. 'Alright, I forgive you for hitting me, Rosie.'

I bristled. 'Don't push your luck. If you want forgiveness, you could maybe start with an apology.'

'How did you get on?' Cora asked Dallin.

'Awful.' Dallin took the lid off and sipped from the flask. 'Actually, that's probably harsh. It went exactly as I expected. They needed a ridiculously long-winded statement, and it'll likely do no good at all. I thought I might be in trouble for a while, because they wouldn't believe that I hadn't been driving. I think I convinced them in the end.' He took another sip. 'This coffee is great, though. I know it's a cliché that police station coffee is so dreadful, but it's a cliché they really lean into.'

'Did they have any ideas about who might've done it? The damage to the tyres, not the coffee.'

Dallin nodded. 'Kids. They think it's kids. Which is a fair enough assumption.'

'You reckon so? *Kids,* all the way out in the boonies? Looking for a car to vandalise?'

'In the what, sorry?'

Cora flapped a dismissive hand. 'You know what I mean.'

'How's the car, anyway?'

'Rosalie got the tyres replaced,' Cora said. 'Priscilla is back how she was. Better than she was, because now she has a fighting chance of passing her MOT.'

'I've got the receipt for you,' I said to her. 'Don't let me forget.' At the end of the road, I turned left, to wiggle through the back lanes rather than do a three-point turn.

'The police made a big deal of that, by the way,' Dallin said. He figured out the lid of the thermos could be used as a cup and carefully poured himself a measure of coffee. 'They reckon we should've left the old tyres on the car in case further tests needed to be done. Even though I'd specifically asked them whether we could remove the stupid tyres or not. Complete shambles, the lot of them.'

His words were harsh but his tone wasn't. He seemed much more upbeat than he'd been all day. As if the conflict had galvanised him.

At the next junction, he looked up quickly. 'You're taking the mountain road, right?' he asked.

The anxiety in his tone made me forget how much he'd upset me recently. 'Yes,' I reassured him. 'Of course.'

He nodded, relieved. He hated the coast road as much as I did.

'I've had a bit of time to think,' Cora said. 'I made a list of possible people who might've done this. It's a rather loose and flappy list at the moment, so I'd appreciate if everyone could help me firm up some of my ideas.'

'Um.' I hated to interrupt. 'I know everyone's angry about this. But the police will sort it, okay? That's pretty much what they do. Someone commits a crime, the police figure it out. That's how it works.'

'That's how it's *supposed* to work.' Cora sat forward in her seat. She looked on edge. 'But suppose for a second we rule out mindless vandalism. What if someone targeted us deliberately?'

I looked at Dallin in the rear-view mirror. 'Did you suggest this theory to the police?' I asked him.

'I raised it, yeah.'

'And what did they say?'

'They asked whether we knew anyone here who didn't like us.'

'And do you?'

Cora scowled. 'We might've annoyed someone without even realising it. By, I don't know, delving into a historical disappearance of a young girl, perhaps?'

She had a point. I shut my mouth.

Cora rubbed her forehead with two fingers like she had a headache. 'Supposing Simone's body is out in the marshes somewhere. There's only two real ways she could've ended up there. Either some kind of tragic accident, or some kind of intentional act.'

Dallin leaned forward as far as his seatbelt would allow. 'You're talking about murder.'

'I've always been talking about murder. Weren't you listening?'

I slowed to approach a roundabout. 'Please sit back properly,' I said to Dallin. 'If I have to stop suddenly, you'll end up in my lap.'

'Wouldn't want that,' Dallin muttered, but he did as I asked.

'I know Simone is dead,' Cora said. 'Because if she was alive she would've contacted me. I thought there was a possibility she'd died in some kind of freak accident in the curraghs, but that was before I saw the place. It'd have to be exceptional circumstances for someone to die of natural causes out there.'

'A woman had a heart attack in Glen Mooar a couple of years ago,' I said, unhelpfully. 'She was out walking and keeled over. No one found her till the next day.'

'And how old was she?'

'Eighty-something, I think?'

'Alright, so, freak accidents do happen. But not often to teenagers in good physical health.' Cora reached to take the coffee flask from Dallin. The motion of the car didn't impede her. 'We have to consider someone murdered Simone. That's not a fun or pretty thing to carry around in our heads, but we can't ignore it. And, likewise, it might've been twenty years ago but that doesn't mean people don't remember it.' She sipped from the flask. 'Someone knows what happened to her. Someone knows we have an outside chance of finding her body. Ergo, someone has a pretty solid incentive to stop us.'

'That's a convoluted way of looking at it,' Dallin said. 'It's just a couple of slashed tyres. Not like you woke up with a horse's head in your bedroll.'

'I tell you what – how about we assume the absolute worst, and if I'm wrong and it was just kids messing about, I'll buy you a Happy Meal to say sorry. How's that?' Cora kept her voice quiet, but I could hear the frustration behind her words. 'So. Who do we know that was, firstly, on the scene twenty years ago and, secondly, knows we're there right now today?'

I turned left at Signpost Corner. There was a postal van

ahead of us and I was placing bets whether it would turn into the housing estate or whether we'd be stuck behind it all the way to Ramsey. 'Dallin was there twenty years ago,' I offer.

'I was eight,' Dallin said with a roll of his eyes.

'The woman has a point, though.' Cora turned so she could face him. 'You might've seen or heard something.'

Dallin scowled at her. 'If I had, don't you think I would've said something before now?'

Cora shrugged and sat back in her seat. 'All I'm saying is, this needs to be our approach. If Simone came through here, someone must've seen her. It's not a bustling metropolis. Even an eight-year-old might've seen more than they realised. Your mother was living here then, wasn't she?'

'Yeah,' Dallin admitted. 'But we asked her. She didn't remember anything.'

That wasn't strictly true, as I recalled. 'She said Simone reminded her of someone,' I said.

Dallin tutted. 'She would say that if you showed her a photo of literally anyone. Try it. Show her a picture of some Netflix actor and ask if she saw them in the Co-op last week. I guarantee she'll say she did. She doesn't want to admit she's forgetful.'

I locked eyes with him in the rear-view mirror. *And how exactly would you know that?* He hadn't spoken to his mother in months. Hadn't visited her in years. What the hell did he know about what she did or did not remember?

'You should make time to talk to our neighbours,' Dallin said. 'Although I doubt they know anything more than Mum. People don't remember stuff from that long ago.'

I raised my eyebrows as he referenced 'our' neighbours. Did he think the house still somehow belonged to him?

'What about that one who was angry at us for going into the wetlands?' Cora asked. 'What was her name?'

'Eloise,' I said. 'She was worried you'd trample wildflowers and scare away the nesting birds, that sort of thing. But she's more the sort to put a passive-aggressive note in the local paper than cut open your tyres. And she's only lived in her house for a few years. I remember her moving in.'

Cora had produced a notebook and pen from somewhere. 'Where'd she live before that?'

'I've no idea. Somewhere in the south of the island, I think.'

'That's, what? Twenty miles away? Not very far. I drive further than that to the local hospital.'

I laughed. 'It's not far in normal terms, no. But by Isle of Man standards, it's a pretty long way. Like, if I was going all the way down to Castletown, I'd make sure to pack some sandwiches. And probably bring my passport.'

Cora scratched the side of her face. 'I still don't think we should rule her out. She might have ties to this area that we don't know about. Who else did you say lives nearby?'

'Nicole and Patrick are the next nearest. They live at the farm down the road. We'll drive past on the way back. The farm's been in their family for generations, so they were definitely here at the time you're talking about.' I accelerated as we approached the derestricted signs just past Hillberry. The postal van was still ahead of us, but it speeded up as well. I was glad I wouldn't be expected to overtake. 'I spoke to Nicole already. She doesn't remember Simone.'

'What about Lenny? Where does he live?'

'Up past Jurby. Right on the coast.'

Cora got out her map and folded it to the correct page. 'Not far from your house,' she noted. 'And you said he visits the area a lot, as a handyman or something, right?'

Dallin snorted. 'As a busybody, sure. I wouldn't believe a word he says, though.'

Cora ignored him. 'I definitely want to talk to him. Do you have his number?'

'It'll be in the phone book.' I glanced at Dallin. 'Or we can drop in to see him. Might be a good chance for you to pay back that money you owe, Dal.'

'What?' Dallin's head came up. 'I don't owe him anything. Who told you that?'

'Oh, sorry.' I smirked. 'I must've got the wrong end of the stick.'

Cora tapped her pencil against her teeth. 'If someone did dump Simone in the curraghs, that doesn't necessarily point to someone local. In fact, it's more likely *not* to be. Someone from a different town, who happened to think of the curraghs as a good place to dispose of a body.'

Dallin grimaced. 'How can you talk about your own sister that way?'

Cora gave him a look. 'If you don't want to discuss the fact that my sister was probably murdered in a swamp, then you're in the wrong car. I'm not going to skirt around the issue for the sake of your sensitivities.'

I was shaking my head. 'Why would anyone pick the curraghs? If you had a dead body in your car—' I glanced at

Cora, but given she'd already told Dallin off, I pressed on. 'If you were driving around and had to dump a body, why go to the curraghs? It'd have to be in the middle of the night, and you've seen how difficult it is to walk around there even in daylight. Can you imagine it at night? Carrying a person?' I shook my head. 'And there's always a chance your car would get spotted. Twenty years ago, the curraghs weren't as popular as they are now, but there'll always be locals walking their dogs and stuff. It would only take one person to wonder why a strange car was parked up in the middle of nowhere.'

'That's a good point.' Cora pursed her lips thoughtfully. 'Hadn't considered that.'

'Also, there're better places to lose a body.' I made a gesture intended to encompass the whole island. 'There's literally a hundred isolated spots along the coast where you could drop someone into the sea. I could drive you up to a place or two just north of my house which have horrendous riptides.'

'Grim,' Dallin said. 'Also, bodies usually wash back up.'

'Not always,' I said. 'In certain places the currents push bodies back onto beaches, but not many. Sometimes they wash up in Wales; more often they never wash up at all.'

Cora tilted her head. 'How on earth do you know that?'

I hesitated before answering. 'Beth was interested in that sort of thing. She ran a blog about mistakes she'd spotted in forensic pathology TV shows.'

'Ah,' Cora said. 'So, if someone did leave Simone in the curraghs, they're more likely to be local. Or at least have an extensive knowledge of the area.'

'And it *did* turn out to be a good place,' I said. 'No one's found her in twenty years. Well, except me, and that was only briefly. It turned out to be an almost ideal spot to hide someone.'

'You're right about how difficult it is to walk in and out of, though. Can you imagine doing that while carrying someone, in the dark? I wouldn't like to try it.' Cora unfolded her map wider. It obstructed my view of the offside wing mirror. 'Some the pathways are different now than they used to be. I suppose there might've been a better path leading in and out of the curraghs. One only a few people knew about. Which brings us back to a local.' She rubbed her face with both hands. 'It's looking more and more likely, isn't it?'

'Unless it really was an accident,' I said.

'I don't believe that.' Cora let her hands fall onto the spread map. She stared out of the side window at the passing hills, just as she'd done on the way down. 'Why would she come here? Why *here*, of all places in the world? Our family don't know anyone. She had no friends.'

'That you know of.'

'Well, there is that, I suppose.' Cora gave a very small smile. 'I guess I don't really know anything about her. But, I mean, she never spoke about the Island, or mentioned any friends who'd moved away that she really missed. The only time I remember her mentioning this place was when she told me the Isle of Man was a made-up place.' She laughed to herself. 'Somewhere we banished men who'd, I don't know, annoyed us excessively. I was a bit sad when I found out it was real.'

'Sorry to disappoint,' I said with a smile.

'It's okay. There're worse places to be hypothetically banished to.' She picked up her notebook again. 'When we talk about "locals", what sort of area does that cover? Is it just people who are right on your doorstep? Or within, say, a mile?'

I had to think about that. 'When I got lost in the curraghs, Mum phoned her neighbours and they spread the word. More than a dozen people turned up to look for me. I think a few came from Ramsey and Kirk Michael. So I guess that's the sort of area I'm thinking of.'

'How many miles is that, do you reckon? About seven?'

'At most, sure.'

There was a certain amount of rustling as Cora refolded the map to a different page.

'Do you really have to do that now?' Dallin asked. He swatted at a flappy fold of map to get it out of his face. 'You're going to cause a crash. Can't it wait until we get back to the house?'

'Who said we're going to Rosalie's house?' Cora said. 'I'm going back to the curraghs.'

I glanced at her. 'To carry on searching?'

'Don't you think we should call it a day?' Dallin suggested. 'We've had quite a lot of excitement already.'

'I'm already way behind schedule. I've lost half a day today, plus the time I lost yesterday. I factored in some wiggle room, but I've used almost all of that already. If I don't get back out and keep searching, I'll never cover all the ground this week.'

Dallin chose his words carefully before answering. 'I know you don't like to change a plan once it's underway. But you have to admit, this all sounded much simpler when we were planning it online.'

'You think I don't know that? I didn't for a second think how exhausting it'd be. Physically and mentally. I mean ... I'm exhausted.' Cora let out a shaky breath; the only outward sign of the stress she was under. 'It's really taken it out of me. Walking around, knowing Simone might've walked the same route ... can you imagine what it'd be like, to be lost and alone out there?' She closed her eyes briefly. 'I can feel her haunting us. Every time we set foot out there, I feel like she's next to us.'

None of us said anything for several minutes. Cora folded her map and flipped closed her notebook. I could almost hear her thinking.

'We did factor in the need to speak to the neighbours,' Cora said at length. 'That's a necessary part of any plan. I could do that this afternoon. Rosalie, would you come with me?'

'Sure. Of course.'

'Thank you. I'd feel better with some moral support.'

The incident with the car tyres had rattled her, I realised. Someone had reached into her regimented world and made her vulnerable. No wonder she'd reacted so angrily.

'What about me?' Dallin asked. 'You got a job for me as well, or can I go back to my tent for a nap?'

'Do you ... want a nap?'

'Well, yeah, if it's an option. I haven't slept properly in two nights and I've spent a very unhappy afternoon talking to the police. Rosalie can introduce you to the neighbours.'

I hoped Cora wouldn't talk him out of it. I liked the idea of spending more time with her on my own.

Cora caught my eye and smiled. I tried to ignore the warmth that bloomed inside me.

As I drove, I sneaked glances at Cora. She was soon miles away again, her gaze unfocused, one hand clutching the other as if holding herself together. It was difficult to read her. She was so obsessed with looking for her sister that it seemed like she had no interest in personal relationships. But nothing got past her. When she'd been in my house, she'd seen and appraised everything I owned. My books, my pictures, my possessions. The wedding photos of me and Beth. She knew as much about me as I'd revealed to anyone.

I wished I could reach over and take her hands; hold onto them myself. It was probably a good thing I was driving. I didn't want to embarrass myself.

'What about dinner?' I said. Heat rushed to my face. 'I mean, do you guys want to come to dinner at my house? We can sit down and talk things over properly.'

Cora gave me a smile that warmed me all the way down to my toes. 'That sounds great.'

Chapter 18

Before we got back to Ramsey, the rain started again, drizzly at first, then increasing to a steady beat that drummed on the roof of the car. Dallin's bad temper returned by the time we approached the campsite.

'Tell you what, just drop me here,' he said as I turned left next to The Raven. 'I'll wait out the rain in the pub.'

I pulled in and let him out of the car. He ran into The Raven with his shoulders hunched. I smiled at Cora, happy to be on our own again.

But it turned out we would have an unproductive afternoon as well. We called at Eloise's house, but she wasn't in, and neither were Nicole or Patrick. Next, we drove up through the winding roads to Lenny's house. He lived on a narrow track near Blue Point beach, right on the exposed northern coast of the island. Here, wind and wave sloughed at the coastline, eroding the crumbling cliffs a centimetre at a time. The land was flat, the trees and bushes stunted by the salt air.

I didn't expect to find Lenny home at that time of day, but to my surprise, his work van was parked on the driveway.

'Bleak kinda place,' Cora said as she got out of my car.

Scrubby gorseland surrounded the house. To our right was the sweep of the exposed coastline. The tide was out, leaving a thick band of dullish sand, dimpled with rocks and puddles, but when the sea came in it would crest up to the foot of the cliffs themselves. From where we stood, I could see the clifftop car park at Smeale, where a few hardy dog-walkers had parked to enjoy the view.

We knocked at Lenny's door and stood shuffling our feet in the cold as we waited. Cora glanced at her watch.

'Is he likely to be out, if he's not taken his van?' she asked.

I had no idea. Lenny might've had two cars – or a dozen cars – for all I knew. I knocked again and, when there was still no response, tried the door handle. It was unlocked.

'Hello?' I called into the hall. 'Lenny? You around?'

No answer.

'He must be out.' I pulled the door closed.

Cora gave me an odd look. 'With the door unlocked?'

'Sure, why not?' Beth had always forgotten to lock our house. On more than one occasion we'd gone out and left the back door wide open. The worst that'd ever happened was a farm cat had got in and eaten my tuna sandwich.

Cora opened the door. 'Hello?' she called, louder. She stepped into the hall.

'Cora—'

'What if he's had a fall? Why else wouldn't he come to the door?'

'He could be on the loo. Or in the shower.' There were a dozen sensible reasons to ignore visitors.

Cora went through the hall, peeking into each room as she passed. I hesitated at the front door for a moment longer before following her. If Lenny had turned up at *my* house, I reasoned, and I wasn't answering the door, he'd be neighbourly enough to check I was alright. Cora could be right – he might've fallen. Once the idea got into my head it wouldn't dislodge.

Cora checked the downstairs rooms then went upstairs, calling to Lenny again. I went into the front room. Lenny's house was just as full of random clutter as mine, but it didn't look like he tidied often. On the sofa, a calico cat watched me with sleepy green eyes. Obviously it didn't care that I'd wandered in off the street.

I could hear Cora moving through the rooms upstairs. The floorboards creaked under her feet. Lenny's house was built of thick, sturdy stone, but inside it was cosy to the point of claustrophobia. The furniture was outdated and shabby. I picked up a copy of the local newspaper from the coffee table. I recognised the front page from several weeks ago.

It didn't feel right to be there without permission. It definitely wasn't right for me to appraise Lenny's possessions. How would I feel if someone did that to me? I left the room, making a conscious effort not to look closely at anything else.

'Cora?' I called. I started up the stairs. It was obvious Lenny wasn't home. I didn't want to invade his privacy any further than we already had.

On the upstairs landing, I paused. Through a doorway to my left, I saw Cora's shadow moving. 'Cora?'

I went to the door. Cora had found what appeared to be

a junk room. She'd lifted a cardboard archive box off a pile against the wall and set it on a broken-backed chair so she could rummage through the contents.

'Cora, what're you doing?'

'Looking.' She lifted a stack of papers, sorted through them quickly, then stuffed them back. She grabbed another box off the pile.

'You can't—'

'I'm not doing any harm.' Cora opened the next box and pulled out more papers. 'I'm just looking.'

I was certain that wasn't harmless at all. But I stood frozen as she rooted to the bottom of the box. 'What're you looking for?'

'I'll know it when I see it.' She found a battered old Filofax and flicked through it. 'I told you, a lead can come from anywhere. It's just a case of searching hard enough.'

'Cora.' I spoke softly, like Beth used to when she had to talk me down. 'This isn't the way to find anything.'

'How do you know? Lenny knows more than he told us. What if there's something here that can lead me to Simone?'

I saw it clearly then, how her obsession affected her. In the same way she would have to search every square foot of the curraghs before she'd accept Simone wasn't there, so she would stay here all day, if I let her, and peruse every single time in the junk room.

I crossed the room to her. She still clutched the Filofax but I took hold of her wrists gently.

'Cora,' I said again. 'This isn't how we'll find her. Come on.'

For a second I thought she would argue. Her jaw clenched and relaxed. But then she let out a breath. A shiver of released tension ran through her hands. Her eyes held mine for a moment then darted away.

'Yeah,' she said with a sigh. 'I know.'

Chapter 19

Before we drove away, I made a quick circuit of the outside of the property, in case Lenny was working in one of the sheds out back. There was no sign of him. The sycamores that bordered his back garden shook and whispered in the rising wind.

When I got back in the car, Cora had taken out the photo of Simone she kept in her wallet. It was rubbed at the corners, as if she'd spent a lot of time taking it out to show to people.

Before she could put it away, I held out my hand. 'Could I see, please?' It'd occurred to me that I'd not taken the time to study it myself.

Cora passed it over. It had obviously been trimmed down from a larger, standard-size picture. I wondered if Cora had done that to make it fit more easily in her wallet, or if she'd deliberately cut someone out of the photo. Simone looked at me from the picture, her eyes cool and her smile distant. I couldn't tell if she was happy or not. Without the context of her surroundings, I had no idea where the photo had been taken.

Now I was looking closer, I could see the definite family

resemblance between her and Cora. The main difference was their noses. Simone's was snub where Cora's was fuller.

I examined Simone's face, frozen forever at age fifteen. I tried not to compare it with my mental image of how I'd pictured Bogbean. But it was difficult. Bogbean had always been a faint presence at my side, a wisp of a girl, with drifting hair. Simone was real.

Her smile in the picture made me think of something. 'Fillings,' I said aloud.

'What?' Cora blinked at me. She'd been lost in her own thoughts.

'Did Simone have any fillings in her teeth?'

Cora's brow knitted in thought. 'I don't know. I think she probably did. We have a history of lousy teeth in my family.'

'The skeleton had filings in two of its teeth,' I said. 'I'm just thinking of corroborating details. If we could find out whether Simone had dental work or not ...'

She tugged her bottom lip in thought. 'I didn't think of that. I guess there would've been dental records from the time, but they probably wouldn't have kept them.'

'What about your parents? Could you ask them?'

Cora took out her phone and started typing a text. 'Hold on, let me ask my brother.'

'You have a brother?'

'Half-brother. Simone always confided in him.'

There was a faint, residual bitterness hidden beneath her words that took me by surprise, more so than finding out she had another sibling. 'Really? Why?'

'God knows.' She kept typing. 'They were ridiculously

similar. Both hated our dad, for different reasons. Both wanted to be anywhere but at home. They used to hang out all the time. If anyone would know a ridiculous detail like her teeth, it'd be him.'

'I ...' *Why hadn't she mentioned him before?*

'It's okay.' Cora gave me a tight smile. 'It's helpful, to be honest. He remembers a lot more everyday stuff about her than I do. It can be useful.'

'Where is he now?'

'Home. He never escaped. I figured, after Simone went, he'd be right behind her. But he kinda swung in the opposite direction. Now he hardly ever leaves the house. He's a proper technological marvel too. Even if he doesn't know something offhand, he'll find out for you.' Cora lifted the wrist with her GPS watch it. 'He got me this doo-hickey. Said if I was going to look for Simone, I should have technology to back me up. That was as close to encouragement as he'd get.'

'He doesn't think you should be looking for Simone?'

'He doesn't think I'll *find* her, not by searching in the real world. He's been looking online for years. And, since he can't find any trace of her, ergo she's not findable. That's how he looks at the world. Plus he's residually mad at me because I've only recently taken up this search. He doesn't understand why I didn't start searching the minute Simone went missing.'

'Why *did* you leave it so long?' It was something I still didn't understand.

Her phone beeped as a text came back. Cora frowned at the screen. 'What side were the fillings on?'

I rubbed the side of my face. Could I trust my memory? I

tried to picture the day I'd found the skeleton. So many times over the years I'd done the same. I could no longer be completely certain what I had or hadn't seen.

And if I wasn't certain, would it be right to tell Cora? I was still scared of giving her false hope. If she latched onto what she saw as a corroborating detail, no matter how small ...

'I don't remember,' I hedged. 'What does your brother say?'

'He's gonna look into it. That means he doesn't remember either.'

'Doesn't he think it's weird you messaged him a query like that?'

'It's the only sort of query I ever send. We don't have a traditional texting relationship.'

I used my phone to take a picture of Simone's photo. 'In case I need to show it to anyone when you're not around,' I explained. I gave her back the photo and started the car. 'I'm sorry this afternoon's been unproductive,' I said as I checked my mirrors. 'This can't be easy for you.'

'It's fine.'

I sneaked a glance at her face. 'Are you sure? How're you holding up?'

'Badly. That's the honest answer, if you're looking for one.' Cora leaned her head back against the car seat headrest. 'It's made everything with Simone feel like it happened yesterday, y'know? I wish I knew if I was getting close or if this is another wild goose chase.'

I pulled out onto the main road. 'How many other places have you visited?'

'In total? Five outside Birmingham. There's only so much

you can do by phone or internet. Sometimes you have to visit the actual place for answers. But, obviously, that doesn't always work out like you expect.' She sighed heavily. 'Every potential lead I've found has turned out to be nothing.'

'I'm amazed you've found so much to track down, after all this time.'

'Yeah, well. A lot of the time I was clutching at straws. I can admit that in retrospect. I would latch onto a story or a hint, and I would spin it out until I was convinced that here, at last, was the answer to my prayers. Did I tell you about the trip to Scotland?'

'You mentioned an exceptionally weird bed and breakfast.'

'Yeah, that was the Scotland trip, about two years ago. I was chasing up a decade-old sighting of someone I genuinely thought could be Simone. It was a woman, the right age, the right description, with a midlands accent, who'd moved to the middle of absolute nowhere in north Scotland. She lived in a caravan and stayed the hell away from everyone. I never would've heard about her except a pair of backpackers got lost in a storm and she let them stay overnight to dry out. They were so grateful that when they got home, they immediately went online to tell everyone who'd listen about the wonderful hospitality they'd encountered. I stumbled across the story. They'd taken a picture outside her caravan, although you can only see the back of the woman's head. I don't think she knew they'd taken the picture, otherwise I'm sure she would've told them not to put it online.'

'Why not?'

Another heavy sigh. 'It wasn't Simone. It was some poor

woman who'd escaped from her abusive husband. She'd set up a new home in the middle of nowhere, figuring no one would find her. And I went rushing up there, asked all her neighbours where to find this woman ... you can imagine how she reacted when I turned up at her door and told her I'd tracked her down from a story online. She flew into a panic. If I could find her, so could her husband.' Cora pressed her hands over her eyes. 'I put the absolute fear of God into her. I never meant to. But she packed her bags that night and disappeared. All thanks to me.' She let her hands fall. 'It's easy to think that this stupid, obsessive quest isn't hurting anyone. But that's just not true.'

I didn't know how to react to that. 'What about the weird bed and breakfast?'

Cora laughed. She shook off her despondency. 'Oh my goodness,' she said. 'Where to even start with *that* place?'

Our half-brother Jason was eight years older than me, only one year older than you.

He wasn't always around. I was glad he lived with his mum, across town, because I was jealous. Jealous that you shared your secrets with him instead of me. Jealous of the way Da spoke about him, always in gentle tones, with none of the exasperation or impatience he reserved for you and me.

But, despite your closeness, you never told Jason about him.

The only person you ever told was me.

And that was only because I found the letter he sent you.

Chapter 20

At five o'clock we gave up for the day and collected at my house for dinner.

People do this all the time, I reminded myself as I checked my reflection in the hall mirror. *And they do it without freaking out.*

But my constant reassurances weren't working. Inside I was a tangle of nerves. It showed in every little thing I did. For example, looking in the mirror five times in the space of an hour. That was unprecedented. There'd been times when I'd gone a week or more without feeling the need to see my own face.

My eyes fell on the pile of post on the hall table. Somewhere beneath it was the Manila envelope that'd arrived that morning. I'd still not psyched myself up to opening this one, although I was certain it contained the same stuff as the last, and the one before that, and the one before that. What I really should've done, I told myself, was dump it straight in the bin. Or, better yet, round up all the other, similar letters that'd been sent to me over the last two years, and burn them in some kind of cathartic bonfire in the garden. It would certainly be healthier than hiding them around the house, which is what I'd done, as if they were something I needed to keep and agonise over. As if I didn't have enough of my own guilt without other people heaping it onto me.

In the kitchen, Cora and Dallin were discussing some television programme that'd aired last year. The argument had the soft, almost-comforting edge to it that told me they'd hashed out these opinions before. Dallin seemed to have left his bad mood in the pub, which was a relief.

No, there was no time to go through my post tonight. It could wait till later. Till forever, maybe.

'You got rid of the steps out to the garden,' Dallin said.

I turned to find he'd come out of the kitchen without me hearing. He held a slim bottle of beer in one hand. There was the slight flush to his complexion which he always got when he was drinking. He made a vague gesture towards the back door.

'The steps,' he repeated, as if to clarify. 'You got rid of them.'

I couldn't stop from rolling my eyes. 'They were like that last time you were here. Mum had the ramp installed. When we were looking for a way to keep her living here. Remember?'

Dallin winced at my tone. 'I don't remember. I mustn't have gone out to the garden that time.'

'How else do you think she would've got outside? It's not like she could've bumped her chair down the steps.'

'Alright, I get it.' Dallin's voice was defensive. 'I thought maybe you'd done it yourself for some reason. I was just asking.'

'Dallin,' I said, then had to stop before I said something

too harsh. 'I've not done much to the house,' I said instead. 'We repainted the bedrooms and put in a new bathroom suite, but that's it.'

'Is Mum okay with you doing that?'

This time I didn't try to hide my exasperation. 'This is a really weird time for you to take an interest in our interior decoration skills. If it bothers you so much, you could've said something earlier. I'm sure Mum would've let you use the house instead of us, if you'd wanted to.'

Dallin looked away. 'Yeah, well. I had no idea she was even planning to move out. I didn't find out until after the fact.'

'And who's fault is that? What did you expect us to do, sit around on our hands waiting for you to come home before we made any decisions about our lives?' I turned to go back into the kitchen, then remembered I had additional things to be mad at him about. 'You set up that website.'

'What?' He blinked at the abrupt change of topic.

'The website. The *forum*, where you met Cora.'

Dallin held up his hands defensively. 'I never set up the forum.'

'But you wrote the page that talked about the curraghs, didn't you?'

'How did you—?'

'I might be a technophobe but it doesn't mean I'm dumb. You used your own email address to register on the forum. It's right there on your profile page. Username "Daytripper". That's you, isn't it?'

In honesty, I never would've put the pieces together if Cora hadn't told me. I'd gone onto the forum when I'd got home, looking for confirmation, and it'd taken me an embarrassingly long time to find the author of the page about the curraghs. And then a while longer to access his profile, because that involved me having to make my own profile for the stupid forum. But, eventually, I'd confirmed what Cora had already told me – someone by the name of Daytripper, using an email even I recognised as Dallin's, was the author of the page detailing my story.

Dallin scrunched up his face in annoyance. But he didn't deny it.

'So—' I held out my hands like he might drop a good explanation into them. 'Why? Why on earth would you put all that personal stuff on the internet?'

'It was all anonymised. There were no personal details.'

'Are you kidding? Every single bit of it was personal.' I lowered my voice so Cora in the kitchen wouldn't hear me. 'It was my personal story. And you put it on some scuzzy website for all the world to see.'

'Okay, first of all, it's not a scuzzy website, it's a perfectly legitimate forum. I've been posting there for years. I've met some of my best friends there. And, second of all—' He kept talking when I tried to interrupt. 'Second of all. Since when was it private? For the last fifteen years you've told it to anyone who'd listen. For all I knew you'd already put it online. Beth certainly blogged about everything else that crossed her mind. Your whole life was online, thanks to her.'

I flinched at Beth's name. 'She didn't— It wasn't—' But I couldn't refute it, could I? Beth had blogged about everything. It'd started as critiques of TV shows then expanded outwards.

Her life, my life, our marriage, our house. Her illness. The last post she'd ever done, the morning of the day she'd died, was four lines, which was as much as she'd been able to write before she'd been exhausted. She'd never kept anything back.

But, on the other hand, I'd always read every single word she'd written before it was posted. On the very few occasions when I'd felt uncomfortable with something she intended to put on her blog, she deleted it. One time that'd happened, it'd been to do with Mum, something minor that I nevertheless didn't want the entire world to know.

The other time had been about the skeleton I'd found in the curraghs. She'd typed up the story but when I read it, she knew, without me having to say, this was the one thing I didn't want to see written down in black and white.

Dallin was right. The feeling was irrational. How was a webpage any different from me telling the story to people in the pub? But still, I couldn't shake the feeling. I didn't like the fact that Dallin had taken my story and put it online in his own words. Was I too sensitive?

'It was never meant to upset you,' Dallin said. His voice was sympathetic now. 'Honestly, I just wrote it up because ... well, someone was talking about unsolved mysteries around the country, and I mentioned the curraghs because, y'know, it's the only one I've heard first-hand. They said I should write it up. Other people would be interested, they said. So I did. It was just a bit of fun. I tried to keep it exactly like you told it. It's not like I exaggerated the details to make myself sound better.'

That was true. I hadn't fully read the webpage this afternoon but it hadn't sounded sensationalised. If anything, from my skimming, it read as a fairly dull summary of the facts.

'People really connected with it,' he said. 'I've got a lot of emails. Not just the randos who comment on every forum post. It struck a chord with people. But it was never meant to be anything more than that. Honestly, I didn't think anyone would read it.' He gave a self-deprecating chuckle. 'But, you're right, I should've run it past you first. It wasn't my story to tell.' He quirked a smile. 'This probably doesn't make it any better, but I genuinely thought you'd never find out. Unless you specifically Googled your own story, I suppose, there was never much chance of you stumbling across that forum.' He did that half-laugh again. 'If you stop and think about it, if Cora hadn't contacted me, none of this would've ever come to your attention. How could I predict that?'

I noticed he wasn't apologising. But then, I wasn't sure if I would accept an apology for this, not when he had so much else to apologise for first.

'To be honest,' Dallin said then, 'I probably should've gone with my first thought when Cora messaged me.'

'Why? What was your first thought?'

Dallin did a shoulder-check, then leaned forwards to whisper, 'I thought she was crazy. Obviously.' His expression was serious now. 'I'm still half convinced she is crazy.'

Chapter 21

I woke the following morning with an ache behind my eyes. I couldn't even blame a hangover, because I stuck to water all night, despite Cora's best efforts.

'Don't you even want a fizzy drink or something?' she asked. Her bag had been stuffed with cans of caffeinated, over-sugared, alarmingly-coloured beverages. 'I've plenty to share.'

I'd stuck to my guns. But that hadn't made me feel better. All I'd been thinking of was the other dinner parties we'd hosted in this kitchen. The times when Beth and I had cooked, each making our personal favourite dishes, both laughing and sniping as we invaded each other's spaces and stole vital utensils and ingredients from the other. By the time our guests arrived, we'd usually made decent headway on the drinks, and were giddy and over-excited by the prospect of food and friends.

Did I miss those days? In some ways, yes, of course I did. I would've given anything to step back into one of those evenings, with Beth at my side, if only for a few hours. But did I want to do them again? That was a more difficult question. Those sociable evenings, full of food and cocktails and friends, felt so long ago they might've happened to another person.

I got up, went downstairs, and put the kettle on. Despite my persistent headache, I was still in that pleasant, half-awake state where the outside world didn't impact on me much. I could pretend that this Sunday morning was no different to a dozen other days I'd spent alone.

There was an empty beer bottle on the kitchen table. Before he'd left last night, Dallin had put the rest in the recycling, but he'd left the last one, like a prize for me to find. I flinched at this obvious reminder of people being in our house.

That was the source of my headache, I realised. Not an alcohol or sugar hangover, but a social hangover, caused by interacting with other people. My brain was cringing from the memory of what I might or might not have said.

Last night, Dallin had tried his best to keep the conversation away from difficult topics, but inevitably we ended up talking about Simone. Cora filled us in on more details about her extensive family. I kept getting confused with who was related to who, until eventually Cora dug out a folder from her backpack and unfolded a large sheet of paper across the kitchen table.

'I knew I'd brought this,' she said. 'This is the closest any of my family's managed to making a proper family tree.'

Cora's family took up the whole sheet. She smoothed the paper flat with both hands.

In the centre of the page was Simone's name. It was surrounded by a box, drawn in black ink, so it immediately caught the eye. Most people would've put themselves at the centre, then drawn their family radiating out from there. But Cora's name was off to the side, almost like an afterthought. It was clear, in everything, she was overshadowed by her sister.

'What's with the lines?' I asked. Almost every name on the page was underlined in different coloured inks. Some were red, others blue, a very few in green. Some had multiple red lines underneath them.

'They show who's talking to one another,' Cora said with a laugh. 'It started as a joke, so I could keep track of which aunts I should be stonewalling, but it's become a handy visual guide.' She put her finger on her parents' names, both of which had blue lines underneath. 'My parents are talking to everyone who's underlined in blue. They're *not* talking to anyone who's underlined in red. They're *really* not talking to anyone with more than one red line.' She took a sip of her beer. 'The ones in green aren't speaking to each other, but we haven't taken sides in the argument, so we're okay to talk to either one, if we want to.' She shrugged. 'Families are complicated.'

I avoided looking at Dallin. 'It's a wonder you can keep this straight in your head.'

'I can't. That's why I drew a chart.'

I put my finger on one of the names. *Florence.* She had several alternating red and blue lines underneath her name. 'What's going on here?'

'That's my Aunt Florrie. She's my—' She peered at the chart as if to remind herself of her own family. 'My dad's step-sister. We weren't speaking to her for years. I can't remember why. Then we patched things up and everyone was friends for a while, until she and my dad fell out again. That's kinda repeated itself for the last few years. Hence all the lines. I really should come up with a different colour-scheme, just for her.'

'What do they argue about?'

'Literally anything. Aunt Florrie has terrible luck with boyfriends. Every single one of them has been an awful decision. I told you about that one guy, who she dated for a couple of years? Ran a garage and thought he looked spiffing in blue coveralls?'

'The one Simone was—?'

'That's the one.' Cora's expression twisted at the memory. 'Florrie insisted he wanted to marry her but – get this – he was already married, with no intention of leaving his wife, so she changed her surname by deed poll to match his, and literally pretended they were married.' Cora shook her head. 'Sometimes, looking at her, I can see where Simone got it from. Aunt Florrie is a series of disasters poured into a Chanel suit. She infuriates my dad something chronic.'

'Family gatherings must be fun,' Dallin observed.

'Fun is not the correct word.' Cora ran her finger over the names at the periphery of the family tree. 'Did I ever tell you about how my cousin Benji got barred from KFC for indecent exposure?'

For the next half hour, Cora told us the various ridiculous things her families had done. Dallin retaliated with some horror stories from his time in Barcelona. It was like they were trying to outdo each other. I smiled at the correct times and wished I had some funny stories about my own family I could share.

Eventually, Dallin succeeded in changing the subject, and Cora folded away her family map.

Now, I left Dallin's beer bottle on the tabletop and instead took my cup of tea out into the garden.

Instead of drinking my tea on the back doorstep, like usual, I wandered down into the garden. It was early and the sun was barely risen. I shivered in my dressing gown. The grass was wet and cold beneath my feet.

I walked across the lawn to the southeast corner of the garden. I was vaguely thinking about the photo I'd seen in Cora's book, of the tree that'd once stood there. I was interested to see if there was any sign of where it'd stood.

Right in the corner was a spill of ivy that'd grown over the back wall and tangled into a huge matted clump. It'd been a while since I'd come down to this shady corner. Mostly it was given over to whatever wildflowers could find a foothold. During the spring, there were clumps of snowdrops, daffodils and bluebells, one after the other, which pushed up through the tangle. But I hadn't realised how much the ivy had taken over. I wondered if I should get the shears out.

I set my cup of tea down on a flat stone at the edge of the lawn. With both hands, I started to pull aside the thick tendrils of ivy. They resisted my best efforts. Over the years, the ivy had put down roots into the soft ground, the space between the stones of the wall, and anywhere else that gave them an inch-hold. I ended up ripping up big handfuls of it. Well, it would undoubtedly grow back. I flung the torn strands over the back wall.

It occurred to me there might be nothing left of the tree.

If it'd been pulled down, the roots dug up, there could be nothing for me to find. I gave up on the ivy and started shoving aside ferns and bindweed.

Eventually, underneath the ivy and bindweed, I found the tree stump.

It was no surprise I'd never noticed it before. Even now, when I'd known it was there, it still took me a solid ten minutes to find.

I pulled the strands of bindweed away. It felt like uncovering history. I felt a small frisson inside me. I'd lived in this house for years, yet it could still surprise me.

The base of the tree stump was blackened with rot. No, not rot. As I pulled away the obstructing vines, I realised the stump had been scorched with soot. It looked a lot like someone had started a fire that burned the bark on one side.

I wondered if Dallin or Mum remembered the tree, or what had happened to it. I made a mental note to ask next time I spoke to either of them.

In the meantime, I picked up my cup of tea and went back into the house.

Cora and Dallin were spending the day searching the curraghs. I'd agreed to meet them at lunchtime to bring food and get updates. It was probably quite telling that I assumed they'd have nothing to report.

For the duration of the morning, I made myself think about anything other than Cora. I spent my time dusting and hoovering the sitting room. It was nice to get back into my rhythm. The sitting room often took an entire day to tidy, since I had to dust under or around every single one of Beth's ridiculous ornaments. Once I got past the trauma of opening the curtains, I could bring my dust-cloths into the room, break out the beeswax, and get to work.

At midday, when I came to the natural halt where I would normally make my third cup of tea, I picked up my mobile phone and found a message from Cora. It was embarrassing how a few simple words from her could make me smile. I hunched my shoulders, still hiding the message from prying eyes.

Want to talk to neighbours again today? My turn to buy lunch.

I read the message three times. Was I reading something into it that wasn't there? Cora wanted to see me. Wanted to buy me lunch. That was pretty clear. Wasn't it? I wished I wasn't so out of touch. The last person I'd flirted with was Beth. And, to be honest, she'd done all the flirting. I'd just been swept along in its wake.

Sounds great, I typed, then dithered about whether I should put a kiss at the end. No, better hadn't. I went for a smiley face instead. Smiley faces were neutral.

I hurried upstairs to get ready.

Chapter 22

When Cora arrived, she was driving Priscilla.

'I've checked the wheels aren't going to fall off,' she said as she leaned out of the driver's side window. 'How strict are the laws over here? Will I get pulled over for not having all my wheels?'

I laughed and got in the passenger side. 'That depends on a lot of things,' I said as I settled into my seat. 'Like if anyone's watching. How's Dallin?'

'Unhappy. He didn't drink much, but you can tell he'd rather have stayed curled up in bed than stomp around in a bog this morning. He still isn't sleeping well, I think. The hard ground disagrees with him.'

'What about you?' I snuck a glance at her. She looked pale, with shadows under her eyes.

'Me?' She sounded surprised at my concern. 'I'm fine. I don't sleep much anyway. Thank you for dinner last night, by the way.'

'No problem. Thank you for coming over.' And like that, I ran out of conversation. I stared at my hands, then up at the clouds. Should I comment on the weather? Or maybe give her a compliment – tell her I liked her hat, or her jumper, or—

I closed my eyes in annoyance. Why was I so bad at talking to people? How did everyone else in the world manage small talk?

Fortunately, the drive to Nicole's house only took a matter of minutes, so there wasn't time for the silence to become awkward. I got out of the car and stretched my back. The front door of Nicole's house was open, and we could hear a radio playing from somewhere inside.

'Looks like they're in,' Cora said. 'Thank goodness. I was beginning to think we'd have to stake out their house to find them.'

I laughed. 'While I was waiting for you to pick me up, I gave Nicole a call to check she was in.'

'See, I should put you in charge of planning everything.'

Together we went up and knocked on the open door. 'Hello?' I called. 'Nicole?'

'In the kitchen,' her cheery voice called back. 'Come on through. Leave the door open, will you please? One of the farm cats has gone to sleep on my bed and I don't want them getting locked in the house.'

I led the way to the kitchen. Nicole's house always looked like an advertisement for the perfect farmhouse. Everything was tasteful and understated. With one exception – Nicole had an inexplicable fondness for bad watercolour pictures. There were five of them in the hallway and, I knew, another four in the sitting room. They all showed the same view of Bradda Head, the admittedly scenic headland above Port Erin which every amateur painter on the Island drew at least once in their lifetime. I was sure Nicole could've found better versions of the hill. When I'd asked her, she'd laughed, and said it was an in-joke of sorts, but never explained further.

'Lovely to see you, Rosalie.' Nicole came bustling around the breakfast island to greet us. Her kitchen was about the same size as mine, but seemed so much bigger because of the floor to ceiling windows that formed the back wall. Through those windows, there was an unrivalled view over the fields. It felt like the whole world was at their back gate. Also, because of the way the house faced, no other houses were visible. I could see why Nicole's family had chosen this spot.

'This is my friend, Cora,' I said. My cheeks reddened as soon as I said it. She wasn't really my friend, I'd only just met her; was I being presumptuous introducing her like that?

But neither Cora nor Nicole noticed. As usual, I was being oversensitive to things no one else was even aware of.

'Cora.' Nicole smiled. 'Lovely to meet you. I've got a pot of coffee on the go, if you fancy it. I've peppermint or camomile if you prefer, Rosalie.'

I smiled. It was little things like that which made you feel welcome. 'Camomile would be lovely, thank you.'

Nicole sat us down at the breakfast island. She was dressed in jeans and a loose blouse, which somehow looked like the height of fashion on her. Her gardening hat was upturned on a small table near the patio door with her gloves folded inside it. Next to it was a wooden rack with a neat row of upside down wellies. When I'd called, she must've been in the garden. I felt bad for interrupting.

'Now, I understand you're trying to track down your sister,' Nicole said. She pulled one of the spare stools up to the counter so she could sit down.

'Pretty much.' Cora glanced at me. For reassurance? I gave her a smile. 'We think she came over here, to the island, about twenty years ago.'

She went through her story again. Nicole listened with a sympathetic ear. Even though I'd heard Cora tell the story several times already, it still struck me how it affected her. She kept her hands clasped tightly in her lap. I dearly wanted to reach over and squeeze her hands. Offer some kind of tangible reassurance.

'This is her,' Cora finished. She placed the photo of Simone down on the counter so Nicole could see.

Nicole put on her reading glasses and leaned forward to examine the photo, rather than picking it up. 'Such a pretty face,' she said, with a soft smile. 'She looks a lot like you.'

'She was about six years older,' Cora said. 'We didn't look a bit alike when we were young. I guess I've maybe grown into my face.'

'It was June 1999 that she disappeared, that's what you said?' Nicole nodded to me. 'After you told me about it the other day, I went looking for my old diaries.'

'You've kept diaries for twenty years?' I asked, amazed.

'They're not like a journal or anything.' Nicole smiled. 'Just a calendar on my computer where I kept track of conferences and holidays and dentist appointments. Y'know, the important things in life. I keep a paper diary as well, but that's just a record of the garden, so I know when and where I've planted.'

I knew she must've had a careful plan to keep her garden looking so amazing. 'So, I suppose they don't say anything about Simone?' I asked.

'They probably don't, no.' Nicole refilled her coffee mug from the cafetière on the counter. 'But I haven't been able to retrieve them yet. I know I kept them on a flash drive, but can I find it now? Of course I can't. It'll be tucked away safe in a desk drawer somewhere.'

Cora cupped her hands around her coffee mug. 'Can you remember anything without the calendar?'

'Well, I was travelling a lot back then. I was a travel rep, did I ever tell you that, Rosalie?' Her eyes twinkled. 'There are some stories I could tell you from those days. But anyway, from what I recall of 1999, a lot of the time I wasn't here.'

'You weren't?'

'I was off in Greece for at least three months, which I think started in August that year. Working at a grotty tourist hotel in Mykonos. Got so horrendously sunburnt I vowed never to set foot outside without a sunhat. Met a very interesting young man called Estoban who showed me which bars would sell you a decent drink.' Nicole's distant gaze came back into focus. 'Don't tell Patrick about that last part, by the way. What he doesn't know won't harm him.'

Cora edged forwards on her seat. 'But you think you were at home in June?'

'As far as I can remember. I have to tell you, it was a terribly long time ago and I'm not sure I remember anything specific.' Nicole's gaze went back to the photo on the table. 'I definitely don't remember seeing your sister. Sorry.'

'She might've changed her hair before she got here,' Cora said. 'Or been dressed differently.' The desperate edge crept back into her voice.

Nicole shook her head sadly. 'If I did see her, however she looked at the time, I don't remember her. I'm sorry.'

'Did you go into town much back then? I mean, is there a chance you could've seen her at the supermarket or—?'

'I genuinely wouldn't remember.' Nicole kept the sympathetic smile on her face, but her tone was clipped. 'Unless she did something extremely memorable, like run naked through the car park, I wouldn't recall. Not after twenty years.'

'We know,' I said, trying to smooth things. 'Cora understands how difficult it'll be. If Simone had done anything to draw attention to herself, maybe people would've wondered where her parents were. Maybe they would've recognised her photo when it was shown on the news.'

'It was never on the national news,' Cora said.

I raised my eyebrows. 'But surely the police would've—'

'I remember it being in the local news. Then it was mentioned in the newspaper about a month later, to jog anyone's memory. As far as I'm aware, it never made it as far as the national press.'

I frowned. Things were maybe different two decades ago, but I could remember, when I was a kid, seeing appeals for information about missing children on the news. Any child who ran off would feature on the news at some point, along with an appeal for them to get in touch. Had no one done that for Simone?

'What about your niece?' Cora asked.

Nicole blinked. 'I don't have a niece. My brother has two kids, but they're both boys.'

'Oh,' Cora said with a frown.

'I tell you what,' Nicole said. She took out her phone and snapped a quick picture of the photo. 'I'll ask Patrick if he remembers seeing or hearing anything about your sister. And I'll phone round a few of my friends. Let me think, who lived in Ballaugh all that time ago?' She pressed a finger to her lips in thought. 'Leave it with me. I'll ask around.'

'Thank you,' Cora said. She attempted a smile in response, but I could see the dejection behind her eyes. As much as she told everyone she knew she wouldn't find answers, each little defeat must've chipped away at her determination.

Nicole gave her back the photo. 'And how's your mum doing, Rosalie?' she asked, brightly. 'Alright, I hope?'

'She's fine. She's doing fine. I'll tell her you said hello.'

'Please do. You'll have to bring her round to see the garden. It's been a while. I've planted up the whole southern bed. Remind me before you go, and I'll give you a bunch of the dahlias to take to her.'

'She'd love that, thank you. I've still got a clump of them growing in my garden from the bulbs you gave me two years ago. They're looking better than ever.'

'Well.' Nicole couldn't hide a tinge of pride. 'Green fingers are their own reward, aren't they? I always loved that little garden of Opal's. I'm glad you're making the most of it. Your mum, she used to grow the most incredible sunflowers. I don't know if you remember? Fifteen feet tall, some of them were, with heads the size of a dinner plate.' She indicated with her hands. 'I had a friend at school who was afraid of sunflowers. No kidding. She said she didn't like the way they looked at her.'

I was ready to make an excuse to leave, but speaking about the garden reminded me. 'Did there used to be an oak tree in our garden?' I asked. 'Down at the bottom, in the southeast corner?'

Something flickered across Nicole's face; there and gone before I could figure it out. Then her smile came back. 'A horse chestnut,' she said. 'Not an oak. Dallin used to collect conkers from it when he was a toddler. Lovely old tree, it was.'

'Why was it cut down?'

'It got hit by lightning.' Nicole's gaze slipped away from me. 'During a storm. The whole thing was hollow, you see, although no one knew that until afterwards. When it caught fire, it went up like kindling. Terrible shame.'

'I don't remember it at all.'

'No, you would've been too young. Dallin was—' Nicole frowned as she counted the years in her head. 'I guess he would've been about eight or nine? But he was away from home when it happened. Actually, I think he was staying at your Dad's house.'

I frowned as I tried to think when that would've been. Dallin had spent almost as much time at our dad's house in Douglas, as I had at Mum's. Possibly it had been during either TT or Manx Grand Prix week, which took up two weeks in June and August respectively, because Mum had gone through a phase of worrying about Dallin living so close to the TT course. Personally, I didn't think Dallin was daft enough, even as a kid, to wander into the middle of a road race, but you never did know.

'Let me get you those dahlias for Opal,' Nicole said. She hopped off her seat and snatched up the secateurs from the side table. 'It was lovely to meet you, Cora. Sorry I couldn't be more help. I do hope you find what you're looking for.'

'Thank you,' Cora said again.

I realised she was still gripping the picture of Simone in her hands. As we left the house, she carefully tucked it back into her wallet.

We stood in the garden for a few minutes while Nicole busied herself cutting a half-dozen long stemmed flowers for me to take to Mum. Cora looked like she had something on her mind. Her lips moved in absent thought.

I nudged her with my shoulder. 'You alright?'

She blinked, coming halfway back to herself. 'Yes. I'm fine. I was just thinking. How old are you?'

I tucked a loose strand of hair behind my ear, and tried to ignore the warmth that rose to my face. 'I'm twenty-six.'

'And Dallin is a few years older than you.'

'About two and a half. Although you wouldn't know it from the way he acts.' I smiled, but Cora was preoccupied.

'This might be nothing ...' She stared to say, but was interrupted by her phone ringing.

It took her a moment to dig it out of her jacket pocket. The ringtone rose louder and louder, as if shouting its urgency. At last she got the phone out, checked the screen, then answered.

'Hi Dallin,' she said. 'What's up?'

There was a tense note to her voice. With a lurch, I realised Dallin wouldn't be calling for no reason.

He's found something.

'What?' Cora turned away from me and put a finger in her other ear, so she could hear Dallin better. 'What's happened? Where—?'

She listened for a moment, her shoulders hunched, her face turned away so I couldn't see what she was thinking. Nicole raised her head as well. We caught each other's eyes and knew we were thinking the same thing. *What's happened?*

'We'll be right there,' she said at last, then ended the call.

'What is it?' I asked. I was half-dreading her answer.

But when it came, it wasn't at all what I expected. 'Someone's been in my tent,' Cora said.

Chapter 23

The campsite was tucked away down the backroad that led to Druidsdale. It occupied a large field behind The Raven public house and was right next to the humpbacked bridge at Ballaugh, where, during the races, motorbikes would go over at enough speed to become airborne for a split-second. A few years ago, one unlucky racer had hit the bridge with too much speed and fired himself into the wall of the pub. Now, during TT week, they put up a load of crash padding at that spot.

I had never been to the campsite itself, aside from my brief visit the day before to drop off Cora's car, but I'd heard other people commending it for being family- and dog-friendly. Those were apparently the most important features in any campsite.

As I turned into the big field, I saw a man sitting on a bench, on the veranda outside the wooden cabin that doubled as an office for the owners of the site. When he saw my car, he dropped the cigarette into an ashtray that was nailed to the arm of the bench.

'You're the owner of the tent, are you?' he asked as I rolled down my window. 'I'd approach with caution if I were you. Your friend's very angry.'

'Where's the site manager?' Cora asked.

'On the phone to the police.' He waved us onto the grass. 'Hope everything's okay.'

I drove at a steady eight miles-per-hour over the grass towards where Cora pointed. Her tent was a green dome-shape that looked comfy for one person but definitely too cosy for two. Mostly I spotted it because Dallin was standing outside with his arms folded and his face like a thundercloud.

'Someone's been in there,' he said. He barely waited for us to get out of the car. 'They've been through all your stuff. It's a mess.'

'Oh my God.' Cora crouched down and stuck her head into the tent. 'Who would do that? Is anything missing?'

'I haven't looked at anything. You should check your stuff though.'

'Is your tent okay?' I asked him.

'Yeah, untouched.' He scuffed the ground with the toe of his trainers. 'I only noticed this because Cora's tent was unpegged at the front. I know she didn't leave it like that this morning.'

Cora sat back on her heels with her rucksack in her lap. 'Looks like everything's here. They just tipped out all my clothes. I didn't leave anything valuable in here. Everything worth more than tuppence is in my pockets. It's just—' Cora let out a breath, '—first my car, now my tent. Why would someone do that? It's not necessary.'

Peering past her, I got a glimpse of the tent interior, strewn with clothes and paperback books. 'I hate to say it, but it could've been kids,' I said. 'They might've crawled in here on the off-chance you had booze.'

'That's what the site owner said as well.' Dallin switched his glare to a collection of ridged tents at the bottom of the field. 'There's a gaggle of twenty feral kids in those tents over there. Some kind of birthday holiday. Some of the older ones might've done it.'

'You don't sound convinced.'

Dallin rubbed the side of his face. He badly needed a shave. 'If this was just some random, one-off occurrence, sure, I'd be happy to write it off as scrotey kids. But yesterday someone ruined two of Cora's tyres. Today, this.' He turned his pale gaze to me. 'I don't like it. Seriously, I do not like it at all.'

'Are you going to call the police?'

'I don't know.'

It was the first time I'd seen him less than completely sure about anything. It unnerved me. 'You should.'

Dallin let out a measured breath. 'It's likely out of our hands anyway. The site owner is making phone calls in his shed over there. Chances are, his first call was to the police.' He gave a hollow laugh. 'They're going to be super happy to see us again so soon. Especially after the names I called them yesterday.'

I walked around the tent. At the back, two other pegs had been pulled loose, as if someone had yanked up the flysheet to check there was nothing hidden underneath.

'If someone was looking for something, what would it be?' I asked.

Dallin lifted his hands in exasperation. 'Alcohol. Phones. Money. Whatever people are daft enough to leave in an unsecure tent.'

'And if they weren't looking for those?'

Cora frowned. 'What're you getting at?'

'Do you have anything specific that someone would look for? Not necessarily something of value, but which someone who knew you might look for.'

Cora narrowed her eyes. 'You think it's the same person who damaged my car.'

'It's a possibility. Two apparently random acts in the space of two days? Both designed to freak you out as much as possible with the minimum of effort?'

'They didn't cause any damage this time,' Dallin said.

'Don't be so sure.' I snagged the inner lining of the tent and lifted it. 'Look at this.'

Someone had slit the groundsheet open in a long, straight gash. The cut was about four inches long. The heavy fabric of the tent meant the damage wasn't visible until I pulled the material taut.

Cora let out a stream of expletives.

'There's another one here.' Dallin had gone to the other side of the tent. 'I hadn't even noticed.'

'No. That's the point.' Cora stuffed her hands into the pockets of her jeans. 'We wouldn't have realised until tonight, when the rain came in and soaked all my stuff.'

It was a nasty, malicious action. 'I think the person lifted the flysheet here,' I said. 'Maybe they planned to cut the fabric from the outside.' I straightened up and looked around. 'There are too many people within sight. They could've been spotted. So they went inside the tent to cut it, where no one would see them.'

'Did they empty the bags so we wouldn't notice the damage straight away?' Dallin wondered. 'Or were they really looking for something?'

'Whatever it was, they won't have found it in my dirty underwear.' Cora tilted her face to the sky. Her anger was bubbling under the surface. It seemed likely she would start swearing again at any moment. 'What the hell did they expect to find?'

In the mud near the back of the tent was half a boot print. I bent to examine it. Obviously, it could've belonged to Cora – or Dallin, if he'd wandered around the tents at any point. But it must've been left recently, because the rain last night would've erased it. The back half of the print was the only bit captured by the mud; the front was on the grass. What I could see of it displayed a wavy pattern, like you'd find on a child's shoe.

I pointed it out to Cora. She took a photo, just in case.

'Something else to show the police,' she said. 'Probably nothing they can use, but at least they won't dismiss us out of hand. Hopefully.'

'We're on private land,' Dallin said. 'That'll make a difference. The campsite owner won't be happy about vandalism, deliberate or random. It'll reflect badly on his business.' He gestured at the other tents. Outside a few, people were sitting, talking. I realised they were casting covert glances in our direction. 'Word spreads fast in places like this. Soon everyone will know what happened. The owner wants people to know he's responding quickly and it won't happen again.'

I ducked my head to look inside the tent again. Now the shock had worn off, I could see the mess more dispassionately. The tears in each side of the tent were not obvious at all. But when it rained again – which it would do at any time – the interior of the tent would end up damp at best, soaked at worst. That sort of thing could send people home very quickly. I'd only been camping a few times, when me and Beth were both younger and more adventurous, and I knew being wet and miserable would take the shine off an adventure fast.

Would it have been enough to make Cora give up and return home? Was that what someone was hoping for?

Underneath a pile of T-shirts, I spotted the corner of something solid. I lifted a shirt to reveal a picture wallet, of the sort I'd sometimes seen people keep in their pockets, when they carried a large number of family photos that they wanted to bore people with. I didn't think anyone still used those these days. You could bore people much more effectively with a smartphone.

The wallet was open to a picture of Cora and Simone together when they were much younger. Since it was obviously personal, I didn't look too closely. But underneath was something else. A square black book with rubbed corners and the word Filofax embossed on the front.

My stomach lurched. *No … she wouldn't have …*

The door fabric rustled as Cora moved to come in. I snatched up the Filofax and shoved it under my coat.

Cora poked her head into the tent. Her eyes fell on the photo wallet.

'You think they looked at these pictures?' I asked.

Cora made a small noise in her throat. 'I keep them in a zip pocket of my bag. They wouldn't have fallen out by accident.' She turned to look at me, very close in the confines of the tent. 'Whoever was in here, they were looking for pictures of Simone. Why would they do that?'

Chapter 24

Later, I was sitting in my car, parked outside the campsite office, when Dallin sought me out. Cora was talking to the police, down next to her tent. It'd been decided to keep Dallin away from the police this time.

Dallin opened the car door and dropped into the passenger seat without asking. He let out a sigh so long and heavy it was like he was deflating. 'I'm exhausted,' he said. 'What a goddamn mess, huh?'

I nodded absently. I was distracted, still thinking about the Filofax I'd found. It was Lenny's, I was certain. Cora must've snuck it into her pocket while I was putting the boxes back. But why?

From where I'd parked, I could see the top of Cora's tent and the police car next to it, but I couldn't see her. Presumably she was talking with the officers somewhere.

'All I want to do is fall into bed,' Dallin said. 'But apparently I can't even do that.'

'Did you check if your tent is damaged too?'

Dallin nodded. 'Nothing's been touched, inside or out. I guess it was just Cora's tent that got targeted.'

'First her car, now her tent.'

'It does look like someone hates her, doesn't it? Cora was talking about some photos that'd been pulled out of her bag. Family stuff. Did you see them?'

'No. I saw the photo wallet, but not what was inside.'

'The police have taken it. They reckon it's the best bet for finding fingerprints.' He ran his fingers through his hair. 'It's weird. Cora never mentioned those photos. I've asked about her family a bunch of times. You'd think she would've brought out the pictures.'

'Not if they were personal.'

'But if she had anything, no matter how personal, that would potentially jog someone's memory about Simone—' He shrugged. 'I don't know. I would've expected her to be showing them to everyone. She's weirdly secretive about her family sometimes.'

'Not everyone likes to overshare.'

Dallin looked at me. 'Is that a dig at me?'

'A little, yeah.'

'You're still angry about the website?'

I sighed. 'I'm still angry about everything. The website is the absolute least of it, and you know it. You can't expect me to forgive you so easily.'

'I've said I was sorry.'

I wasn't entirely sure that was true, but I let it pass. 'Why did you hate us, Dal?' I asked.

'I never hated you,' he said with surprise.

'No, but you hated *us*. Me and Beth, together. You hated the idea of us being together, and living in Mum's house.'

'That's not true at all.'

'Isn't it? The minute you heard Mum say she was renting her house to me and Beth, you were gone. Pretty much the same day. That looks a lot like you hated us.'

'Rosie,' he started, then sighed again. 'Listen, it was nothing to do with you. It was a really difficult time. I didn't know how to process how I was feeling. Losing Dad ... and then Mum having to give up the house she loved and go live in that pokey little flat, just because we couldn't figure out how to install a stairlift ... that's the sort of thing that happens to old people. She's not even sixty. I hate that she was forced out of her home.'

'And you thought the best way to express that was to move to England? Don't you think she needed your help more than ever?'

'She had you. And Beth.' As always, he said her name carefully, like it was something made of glass, or knives. 'I tried talking to Mum about moving back in with her. Getting a load of work done to the house, to make it suitable for her. But she'd already made her own plan. She wanted you to live in that house. More than she wanted me living there.' He rubbed the side of his face. 'Don't pretend it isn't true. She said you would take better care of the garden.' He rolled his eyes. 'Like that's a proper excuse for anything. She just didn't want to admit she liked you better than me.'

I said nothing. In point of fact, I remembered those conversations between me and Mum and Dallin. I'd been just as resistant to the idea of her moving into a flat. It'd be such a huge wrench. But she'd been adamant. She wanted to remain independent, even if that meant leaving her beloved home, and I'd supported that decision. Only once had I asked her why she'd rented the house to me and Beth instead of to Dallin.

'I could never have asked him to pay rent,' Mum had said. 'It would've never worked out, for either of us. The only other thing I could've done was sell the house and split the money between the two of you. But I knew what would happen if I did.'

I knew as well. Mum couldn't bear the idea of losing the house and seeing Dallin squander the profits. So she'd found a compromise she could live with – she knew me and Beth would use the house as a home, and love it as much as she had. Apparently that wasn't what Dallin had hoped for. I uncharitably wondered what plans he'd had for the money we would've made from selling.

'Anyway, it doesn't matter, does it?' Dallin said at length. 'Things never work out as anyone plans. Your whole life can go awry in a moment.'

I laughed without humour. 'Yeah, tell me about it.'

'I just never understood ... how come you're not more *angry?* I'm furious, all the time. But you're just—' He gestured at me. 'You've just accepted it.'

'Is that what you think?'

'Come on, Rose. How can you *not* be angry at Mum for what happened to Dad?'

And there was the truth, at last. I felt a weird kind of satisfaction that he'd finally admitted it aloud. 'It was an accident, Dal,' I said. 'We all know that.'

'Mum was driving. Whatever happened had to be her fault.'

'Possibly. We'll never know, will we?'

Mum had no memory of the accident. No memory of that entire day, in fact. The police found Mum's car, on its roof, halfway down a steep embankment on the coast road to Douglas. Another twenty feet and the car would've pitched over the cliff into the sea. No one ever pieced together exactly what happened. From the marks on the road, it looked like she'd swerved, but for what reason we'd never know.

Dallin was shaking his head. 'It must've been—'

'There's no *must* about it. For all we know, another car forced them off the road. Or a duck ran out in front of them. Or they had an argument and Dad grabbed the wheel.'

Dallin stared at me in shock. 'Dad would never—'

'That's the point though, isn't it? We don't know what they did. We have to accept that.'

Which was fine for me to say, of course. But when I catalogued the ghosts at my shoulders, Beth and Bogbean, why did I never include my dad with them? By all rights, he should've been right there, in my thoughts and memories always, and yet I hardly ever caught myself looking around for his shade. Why? Because I was angry with him too. I knew I had no right to be, but some things defied rational thinking.

What if he *did* cause the crash? Him and Mum always argued when they were in a car together. It was as inevitable as the tides. Even after fifteen years of separation, they still picked fights with each other. On more than one occasion I'd seen her take both hands off the wheel to harangue him.

So, yes, the same dark thoughts had crossed my mind. *What if? What if?* I didn't want to believe Mum would've done anything to hurt Dad.

But *what if?*

'It's your fault as well,' I said. I didn't mean to say it aloud but it slipped out as I was trying to suppress those other, darker thoughts.

'What?' The stricken look on Dallin's face made me wish I'd kept quiet.

'Mum only went to pick up Dad from Douglas that day because you were too hungover to do it yourself,' I said. 'If you'd just got out of bed that morning ...'

I didn't finish the thought. My awful words hung in the air between us.

'Is that really how you feel?' Dallin asked, his voice subdued.

'No. Of course not.' The lie came easily. 'If we're playing the blame-game, we can point the finger at anyone. The crash could've been the fault of Mum, or Dad, or you, or me, or the universe, or no one or everyone.' I rubbed my forehead. 'Or it could've been an accident. A stupid, unfathomable accident that makes no sense no matter how much you want it to.'

I thought about Cora, so desperate to know what happened to her sister. I could've been like that – obsessing over what caused my mum to crash the car, or what had sparked the cancer in Beth's young body. If I'd asked the right questions, harassed the right people, could I have discovered why exactly these terrible things had happened to us?

When I closed my eyes I thought I felt Beth's hands on my

shoulders. *Don't hold onto it,* she would've said. *Some things ground you; others drown you.*

There was another silence, longer this time. But the air felt clearer. I blinked away my tears.

Eventually, Dallin said, 'Have you considered having the garden remodelled? It must be a lot of work for you on your own. Have you thought about putting down decking?'

I laughed at the side-stepping of topic and shook my head. No, I hadn't considered remodelling anything. For a start, I didn't have the money. I also didn't have the mental wellness. I was struggling just to keep things ticking over from one day to the next. The slightest deviation to my routine left me discombobulated for days. What would happen if I got a load of workmen in to tear up the garden and remodel it? Just the thought gave me a tight feeling in my chest.

'Do you remember the big tree that used to be in the garden?' I asked. I wasn't really interested, I just wanted to distract him from proposing changes to my home.

'Which one?'

'The big horse chestnut. It was down by the boundary wall. Nicole says it got struck by lightning when you were a kid.'

'Oh, shit, yeah. I remember. It caught fire one night. Proper horrifying. I was asleep in bed when I heard people shouting. When I looked out of my window the whole garden was lit up. Like something from a movie. Flames climbing all the way up one side of the tree. Mum came pounding up the stairs and bundled me out of the house – picked me right up and hauled me out of there. It must've been adrenaline or something, because I was pretty heavy by then. It'd been years since she'd carried me anywhere. But anyway, yeah, I remember sitting out on the road in front of the house in my pyjamas. I think Mum must've been scared the tree would fall onto the house; that's why she got me out of there so fast.'

Nicole had said Dallin wasn't home when it happened, but I guessed it was so long ago, it was no wonder memories got mixed up. 'Why did no one tell me about this?' I asked.

'I told you a bunch of times. It was literally all I talked about that summer. Mum sent me to stay with you and Dad for a week afterwards, in case I'd been traumatised, I guess. When I got back, whatever was left of the tree had been chopped down. There was only a stump left.' Dallin looked at me quizzically. 'Don't you remember it at all? I swear I told you.'

I shook my head.

'I guess you were pretty young. About five or six, maybe? Mum never liked talking about it. I think it traumatised her more than it did me. I got into the habit of not mentioning it.'

I thought hard but no memories surfaced. Dallin was probably right – how much did I really remember from when I was young? My memories of early childhood were scrappy and piecemeal. Like most people's, I suspected. There were more important things that I'd forgotten. My grandfather, for example, who died when I was three. Three whole years, and I didn't have a single memory of him. At least I could picture my dad, if I closed my eyes.

But still, it was weird, to think I'd been living in that house all this time and never known about the tree. It made me wonder what other secrets were buried in my garden.

'Something else we're not mentioning,' Dallin said then. 'I think we should tell Cora to give up on this search.'

I turned to look at him. 'You really feel that way?'

'Don't you? This search is a loss. She won't find anything.'

'What makes you so certain?'

'I don't know. Nothing. Everything.' Dallin pulled down the sun visor so he could check his reflection in the vanity mirror. 'She's not telling us the full story about her sister. Have you heard the way she talks about her parents? There's something not right there.'

I frowned. Had I noticed anything odd in Cora's comments? 'They don't get along,' I said. 'That's not so unusual.'

'It's more than just not getting on. She's angry as hell at her parents. She blames them completely for Simone's disappearance. In fact, I think she blames everyone she knows. She keeps saying if only everyone had looked harder for Simone, maybe they would've found her in time.'

It was a fair enough sentiment, I thought. 'She's been through a lot. It'd be weirder if she wasn't angry.'

'Maybe. I'm just saying, I've only known her a few months, but it's long enough to suspect she's plastered over a lot of cracks. I'm worried she's not stable.'

'She's fine.' I came to Cora's defence automatically. 'This is what people look like when they're grieving. It's normal.'

Dallin didn't answer. Silence filled the car, broken only by the barking of a dog outside a tent further down the field.

'Anyway,' I said at last. 'Someone obviously thinks Cora is

onto something. Otherwise, why would they be trying to scare her away?'

Dallin smoothed his hair forwards with both hands. 'I don't think they are. I think she's had a run of bad luck, that's all. Two bad things happening in two days can look a lot like a conspiracy, if you're of a certain mindset, which Cora is.'

I stared out towards the tents. I still couldn't see Cora. 'She won't listen to you if you tell her to give up.'

'I know. And I'd feel bad leaving her, after I promised to help, but I can't stay here if I don't believe in what she's doing.'

It took me a moment to understand what he was saying. 'You're leaving?'

'Don't make it sound so dramatic. I'm here voluntarily. I said I'd introduce Cora to you and Mum and anyone else who could help her. And I've done that. My usefulness doesn't extend to much more. What am I going to do, trail behind her in the curraghs for the next four days on the very slim off-chance I might spot something she doesn't?'

'Has she asked you to do that?'

'She never asked for anything, not directly.' He raised his hands, then let them fall. 'She has something about her that makes you want to do more for her, y'know? When she told me she intended to come here ... it stood to reason I should go with her, right? I mean, this is as close to a hometown as I've got.' He pursed his lips. 'I thought she needed me, y'know? I thought I could be helpful. Stupid, really. She doesn't even need me for moral support. She found you for that.'

I studied his face, in an attempt to make sense of the

conflicting emotions there. 'Are you mad that she won't share a tent with you?'

He evaded the question, which was confirmation enough. 'Why're you helping her?' he asked. 'What're you hoping to get out of it?'

'Why do I need anything out of it? Cora wants our help. That should be reason enough.'

'She doesn't need us.' Dallin's lip curled. 'I felt weirdly indebted to her because I'm the one who told her about the curraghs. She never would've come here if it wasn't for me. But you don't even know her. Why're you still following her around like a puppy?'

That was harsh, intended to get a response. I didn't rise to the bait. 'I'm not doing it for her,' I said. 'I'm doing it for me.'

'How so?'

'Don't you think I've been haunted by this as well? I found a human skeleton when I was ten years old. *Ten,* Dallin. Have you ever thought about how that screwed me up?'

'Yeah, but you—' He bit his tongue.

'But I what?'

'Nothing. I was—'

'But I made it up, is that what you were going to say?'

Again, that incriminating silence. After far too much of a pause Dallin said, 'That's not what I meant.'

I slammed my hands on the steering wheel. 'Seriously? You still don't believe me? You genuinely think I made up a story when I was ten and I'd rather put everyone through *this*—' I gestured expansively, 'than admit it wasn't true? That's what you think of me?'

'I don't think you made it up.'

'You think I exaggerated it? I was mistaken? I found a pile of rabbit bones and mistook them for a person?'

With absolute sincerity, Dallin said, 'You have to consider it's possible.'

I stopped myself from slapping the steering wheel again. All it'd done was hurt my palms. 'Get out,' I said.

'There's no evidence to back up what you saw! Trust me, I've looked. I've spoken to everyone who might know a single thing about the case. There's nothing. I barely even remember it myself. That's one of the reasons why I started that stupid bloody website in the first place – to see if anyone would come forward with more information about the curraghs. I *wanted* to believe you, Rosie.'

I let out a breath. 'Get out of my car. I'm done with you.'

It seemed like Dallin would argue, but then he sighed and opened the car door. 'I don't doubt what you think you saw, Rosie,' he said. 'But that doesn't necessarily mean—'

I cut him off. 'You know what? I don't care that you've never believed me. No one ever did. But you've told the story to Cora like you completely believed it. Like it was the definite truth. She trusted you. Pinned all her hopes on you. That's a lot worse than thinking I've made something up.'

I started the engine. He still had the car door open, but if he didn't move, I was going to drive forwards, whether he was still holding the door or not.

'You want to know why I think she's wasting her time out here?' he asked.

'Do please tell me.'

'I don't think Simone ended up here at all. I think she made a full break from her old life and is living somewhere far away from her family. Probably with that fella she ran off with. Or, if she really is dead, I reckon Cora should be looking closer to home for a culprit.'

I stared at him for a moment longer. But he was finished talking. With another sigh, he shut the car door.

I turned the car around on the grass and drove away from the campsite.

The letter was rough, littered with misspellings; the effort of someone used to working with manual tools rather than a pen. At first reading, I thought they were from someone at school. Some ridiculous boy who'd fallen for your charms.

There was no name on the letter, of course. He wasn't that stupid.

He talked about how torn he was. How much he wanted to be with you. There were details included that gave me a sick thrill to read.

'I wish I could just run away with you,' he wrote.

I stood in your room and read the letter three times. My fingers trembled.

He wanted to steal you away from me.

I could prevent it, of course.

All I had to do was tell our parents. The proof I needed was right there in my hands.

Chapter 25

I hadn't told Dallin the whole truth. I wasn't helping Cora just because I wanted to lay to rest the ghosts in my head. It was more complicated than that.

Although I didn't want to admit it, especially not out loud, I felt like the past few days had done me good.

For the last year, I'd held rigidly to my self-imposed routine, leaving the house only once a week on my prescribed outings to visit Mum and do my shopping. Except for occasionally driving to the Spar shop in Ballaugh when I ran out of bread midweek, the idea of going out at other times had never entered my head. Everything I needed was contained within the house and its garden.

So this week had been a big step for me. I'd gone out every day. I'd met new people. I'd gone into the garage in Ramsey and interacted with other humans. I'd visited my neighbours. Most astonishingly of all, I'd invited people into my house and prepared a meal for them.

Maybe this wouldn't have sounded like a big deal to anyone else. But for me it was massive. Any of those small steps would've seemed unthinkable even a week ago.

For the first time in ages, I had a purpose.

Maybe Dallin was right, and Cora didn't technically need me to drive around for her and introduce her to my neighbours. She was more than capable of doing it herself. But she'd made me feel useful. She'd given me a reason to get out of bed.

I thought about that as I drove home.

Eventually, Cora's search would come to an end. Either she'd find what she was looking for, or, much more likely, she would give it up for a lost cause and go home. Either way, in a few more days, I would lose her. She'd return to her old life and I'd go back to mine. I wondered if the advances I'd made over the last few days would stand up to her being gone. More likely I would retreat, maybe even further than before, until I was tucked up like a hermit crab in the safe confines of my empty house.

When I got home, I waited for half an hour to be sure of my feelings, then called Cora.

She didn't answer straight away, and when she did, she sounded distracted. 'Hello?'

'Hi. It's Rosalie.' Which was dumb, because she could see my number on her screen. 'Are you okay?'

'Yeah, we're fine. The police are just about done here.'

'Sorry I left.'

'Don't worry about it. Not much point us all standing around in the cold, is there?'

Before I could talk myself out of it, I said, 'Listen, I know you might not want to stay in your tent now that, y'know.' *Now someone had knifed several big holes in it.* 'So I wondered if, I mean, if you needed somewhere to stay ...' I closed my eyes and gripped the phone tighter. 'If you wanted to stay at mine. Don't feel you need to say yes. But I've got a spare room and, well. It seems daft to leave you sleeping out in the cold when I've got a whole house to myself.'

Cora laughed. The sound was gentle and warm. 'Oh my God. That's so sweet of you. I don't want to impose on you.'

I thought about the stolen Filofax, which was now hidden in the glovebox of my car. I needed to ask Cora about it. But not over the phone.

'It wouldn't be an imposition, not at all,' I said. 'Dallin can stay too. I mean, if he wants to.' It took a lot out of me to extend the invitation to Dallin, but what was I supposed to do? I couldn't invite Cora and not him. Could I?

'Honestly, I can't think of anything better than a real bed,' Cora laughed. 'You can't see it right now, but I'm making kissy motions in your general direction.'

The warmth in my stomach told me I'd done the right thing. 'I'll get the kettle on, shall I?'

'You're an absolute star, Rosalie. Give us half an hour to pack everything up. Oh, I tell you what, shall we swing through Ramsey on our way? We'll grab a takeaway.'

I found myself smiling along with her. 'That sounds great.'

It was closer to an hour and a half by the time Cora arrived. She met me at the door and pulled me into a hug.

'Sorry we're late,' she said. 'I had to argue with the campsite owner over how much we owed him. How much *he* owed *us*.' She carried in two plastic bags loaded with takeaway containers. 'We paid for seven nights. We only stayed for three. Ergo, he owed us a refund for the four nights we weren't able to stay. I'm surprised he put up as much resistance as he did. You would've thought he'd be happy for us to leave quietly, rather than make a scene in front of his other paying guests.'

Cora went into the kitchen and set down the bag on the table, then retrieved a stack of plates from the cupboard over the sink. It should've been weird to see her pottering my kitchen like it was her own, but I found myself smiling. The house did look better with people in it. I couldn't believe it'd taken me so long to realise.

Dallin brought up the rear, hovering for a moment on my doorstep like he was half-afraid I might slam the door in his face. I stepped aside to let him in.

'Thanks,' he muttered.

I shut the door behind him. Honestly, I would've preferred to leave him outside. I was a little surprised he'd actually accepted my invitation to sleep here. I'd figured his pride would've stopped him.

As I went into the kitchen, I glanced out through the windows, where rain was splattering the paving stones of the path. Maybe it was the weather more than his pride that'd been the deciding factor.

'We bought a variety of things from the Thai place,' Cora said. 'I know nothing about Thai food so I just pointed at the most interesting names. Anyway, enjoy.'

Dallin pulled his chair up to the table. 'For someone who loves planning so much, you're surprisingly laisse-faire at coordination,' he said.

'I'm not flaisse-dah,' Cora objected. 'I have a system that works totally fine for me. Anyway, I asked you at the outset what you wanted to eat and you said "anything".' She gestured at the plastic takeaway containers she'd pulled from the bag. 'This is anything. I intend to eat most of it anyway.' She took cutlery out of the drawer by the cooker. 'I have fear-of-missing-out when it comes to food,' she told me. 'I'm always scared the other person is eating something better. Hence why Thai is a great idea.' She came to the table and pulled the lid off a container of noodles. 'You can pile a bit of everything on your plate and it still tastes amazing.'

I glanced at Dallin as I spooned jasmine rice onto my plate. He'd taken one container of rice and one of curry and made a pile on his own plate, conspicuously not sharing. I smiled to myself. As a kid, Dallin had always hated sharing food. He'd always say, 'If I'd wanted what you're eating I would've ordered what you're eating.' One time, when I was fourteen, we went out for a birthday meal – him, me, and Mum – to my favourite tapas restaurant. It still made me laugh to remember the look on his face when we all started reaching over to take bits of each other's dishes.

'I've made up the bed in the spare room,' I said, reaching past Dallin to grab a tub of what looked like Pad Thai. 'You'll have to ignore the *Jurassic Park* bedcover.'

Cora's hand shot up. 'Dibs that one.'

'Why do you have dinosaur bedcovers?' Dallin asked me.

'Because dinosaurs are great,' Cora said. 'Duh.'

'We were looking for single bedspreads for the spare room,'

I said. 'All of them were so dull. It was Beth's idea to look in the children's section instead.'

It'd made Beth laugh whenever one of our friends had stayed the night. We tried so hard to be grown-up in other ways. Moving in together, getting married, decorating the house in tasteful, pastel colours. But there were times when we couldn't help being daft. Dinosaur bedsheets were the least of it.

What I didn't tell Cora – what I would never tell anyone, as long as I lived – was what Beth had accidentally said when we were putting the covers on the bed for the first time, when she'd said, 'This baby room will look great.' She'd corrected herself straight away, of course. 'Guest room. *Guest* room.' But the thought was out there. Spoken into the world. There was no putting it back.

Cora grinned as she forked up more noodles. 'Sounds perfect.'

'Which one is the guest room?' Dallin asked.

I kept my eyes on my plate. 'It's the one at the back. Same as when you lived here.'

'Oh. So, what happened to—?'

'We turned your room into a study. The sofa bed is still in there.'

Dallin's eyebrows went up. 'Not the *old* sofa bed? The one we used to have?' He laughed. 'That thing was all lumps and broken springs before I left home. What's it like now?'

'You can go back to your tent, if you want,' Cora said with a straight face.

I smiled down at my food. It was nice to have someone to back me up again. One more thing I hadn't realised I missed.

My thoughts soured as I remembered I still had to ask her about the Filofax. I'd tried and failed to come up with an innocent explanation for its presence in her tent.

'Anyone want a drink?' Cora asked. She'd bought a number of beer bottles, which she'd asked to put in the bottom of the fridge. Now, she retrieved two from where they nestled amongst my salad groceries. 'Sure you don't want one, Rosalie?'

I shook my head. Just the food alone was making me a little giddy. After months of avoiding sugar and salt and processed food, I was overloading my system. A tingle of worry started up in my stomach. *I shouldn't be eating this stuff. It'll send my brain chemicals haywire.*

On the other hand, the Pad Thai was delicious. All those sugars and salts and stimulants and e-numbers were amazing.

'This is nice, huh?' Cora said. 'So glad to have a roof over our heads and some hot food. It's been a week since I was last warm.'

'Yep.' Dallin swigged his beer. 'It all worked out for you, didn't it?'

'How d'you mean?' Cora speared some more noodles.

'Just, y'know.' Dallin gestured around the kitchen with his fork. 'You've been saying for days how nice this house is. I'm glad you finally got your foot in the door.'

The table went quiet. 'Hang on there,' I said. 'You guys are my guests. Both of you. No one's got any foot in any door.'

'I'm just saying, is all,' Dallin said. 'It's funny how it worked out.'

'No, it isn't.' Cora didn't look up from her food. 'It was a bunch of unfortunate events that I'd rather not dwell on right now, if you don't mind.'

'Sure. Fine.' Dallin kept quiet for a full fifteen seconds before he added, 'So, Rosie, did you get the money back for the tyres?'

I glanced at Cora. Did I imagine a guilty flinch? 'C'mon, Dallin,' she said easily. 'When have I had time to get to a cash machine? You know I'll sort it out as soon as I can.'

I ducked my head in embarrassment. I hadn't even got round to giving Cora the receipt for the tyres. Why was Dallin making a big deal of this now?

'Oh, of course,' Dallin said. 'I take it you'll pay me back for this food at the same time?'

I shot him a glare. 'Dal, what the hell?'

'I'll get it for you,' Cora said. 'If I'd known it was such a big deal I would've gone to a cash machine while we were in Ramsey.'

'Look,' Dallin said with annoyance, 'I'm just making the point that we're all putting ourselves out for you. A little acknowledgement wouldn't hurt.'

Cora set down her fork, wiped her mouth, then looked at him. 'What sort of acknowledgement would you like? Hmm?'

Dallin wavered for a second. 'You could start by telling us the truth about your family,' he said. 'If you're so intent on winning over my sister, how about you tell her everything?'

Cora turned her level gaze to me. 'What would you like to know, Rosalie?'

I sat, frozen, wishing I was anywhere but there.

'Tell her why you didn't look for your sister sooner.' Dallin gestured with his beer. 'Why it's taken twenty years to get here.'

'Is that what you'd like to know, Rosalie?' Cora asked.

I didn't answer.

Dallin folded his arms. 'Cora was married. She was too busy playing happy homes to look for Simone until now.'

Cora took her time before responding. 'That's half right, yes.'

'Which half?'

'I was married, for six years.' Addressing me instead of Dallin, she said, 'I got married at eighteen. It was one of those mistakes that's only obvious in retrospect. I cut all ties with my family. My husband didn't like me even talking about them. Any time I spent thinking about Simone was time I wasn't devoting to him.' She reached for her beer. 'Afterwards, I started volunteering at the women's refuge that'd saved me. And I started looking for Simone again.' She cocked her head at Dallin. 'Is that everything you wanted to know?'

Without waiting for an answer, Cora stood up and took her beer over to the window. The sun was heading down towards the horizon, although it was still hidden behind the clouds, casting everything in a diffuse grey light. At that time of day, the curraghs looked close enough to touch, like their branches might scrape against the back wall of the garden each time the wind blew. I wished I'd thought to close the blinds earlier. If I got up now it would be too obvious.

When I was sure Cora wasn't watching, I kicked Dallin in the shins under the table.

At the window, Cora peered round towards the front of my

house. Because of the way the kitchen stuck out from the rest of the house, it was possible to see the road and part of the driveway out front. I assumed Cora was checking on her car. After the last few days, I would've been paranoid too.

An odd look passed over Cora's face. She dumped her beer on the table and went racing for the front door.

'Cora!' I called after her.

We both got up. Cora was already out of the front door and halfway down the driveway.

'What the hell do you think you're doing?' I heard her yell.

I made it to the front door in time to see Cora shooing someone away from her car.

It was Eloise. Her hair was stuffed into a multicoloured wrap and she looked to be wearing at least three jumpers, one on top of the other. She held up her hands to ward off Cora. In one hand Eloise held a square of paper, which flapped like a white flag.

'What're you doing here?' Cora demanded. 'What do you want?'

Eloise's mouth opened and shut. When she spotted me, she waved a hand in my direction, like I might be inclined to calm Cora down.

'Well?' Cora asked.

Eloise drew herself up. 'I was leaving you a note,' she said in a wavering voice. 'But now you're here I supposed I can just tell you in person.'

Cora snatched the sheet of paper out of her hand. '*Stay out of the curraghs*,' she read. '"*You don't know the damage you're doing.*" Well, that doesn't sound threatening at all.'

'It's a simple enough fact.' Eloise clasped her hands, so tightly it looked like her fingers were braided. 'Don't think I don't know what you've been doing.'

Cora drew in a sharp breath.

'Each time you go stomping off away from the path, you're causing untold damage,' Eloise said. 'Do you have any idea how many species of flowers need this place to live? Let alone the nesting birds. How can you be so careless?'

Cora read the note again. There was a look in her eyes I hadn't seen before. 'Was it you?'

The question confused Eloise enough that she forgot what she was saying. 'What?'

'Was it you who cut the tyres of my car?'

Eloise took a step away from her. 'You've got no right to be doing what you're doing. Why can't you stay on the paths like you're supposed to?'

'What about our tents?' Cora closed in on her. 'Was that you too?'

Eloise had a panicked look in her eyes that reminded me of a cornered animal. I stepped down onto the driveway, intending to get Cora to back off, but before I could open my mouth, Eloise took us all by surprise. She kicked Cora hard in the knee, then turned and sprinted away like a jackrabbit.

Cora cried out as her knee buckled. By the time I reached her, Eloise was way up the road, head up, legs pumping like a champion sprinter. I swore I'd never seen the woman move so fast in her life. She didn't look back, not once. In a moment she vanished from sight around the corner.

I helped Cora back to her feet.

Chapter 26

I didn't have any ice in my freezer, so we had to pop a bag of frozen peas onto Cora's knee.

'It's fine,' Cora kept saying each time I fussed. 'There's no damage. It just hurts. Give me ten minutes and I'll be fine.'

Dallin tilted his chair back onto two legs, his foot propped against the kitchen table. 'At least now we know who's to blame for your spate of bad luck.'

I shook my head. 'I don't believe Eloise would've damaged your tent,' I said. 'She's eccentric, but she's not dangerous.'

'Tell that to my knee,' Cora muttered. She lifted the pack of peas so we could all see the bruising that was already colouring the top of her shin.

'Keep the peas on it,' I admonished her. 'They won't do a bit of good if you're waving them around.'

Cora grumbled something else. But she put the peas back on her leg.

'Do you want to tell the police?' I asked. I smoothed out the note Eloise had intended to put on Cora's car. Not matter how many times I read it, I still couldn't figure out if it was threatening or not. *Stay out of the curraghs* ... That could've been a threat, if said by the wrong person. *You don't know the damage you're doing.* That sounded more like an exasperated plea. Eloise had signed it from 'a concerned neighbour'. Any way I read it, it was still ambiguous.

Cora shook her head in answer to my question. 'We already told the police Eloise was angry about us going into the curraghs. Told them twice in fact.' She got out her phone and started typing with one thumb. 'I don't know if they talked to her. They thought it was a big jump from words to tyre-slashing.'

'It's odd,' Dallin agreed. He tilted his chair back and forward on its back legs. 'People usually escalate their behaviour. You'd expect the note first. It'd be weird to start with an act of violence and then give us a warning.'

'May I remind you the woman kicked me in the knee?' Cora scowled at her phone. 'What's her full name?'

I had to think for a minute. 'Purcell. Like the composer, not the washing powder.'

After some more one-handed typing and quite a lot more scowling, Cora said. 'She's about forty-five, is that right?'

At a guess, I would've said Eloise was younger, but I was notoriously rubbish at estimating ages. 'I'm not sure,' I said. 'Maybe?'

'She looked about that age to me,' Cora said. 'At a very charitable guess.' She thumbed through another screen on her phone. 'I reckon this is her.'

She turned the phone around to show us a black-and-white photo, one where Eloise looked at least ten years younger. It was on a poetry publication website. I automatically noted the professional formatting.

'Says she's based in Peel,' Cora said. 'That's south of here, isn't it?'

'South, and west a bit. It's on the coast.' I peered over her shoulder. 'How old is the webpage? She moved up here just before I did. About seven or eight years ago.'

'This looks like a pretty old site.' Cora scrolled a bit more. 'Last updated almost ten years ago. Still, it's something to go on.'

She pressed her legs together so the left knee held the bag of frozen peas against the right. That freed up her other hand so she could type with both thumbs. I watched, intrigued by how fast she could go.

'What's she looking for?' Dallin asked.

'I'm backtracking.' Cora answered without looking up. 'Ten years ago, Eloise Purcell was in Peel. Where was she before then?'

Dallin said, 'She doesn't look the sort to have a big online presence.'

'She doesn't.' Cora flashed a humourless grin. 'But people don't realise how much information they put onto the internet, whether they mean to or not. You of all people should know that.'

Dallin stopped rocking his chair. 'What d'you mean?'

'You should take a look at your own online presence sometime. I don't know if you intentionally meant for your details to get attached to quite so many unsavoury websites, but you should perhaps consider changing your password.' Cora scrolled past another page. 'Or getting a different email address. And perhaps not putting your actual birthday online.'

Dallin's mouth twisted. 'You're just trying to wind me up. Why would you go digging around in my personal life?'

Cora smiled, but it wasn't the sort of smile that suggested she was joking. 'I met you on the internet. I drove two hundred miles to a ferry port with you, then all the way up here into the middle of nowhere, with nothing but your promise that you were a nice person. You bet your life I checked you out first. Just like you did with me.'

'Thanks a bunch.'

Cora shrugged. 'I'd rather be paranoid than murdered in a layby.'

Dallin set his chair back onto four legs. There was a bit of colour to his cheeks. 'It's not what you think,' he said to me. 'The websites I'm registered on. It's a bunch of conspiracy forums. I wanted to see what else was out there. Most of them won't let you browse without creating a profile.'

I smiled at his discomfort and said nothing, letting him think we didn't believe him. To be honest, I knew how awkward it was to get onto those forums, having experienced it myself while trying to look at his profile page. Who'd have thought a bunch of conspiracy fans would be so paranoid?

'Here we go,' Cora said then. 'Eloise Purcell was at high school in Peel, went away to university for a bit, then came back to work as a teaching assistant at – ding ding ding – Sulby Primary School. That's right around the corner from here, isn't it?'

I peered at the screen of her phone. She'd found an archived page that contained a list of teaching staff from the primary schools on the island. Halfway down the page was Eloise's name.

'I assume that's the same person,' Cora said. 'It's a distinctive enough name. So, if she was working at the local primary school in her mid-twenties, it's likely she would've been living nearby.'

I crinkled my nose. 'Maybe. She could've commuted in from Ramsey or Kirk Michael.'

Cora leaned over the phone. 'The dates match up,' she said with an edge of excitement to her voice.

'What dates?'

She turned the phone to show me, but I still didn't see anything apart from a list of names and the year they'd joined the school. 'She was here twenty years ago. She was in the area when Simone disappeared.'

Chapter 27

I tried and failed to talk Cora out of going straight round to Eloise's house. The way I saw it, it'd do very little good for us to turn up on her doorstep looking belligerent and, in Cora's case, a little drunk as well.

'I just want to talk to her,' Cora said. 'We're not going to cause a scene. I need to know if she remembers anything.'

Nothing I could say would persuade her otherwise. In the end I went out to the hall and pulled on my boots.

'What're you doing?' Cora asked. She'd already bundled herself up in her duffle coat.

'I'm coming with you,' I said. 'Eloise is way more likely to talk to you if I'm there too.'

Dallin wandered into the hall from the kitchen. At some point he'd opened another beer. He stood watching us as Cora struggled into her boots.

'Are you coming?' I asked Dallin.

He gave a careless shrug. 'Doesn't seem like it needs all of us. I'll hold the fort here.'

I didn't particularly want him being in the house on his own. But I couldn't put the feeling into words. It was the idea of him being unsupervised here. Looking at my stuff. Touching Beth's ornaments.

I concentrated on lacing my boots, glad none of this showed on my face. Even I could tell those thoughts were irrational.

'Don't eat all the food before we get back,' Cora said.

We walked round to Eloise's house. I could've driven, but it seemed daft to take the car such a short distance. Besides, it was nice to be out in the evening air. The wind had picked up, tousling my hair forwards over my face, and making the trees chatter loudly as they moved. A slightly wild evening, one which felt like it could tip over into a storm with little provocation. I liked it. The noise of the wind and the trees left little room in my head for anything else.

'Is the weather always like this?' Cora asked me.

'Like what?'

'So ... changeable. It was raining this morning, bright sunshine at lunchtime, now this. And I'm sure the forecast predicted thunder for tomorrow.'

'That sounds about right,' I said with a smile.

'It's crazy. Is it always like this?'

'Living on an island, the weather's always going to be changeable. You get all four seasons in a day sometimes. Hot, cold, rain, sun, sleet, hail. It happens more often than you'd think.'

'How do you get used to it?'

I frowned. 'I don't know. I don't suppose we have any choice in the matter. The weather will always do its own thing, regardless of how we feel about it.' I waited a beat, then asked, 'Why did you take Lenny's Filofax?'

Cora gave a rueful smile. 'I wondered when you'd bring that up. I knew you'd taken it from my tent.'

'You did?'

She shrugged. 'It was there when I first checked if anything was missing. It was gone five minutes later.'

I studied the side of her face as we walked. 'You shouldn't have taken it from Lenny's house.'

'It looked important. You didn't give me time to check it out properly.' Cora side-eyed me. 'Where is it now?'

'In my car.' I knew what she was really asking. I should've given it back to Lenny straight away, but I couldn't think how to explain to him why I had it.

'Did you read it?' Cora asked.

'Of course not.'

'You should.' Cora pulled up her hood against the wind. 'There's some information that concerns you.'

'What information?'

We'd reached Eloise's house. No lights were on. Her car wasn't parked on the drive.

'I'll show you when we get back,' Cora said. She looked at the dark house. 'What d'you think? Out, or hiding from us?' She went up and banged on the door anyway.

Personally, I didn't think Eloise was in. She tended to walk most places, so if she'd taken her car, she must've gone further afield.

A light came on when I went to the side of the house, but it was an automatic burglar deterrent above the side door.

We'd had one on our own house, until we'd got fed up of it being tripped by cats or stray animals, or possibly wallabies.

I peered in through the frosted glass of the side door. No lights inside, no sign of movement. I hesitated before trying the handle. I was secretly glad to find it locked.

There were two pairs of wellies next to the step by the door, turned upside down on a wooden stand so the rain would clean off the mud. I bent to look at the undersides of the boots. All had fresh mud stuck in the treads, but none showed the distinctive wavy pattern I'd seen on the prints next to Cora's tent.

I heard Cora banging on the front door again. Still no response.

'She's definitely not in,' I said when I returned to the front of the house.

'How can you be sure?' Cora asked. 'She might've spotted us coming and hidden.'

'You're standing in her flowerbed. If she was here, she definitely would've come out to shout at you.'

Cora swore under her breath and stepped back onto the path.

'Plus she has a noisy dog called Butterscotch,' I said. 'At a guess, she's taken him for a walk.' I looked up at the dark house. 'We should go home. Come back and try again in the morning.'

This time she didn't argue with me.

When we got back to my house, Cora stayed outside to check her car.

'Making sure the crazy lady didn't touch it,' she explained.

Dallin was in the sitting room. I'd known, as soon as I left, he'd go into the one room I'd deliberately closed the door to. But still, it gave me a thrill of panic, to walk in and see the living room with the lights on. He was sat on the sofa with a beer in one hand and a photo album in the other.

Without commenting, I took the album off him and snapped it closed. I didn't look at him. I also tried not to look at all of Beth's ornaments. 'Come back in the kitchen,' I said.

I didn't wait for him to argue. Instead, I walked off into the kitchen and sat down, like nothing untoward had happened. At that point I realised I was still clutching the photo album. I didn't know what to do with it. Holding it to my chest would make everyone realise it was secret and private. Putting it down on the counter would be an open invitation for everyone to look at it.

I glanced at the cover. It wasn't even one of the important albums. A load of photos from a trip we'd taken to Malta, when Beth's digital camera had packed up and we'd instead bought a handful of cheap disposable cameras. As a result, that holiday was one of the few immortalised in hardcopy. The rest were in a digital folder on my laptop.

After a full minute, just long enough to make it clear he was doing it of his own volition, not to humour me, Dallin followed me into the kitchen. He went to the back window and stood looking out at the garden.

'I still say it's kinda convenient, when you think about it,' he said after a while.

I blinked. 'What?'

'Cora suggested from the outset we should ask to stay here. I told her you'd rather not have houseguests.'

The presumption annoyed me, even if it was correct. 'So?'

'So, it's interesting, don't you think, how her tent got damaged like that? Just hers, not mine. And you just so happened to offer her a room for the night.'

I rolled my eyes. 'Nobody's that weirdly manipulative,' I said. 'Cora hasn't once said – or even suggested – she'd want to stay here instead of a tent. In fact, it sounds like you're the person who's been having trouble sleeping on the ground. Hey, maybe *you* cut holes in her tent, because you knew I would invite her to sleep here instead, and I'd have to invite you as well.'

Dallin got an odd look on his face. 'You really think I'd do that?'

'I don't think anyone would do it. It'd be crazy. And it's kinda ugly of you to suggest your friend might be crazy.'

Dallin turned back to the window. 'She's not my friend,' he muttered, just loud enough to hear.

Whatever. I stayed at the table, hunched over the photo album, my hands gripping it so hard the edges bit into my fingers.

'By the way,' Dallin said. 'This fell out of your photo album.'

I turned my head, slowly, like in a bad dream. Dallin was holding up a folded square of photocopied print. Fluorescent yellow lines picked out a sentence here and there. He also held the Manila envelope the letter had come in, identical in all respects to the one that still sat on my hall table, except this one was battered and creased at the edges where I'd jammed it between the pages of the photo album. I recognised the paper and the envelope perfectly well.

Dallin turned it in his fingers as if examining it. 'Who's been sending you excerpts from medical textbooks? Weirdly annotated excerpts, at that.'

I couldn't find my voice. Someone had stolen it away.

Dallin held the paper up to read something on the back. As if he hadn't already read it before I got home. 'I mean, I don't want to imply too much into this, but is there some reason why someone's highlighted and underlined the word "murderer", right here?'

Before I could even begin to think of an answer, Cora came in, and Dallin, thank God, shut up.

Chapter 28

At approximately three o'clock in the morning, the wind changed direction and caused the rain to drum loudly against my window. It lasted only a couple of minutes but that was enough to wake me up.

I lay in bed, listening to the swoop and wail of the wind. When I was younger, I'd imagined the wind would lift the whole house, tearing loose its roots and pitching it into the sky like Dorothy's farmhouse. The thought had never particularly scared me. I couldn't imagine the storm would hurt me. It would just pick me up and take me someplace new.

When Beth had been here, when a storm woke up one or both of us, we would roll over and find each other. I would scoop her into my arms, or she'd gather me into hers, and we would lie there, awake, listening to the wind and the rain outside. Neither of us would speak. We were secure in the knowledge that our house was safe. That we were safe. Nothing could touch us.

Now, when I rolled over, I found nothing but an empty stretch of cold sheets. Those were the worst moments. In my half-awake state, I sometimes forgot she wasn't there, and startled awake to find her side of the bed cold and untouched.

I reached out and pulled Beth's pillow to me. I clung to it like a comforter.

Murderer.

Outside, the rain spattered against the window again.

It didn't look like I'd be getting to sleep anytime soon. I got up and padded on bare feet to the bathroom.

On the landing, I paused. The only light came from the lamp in my room. None shone from underneath the door to the spare room, or to Dallin's old room. I hoped my guests were sleeping better than me.

Sleeping better than they would in that tent. The thought made me remember Dallin's words. Of course, I didn't believe Cora would've damaged her own tent. That was just Dallin putting weird ideas into my head.

It bothered me he'd been thinking like that. All those half-dropped hints about Cora being manipulative and borderline unhinged ... what exactly was he basing that on? I hadn't seen her acting particularly crazy. Obsessive, sure; determined, definitely. But those weren't particularly odd traits. I did strange obsessive things myself. The difference was I knew my tidying rituals and fear of the outside world were stupid, but I did them anyway, because I wouldn't know how to cope without them.

It bothered me a lot more that he'd found one of the clippings Beth's parents had sent me.

I should've hidden them better. Or burned them without

opening the envelopes. I wished I'd found a way to deal healthily with the guilt they'd brought.

I stood there on the landing for longer than intended. Although I strained my ears, I couldn't hear any sounds from inside Cora's room. She was probably fast asleep.

For a moment – a very brief, fleeting moment – I considered pushing open the door and peering in to see if she was awake. But to what end? I couldn't think what I would say to her. How I would frame the thoughts swirling in my head. Even if she felt the same way I did ...

I remembered what she'd said, about her ex-husband.

Resolutely I turned away. No, it was a nice daydream, but I knew there was no way I could have that conversation with Cora. Not with the ghost of Beth hovering over my shoulder at all times.

In the morning, Cora cooked breakfast, which was a feat in itself given that I hadn't thought to buy any breakfast items when I did the shopping. Usually I only had toast and tea. I never woke up hungry. So I was surprised when I got up, smelled something delicious, and immediately felt my stomach growl.

I put my dressing gown and slippers on before I came downstairs. Beth had said they made me look like a granny, but they were warm and they meant no one had to deal with seeing my bare feet first thing in the morning.

'Morning, sunshine,' Cora said as I came into the kitchen. She'd scrambled what looked like two dozen eggs in the cast iron skillet. 'Are you hungry?'

By rights I shouldn't have been, but my stomach grumbled again. 'Apparently so,' I said.

Cora favoured me with a smile. 'Sit yourself down. Eggs will be done in a minute.'

Dallin was already at the kitchen table, his hands wrapped around a cup of strong coffee, his shoulder hunched. He didn't look particularly happy to be awake. On the table in front of him were spread Cora's maps and charts.

He raised his eyes to mine as I sat down opposite, but didn't say anything. He didn't need to. He now knew I had a secret I didn't want to talk about.

'I need to get out early,' Cora said. 'I've drawn up a revised schedule, but even so, I need to boogie if I've any hope of sticking to it.'

I looked at the nest of red lines she'd drawn across the photographs of the curraghs. 'Do you need me to come with you?' I asked. I crossed my fingers the answer was no. Outside, the rain had turned to miserable, persistent drizzle. I didn't want to be out there today.

'Not unless you want to,' Cora said. 'We should have it covered.'

'Are you going to Eloise's house this morning?'

Cora's shoulders stiffened. 'I've thought about it. I was ... maybe a little short-tempered last night.'

'Maybe a little,' I agreed.

'I'll call by her house on the way to the curraghs. If she's not there, I'll try at lunchtime. Eventually we'll catch up with her.'

I was glad Cora's temper had cooled. After the way she'd

acted last night, I'd been worried what she might do when she found Eloise.

Cora brought a pile of toast to the table. 'Can we maybe ask you to look into something else for us?' she asked me.

'Sure.'

'We need to speak to anyone else who was living in this area twenty years ago. Could you see what you can dig up?'

'I can give it a go,' I said. 'I'm not really a computer whiz though. Not like you.'

'I'm nothing like an expert. All I know is a few tricks my brother taught me. You've got something I haven't, though,' Cora said with the ghost of a smile. 'Friends. You can make phone calls and speak to people. They're less likely to speak to me, no matter how nice I ask them.' She came back to the table with a dinner plate loaded with scrambled eggs. 'Help yourself,' she said. 'We had a bunch of eggs that we bought the other day. They need using up.'

'Looks great. Thank you.' I avoided looking at her directly. Whenever I did, I felt the guilty spark of standing outside her bedroom door last night, straining my ears to see if I could hear her breathing.

What would've happened if she'd opened her door?

I kept my eyes down so no one would see the heat that'd risen to my face.

'When you're searching online,' Cora said, 'don't limit yourself to people who lived in this area. If possible, check out people who worked in the local shops and pubs, stuff like that.'

I seriously doubted I could find out much. Cora had found

Eloise's details easily enough yesterday, but my experience with websites – especially Manx websites – were that the pages I looked for either didn't exist or didn't carry any of the information I wanted.

'I probably won't find anything useful,' I said carefully.

'I'd appreciate it if you try,' Cora said.

'I just—'

'Look, I know no one's going to say, *for sure, I remember your sister, she got killed and dumped in the swamp and, as a bonus, I totally know who did it.*' Cora was turned away from me, scraping the burned-on egg bits out of the pan, so I couldn't see her expression. 'But someone might remember *something*.'

'Hope springs eternal,' Dallin said. He sipped his coffee like it was the only thing keeping his eyes open. 'It could be she *was* here, on her way somewhere else. She could've gone to a different part of the island. Or back to England. If you can find a trail to follow ...'

'So, you think she might still be alive?' I asked.

'In the absence of solid evidence, we have to consider every possibility, don't we?' Dallin said. 'So, yeah, I reckon there's an outside chance she might be living a full and rich life somewhere.'

Cora shook her head without looking up from the pan. 'If she was alive, she would've contacted me. There's no way she would've stayed lost for all this time.'

'Unless she has amnesia. She could've fallen and hit her head and forgotten who she was.'

'Now you're being silly.'

'I'm making the point we simply don't know what she did.' Dallin drank some more coffee. Behind his sleepy, grumpy demeanour, I could see the wheels turning. He knew this was his best chance to talk Cora around. 'There could be reasons why she's not contacted you, Cora. She could've married an unsuitable bastard and been too afraid to tell anyone. She could've been kidnapped. Or brainwashed. Or—' He made a circular motion with his hand as he sought another possibility. 'Rosie, help me.'

'Oh no,' I said. 'You can dig your own way out.'

Cora at last gave up on the skillet and came to sit down at the table. We ate toast with thick wedges of butter and hot scrambled eggs on top.

'I'm coming around to the idea of breakfast,' I said. 'Never been a fan of it before.'

'You just needed someone like me to cook for you,' Cora said with a smile.

My cheeks went red again. I mumbled a rubbish response into my half-finished meal.

Was she being serious? Did she mean anything by it? Or was it just a glib comment? I snuck a few glances at her as I ate the rest of my eggs. Cora seemed unfazed. She was reading a page of the scribbled notes in one of her notebooks.

I tried to think of something else to say, to keep the conversation alive, but my brain had stalled. All too soon, Cora finished eating and stood up.

'Oh, I forgot,' she said. 'Could you check some of this as well?'

From her pocket she produced Lenny's Filofax. I wanted

to groan. She'd obviously taken it from my unlocked car last night. I knew I'd been wrong to tell her where it was.

Cora laid the book down next to me. She'd bookmarked a few pages with scraps of paper. I frowned.

'We'd better get moving,' she said to Dallin.

'Right behind you,' Dallin said. To my surprise, he finished his coffee and stood up. I hadn't realised he was going with Cora.

He winked at me, and I was suddenly glad I wasn't going to be left alone to make conversation with him. I was pretty sure what he'd want to talk about.

Chapter 29

The internet was a wonderful and confusing thing. It always baffled me how everything a person could ever want to know was on there, and yet I could spend hours randomly clicking around without finding a single useful thing.

I think the problem was *too much* information. Even the simplest search dragged me down a rabbit-hole of interesting but irrelevant pages. I never understood how Beth could find and narrow down the information she wanted for her blog posts.

This time, at least, I had something to focus on. It helped take my mind off everything else. I'd managed to avoid Dallin's questions last night and again that morning by the simple trick of staying in the same room as Cora at all times. I'd guessed correctly he wouldn't want to ask me anything difficult while she was around.

My gaze fell on the Filofax. Cora obviously wanted me to read it. With reluctance I opened it to the first of the bookmarks.

The page was sparsely filled with a column of numbers and various comments written in Lenny's surprisingly neat handwriting. I immediately saw why Cora had flagged that page. Halfway down was Dallin's name. The note next to it said, '£2000 – Drainage'.

I sighed. Was this evidence of the money Dallin supposedly owed? I wasn't sure I could cope with untangling the cryptic messages right then.

Instead I pulled my laptop closer and opened a new search window.

The first thing I did was look for Eloise online, trying to replicate what Cora had found last night. I could only do so because I knew to search with the name of the primary school. Even so, I had to wade through pages till I found what Cora had alighted on so easily.

Not for the first time that morning, I wondered whether Cora had given me this task simply to keep me indoors, to give me an excuse not to traipse around the curraghs with them. Looking out at the dull, unappealing weather, I couldn't be entirely upset.

I glanced at my mobile phone. Cora had promised to text me if they spoke with Eloise. So far nothing, which meant Eloise probably wasn't in.

I did a quick Google search of Nicole instead. It took me two attempts to spell her middle name correctly. *Vanaella*, which always made me think of a perfume, or a macrobiotic yoghurt. The first thing that popped up was her Facebook page. It seemed to consist of cute dog pictures.

It made me feel a little seedy, to sit there and Google my neighbours. Like I was prying into their lives. It also made me aware of how long it'd been since I'd last been on social media. My laptop automatically logged me into Facebook when I went onto Nicole's page. At the top, an alert in red told me I had 99+ updates from friends.

The thought made me nauseous. All my friends and acquaintances – many of them people I'd never met in real life, only online – were steadily going on with their lives, while mine had stalled. Did they ever think about me? A glance at the message alert suggested they did – I had over fifty unread messages. My stomach turned over. A lot of those would've been sent soon after Beth died. People offering sympathy, or help, or a someone to talk to. I remembered the influx of text messages to the same effect. Eventually everyone got the hint. The messages tailed off.

I hadn't wanted to answer them then and I didn't want to answer them now. I didn't even want to think about the people I'd used to know. My friends were all Beth's friends.

Quickly, I clicked to a different page before I could give into temptation and look at the messages. I knew with absolute certainty that no good would come of it.

Nicole didn't have a lot more to discover. I tried a couple of the tricks Cora had suggested, and found out Nicole had gone to high school in Ramsey. She didn't have any relatives listed on social media, so it seemed Patrick had resisted its siren call. She definitely didn't have a niece, in Birkenhead or otherwise, so goodness knows who Mum was talking about. Nicole was also a few years older than she'd told me, which was probably not helpful but did make me feel like I'd uncovered one secret. I hit a dead end because I couldn't remember her maiden name.

Cora had also left me the contact number of her brother, in case I got completely stumped, but I didn't want to give in quite so soon.

Mum will know Nicole's maiden name. As soon as I thought it, I slapped my forehead in annoyance. Why hadn't I thought of that before? Mum knew everyone. She would've made a far better detective than me.

I hummed to myself as I went to put the kettle on. I had a plan now. A good cup of peppermint tea, a sit-down on the hall stairs, and a nice long natter with Mum would dredge up more results than a whole morning at my keyboard.

Before I could set foot in the hall, the phone rang.

My first, slightly irrational thought was that Mum had somehow known I was going to call and pre-empted me. My second, only a bit less irrational thought, was it was Cora, and something else awful had happened. But it also could've been Dallin, which would make sense if something had happened to Cora ...

I snatched the phone from its cradle. 'Hello?'

'Oh, hello Rosalie, sweetheart. It's Nicole.'

My brain was still running through anxious what-if scenarios. It took me a moment to adjust to the notion that Nicole probably wasn't phoning with a problem. 'Hi. Hi, Nicole. How're you?'

'I'm just fine, thank you. I've been thinking about what your friend was saying, about her sister that disappeared?'

'Yes?'

'I said I'd give you a call when I got into my old calendars. Well, that's the news, I got into my old calendars. It turned out Patrick had moved them up into the attic for me. Trying to be helpful, obviously.'

I sat down on the third step of the stairs and pulled my knees up. The phone cable stretched out from where it was plugged into the wall. 'Uh-huh,' I said, not sure what response she was looking for.

'I got my dates confused,' Nicole said. 'I thought I went away after June that year, but I actually went at the beginning of May. I wasn't on the island at the time your friend's sister came here.'

'Oh.' I rubbed the side of my face. This didn't sound like earth-shattering news. 'What about Patrick? Was he on the island at the time?'

'He was, yes. He was home alone.' Nicole laughed. 'They don't cope particularly well when you leave them unattended, do they? No matter that he'd spent plenty of time away the year before when he was pretending to run a business. But apparently they still need someone to remind them to put socks on in the morning, don't they?'

'Have you asked him about Cora's sister? Does he remember seeing her at all?'

'He says he doesn't remember her. The name doesn't ring a bell.'

'What about her picture?' I remembered Nicole had taken a photo of Simone's picture.

'He didn't recognise that either. Sorry.'

'Do you want me to come over? Perhaps I can jog his mind.'

'He's out in the fields at the moment. I can get him to call you when he gets home? I think he's got his mobile but good luck getting him to answer it. It's always either on silent or he's left it under his pillow at home.'

We chatted for another couple of minutes – or rather, she chatted, and I made appropriate affirmative noises in the right places, all the while thinking of my tea which I'd carelessly left on the kitchen counter. No matter how much I stretched the phone cable, I couldn't reach it.

Eventually, Nicole said, 'Anyway, I must let you go,' and made me promise to bring my friend round again before they left. I could hear the gentle inflection in her voice when she said Cora's name, and it made me wince. I said goodbye as quickly as I could, before she could start telling me how it was *so nice* I'd made *a new friend*.

I went back and got my cup of tea, but then, on impulse, I stepped out of the back door and stood on the path for a moment. I turned away from the curraghs and instead looked off to my left, towards the fields that bordered the road.

It wasn't my imagination. I could hear the drone of a motor.

I abandoned my tea again on the kitchen counter and grabbed my coat instead.

The drizzle had increased to the sort of sprinkling rain that felt light and gentle but soaked through my coat surprisingly fast. I pulled up my hood and walked a little faster.

When I rounded the bend in the road, the noise of the motor grew louder.

I bobbed up and down, trying to see over the hedge at the side of the road. Obviously I was too short. I hurried to a gate further down the road. My legs ached as I hauled myself up the grass verge to the gate. The past few days had seen me do more exercise than I usually got in a month. Right at that moment, I didn't see it as a positive.

From my new vantage point next to the gate, I could see into the field beyond. At the far side of the field, a figure turned his quadbike around, heading along the hedgerow. This was the only bit of land that Nicole had retained from the sprawling farm her family once owned. At present it was empty, although I'd heard Patrick make vague plans to rent it out as a paddock for a friend who had too many horses and not enough space. Until then, Patrick used it when he wanted to mess about on his quadbike, like now.

I leaned on the fence and waited for Patrick to circle around. There was no point shouting or waving. He wouldn't hear or see me. I tilted my face up to the drizzle.

The engine noise changed as the quadbike reached the end of the field and turned about. I leaned out over the fence and waved. Patrick acknowledged me with a nod of his head.

He brought the quadbike to a stop next to the gate. The bike was a dirty, patched-together vehicle, made of old parts that he'd bodged together. For what he'd spent on spare parts he probably could've bought a sparkling new quadbike instead. But I knew why he hadn't done that. It was about the build, and the work, not just the finished result.

'Morning,' Patrick said. He switched off the rattling engine so we could hear each other.

'How's it going?' I asked, with a nod to the quadbike.

'Ah, it's running a little rough today. The wet weather, isn't it? Everything seizes up more often when it's cold and wet. Me included.'

Patrick stepped off the bike. He was a tall, lean man, with a slightly lopsided face that made me think he might've been a boxer in an earlier life. In deference to the chill air that morning, he wore a fleecy jacket over a Mad Sunday T-shirt. He flexed his cold fingers inside their padded gloves.

'Everything okay?' he asked.

'Oh, yes, everything's fine. I was just hoping to catch you. Did Nicole get a chance to ask you about the girl we're looking for?'

Patrick's brows knit together. 'What girl?'

'Oh. Um. I've got a, um, friend visiting from England. She's looking for her sister, Simone. Simone went missing over here about twenty years ago.'

'Is that right?'

'Did ... Did Nicole ask you about it?'

Patrick's expression was bemused as he shook his head. 'Can't say I've heard anything about it. Sorry.'

'Oh.' Heat touched my face. I could've sworn Nicole had said she'd spoken to Patrick already. 'Well, that's the whole story, really. Cora's looking for her sister. She asked me to go around the houses and speak to, you know, everyone.' I got out my phone. 'I can show you a photo.'

Patrick politely looked at the photo before he shook his head. 'So, she's got you asking us all whether we remember someone from twenty years ago? How come she's not looked for her before now?'

'Cora *has* been looking for her. Just ... I suppose it's been difficult, to find leads for something that happened so long ago. She's only just heard a hint that Simone might've ended up here.'

Patrick raised his eyebrows. 'Must've been a hell of a good hint.'

'It wasn't. Not at all.' I didn't really mean to say it that harshly, so I tried to soften my words with a smile. 'But Cora's desperate by this point. She's willing to look everywhere, I think.'

'Hmm.' Patrick straightened up. 'I don't know what to tell you. Nicole's probably the person to ask. Offhand, I wasn't living on the island then.'

'You ... weren't?'

He gave a lazy shrug. 'I used to own a couple of businesses in the southeast. It was around about that time. I spent most of my time over there.'

'Oh.' Again, that didn't accord with what Nicole had mentioned. 'Nicole said she was away a lot as well, travelling for her job. She looked it up on her old calendars.'

'Well, there you go.' Patrick smiled. He turned back to his quadbike as if losing interest in the conversation. 'She'd be able to say with more certainty than me. She's always kept those calendars. If she says she was away, she probably was.'

'She also said you were home then. It would've been about June 1999?'

But Patrick was already shaking his head. 'I couldn't genuinely tell you what I was doing this time last week, let alone twenty years ago. If Nicole says I was here, well, she's probably right. She's the one with the calendar. But honestly? I don't remember.'

I still had my phone in my hand. I unlocked the screen again and Simone's face appeared, still with that disaffected smile. I held it out to Patrick. 'Can you take another look, please? Just see if it jogs any memories. I know it's a crazy longshot.'

Patrick chuckled. He pushed the phone back towards me without looking at the screen. 'She doesn't look like anyone I remember,' he said. 'I'm sorry I can't help your friend.'

I nodded and put the phone away. Already I was getting used to that response. People wanted to help us. But they couldn't. It was too long ago. I should've stuck with my gut feeling, stayed at home, and phoned Mum, instead of thinking I could dredge anything up by running around in the open air.

'Do you think Nicole—?' I started to ask, but got distracted.

Further up the road, someone was walking with their head down and their hands pushed deep into the pockets of their jacket. An angry, sullen youth. It took me a moment to realise it was Dallin. He might not have been a teenager for ten years or more, but he'd retained that air of annoyance, like the entire world was against him. He looked so solitary that I considered letting him walk past unnoticed.

Except he was obviously heading to my house.

'I see my brother,' I said to Patrick, by way of a goodbye, then set off up the road.

Before I got more than ten paces, I realised Dallin could easily outdistance me. He'd inherited a long-legged, stork-like stride from somewhere on our father's side.

'Dallin!' I called. 'Dallin, wait up?'

For a second I thought he might ignore me. It would've fitted the angsty aesthetic he was cultivating. But after a few more paces he stopped and turned around.

I slowed down. No point giving myself a stitch catching up with someone who didn't want to be caught.

'Where've you been?' he asked when I got closer.

'Where've *you* been? Weren't you supposed to be with Cora?'

Dallin pulled a face. 'I'm deeply regretting ever getting involved with that woman. You can't believe a single thing she says.'

'Is this because she dragged you out of bed this morning and guilted you into going out to the curraghs with her?'

'Listen, I know you've been fooled. She's persuasive, and manipulative, and all that stuff. She fooled me too. So, y'know, it's nothing to be ashamed of.'

I frowned at him. 'Dal, honestly, you're not making any sense.'

'I told her. Like you said I should.' Dallin turned away and started walking towards my house. I followed him because I wasn't sure what else I could do. It was *my* house, after all. 'It went precisely as I expected.'

'What did you say to her, exactly?'

'I told her we should cut our losses.' Dallin kept walking. 'I know she's gone to a lot of effort to get here, but it's going to be for nothing, and at some point she'll have to accept that. No one here remembers her stupid sister. And even if they did, they don't care. Also, I am one hundred per cent certain Cora's lying to us.'

'About what?'

'Seriously, would anyone go to this sort of effort for a relative who ran away from home twenty years ago? There's something else she wants. Something other than the resting place of her long-absent sister. She's got an ulterior motive. Don't tell me she hasn't.' Dallin paused. 'I asked her outright if she'd cut open her tent on purpose, so she could have a roof over her head instead of sleeping on the ground.'

I let out an explosive breath. 'Why are you like this?'

'I wanted to see what she'd say.'

'Why?'

He blinked. 'Don't you want to know if she's the type who'd do that?'

'What for?'

'Well ... so you would've thought twice about inviting her into your house?'

'She could've easily found a hotel if she'd needed to. Or just gaffer taped the cuts in the groundsheet. It would've only become a problem if we hadn't spotted it before it rained.'

'Sure. And when it *did* rain last night, if she'd called you in the middle of the night, distressed and in need of rescue—'

I took a deep breath, held it, while annoyance swirled and built inside me, then let it go. 'She never once asked about wanting to stay in my house. Didn't even hint at it.'

As I said it though, I remembered the various conversations we'd had. The times she'd said how exhausted she was. How she was worried about Dallin – not about herself, only him – because he wasn't coping well sleeping on the ground.

'She was fine in her tent,' I said. 'You were the one who hated it.'

Dallin got an odd look on his face. 'Who told you I hated camping?'

'Cora said you were having trouble sleeping.'

'Not me. I can sleep anywhere.' Dallin's frown cleared. 'You see what I mean? Cora lied to you. She hoped you'd invite me, and by extension her as well, to stay at your house. Except you didn't take the hint, because you have no people skills.'

'Says you.' But the barb stung. Had Cora really been dropping hints? If she'd just asked me outright, I would've fallen over myself to invite her to my house ...

But, honestly, was that true? Up until yesterday, I'd frozen in terror at the thought of merely having people for lunch. Would I really have welcomed houseguests with open arms?

I was worried Dallin was right. About that one part, not the rest.

Since I couldn't think of a rebuttal, I shut up. We walked in silence for a while.

'So,' Dallin said at last, 'what's with all the weird ceramic animals in your sitting room?'

'They were Beth's.'

'And the porcelain teddy bears wearing those little hats?'

'Also Beth's.'

I concentrated on my feet. If I disassociated myself enough from Dallin's stupid questions, I could pretend it didn't hurt to talk about Beth, or her quirky obsession with tacky ceramic knick-knacks.

'When did she start collecting those? She never liked that sort of thing before.'

Before. As in, *before she met me.* Another barb that hurt just as much as the others. 'A lot of them were her grandmother's,' I said shortly. 'They got passed on to her. She started collecting from there.'

Another minute passed in silence. We were almost at my house. I was still debating whether to let Dallin back in the house. But all his stuff he'd brought with him was upstairs in his old bedroom. If I was going to throw him out, it would need more planning.

'What about that letter you had tucked into a photo album?' Dallin asked then. 'What was that about?'

I'd known the question was coming. But somehow I'd hoped I could keep avoiding it. Even now, I thought we could reach the house, and I could find a displacement activity. Put on the kettle, or go out into the garden, or start another argument. Maybe throw something at him. Anything to keep from having to answer the question.

In the end though, I knew I couldn't run or hide or incite a random unprovoked act of violence.

'Did you read it?' I asked.

'Not all the way through. I skimmed it. The highlighting helped give me the gist.'

I pulled my jacket a little tighter around myself. 'It's from Beth's parents.'

Dallin blinked. 'Her parents?'

'They've been sending me clippings like that for a couple of years now.'

'Why would they do that?' Dallin frowned. 'I remember her folks. Mum used to sing in the same choir as them. Neither of them were particularly into, y'know, science and medicine. Why would they send you clippings from medical journals?'

I sighed. 'You didn't read the page properly, did you?'

'I said I skimmed it. It was talking about abnormal brain chemistry and stuff, wasn't it?'

'If you want to read it like that.' I avoided his gaze. 'Beth's parents never liked me. No, that's not completely true. They liked me well enough as Beth's *friend.* Even when—' *Even when me and Beth started dating, when we got engaged, when they politely declined an invitation to our wedding.* 'They always acted like me and Beth were just friends. They refused to acknowledge anything else. It was upsetting, obviously, but we thought that, given enough time, we could talk them around. Except ...'

Except, of course, we didn't have nearly as much time as we'd thought.

'We reconciled with them a bit, when Beth got sick. It pulled everyone together. Sort of. At least, as far as Beth was concerned, we were building bridges. The letters started arriving not long after that. Beth never knew about them.'

We'd reached my house. I got out my keys and used them as an excuse to focus on my hands rather than looking at Dallin.

'The first letter—' But I couldn't put into words how the first letter had made me feel.

It'd comprised five A4 sheets of paper, printed off the internet, and a cover letter in my mother-in-law's neat handwriting. I still shuddered to think of the gentle, faux-concerned words. *Thought this information might help you. Just out of concern for our darling daughter. Something for you to consider.*

'They blamed me,' I said as I pushed open the door. My voice had taken on that flat tone that made it sound like someone else was talking. Like someone was describing people and events with no connection to me at all. 'There was something wrong with my brain chemistry, they said. Something that caused this ... delusion that I was in love with Beth. I'd tricked Beth into believing it as well. I'd made her sick. And that's what made her ill.'

'No way.' Dallin almost laughed. Not because it was funny, I knew, but because it couldn't be true.

'Oh, they have evidence to back it up.' I went through to the kitchen and filled the kettle. 'They became quite the experts.'

'Beth's parents believe *you* made her ill?'

'Google it. I'm serious. Google "does homosexuality cause cancer" and see what pops up in your browser.' I switched the kettle on. 'Go ahead, have a look. I'll wait. You might have to click to the second or third page of search results before you find the bad stuff, but it's there.' I took two cups out of the cupboard. 'You can find evidence of anything you want to believe, if you're really determined.'

'And they've been sending you the print-outs.' At last, Dallin's tone softened.

'It stopped for a while after Beth died, then it came back with a vengeance. They're one hundred per cent convinced I murdered their daughter.'

'Jesus.' Dallin rubbed the side of his face. 'You never

would've thought it to look at the pair of them. They always acted so normal.'

'People always seem normal. Until they're not.' I spooned instant coffee into a cup for him. I very nearly made some for myself as well. At the last instant, I dropped in a peppermint teabag instead.

Dallin rapped his knuckles on the counter, twice, slowly, like either it was helping him think or he had an important point to make. 'I'm guessing they never came to your wedding, hey?' he asked.

'They also tried to bar me from her funeral.' I stirred the herbal teabag seventeen times more than it needed. 'They asked the minister if he could omit any mention of me. Thank God he refused.'

Dallin rapped the counter again, harder this time. *Anger,* I realised. He turned away then immediately turned back. 'I'm sorry,' he said.

Good. 'What for, precisely?'

'For – for not coming home. I'm sorry. I didn't realise you were dealing with all this. I should've come back for the funeral.'

'And the wedding.'

Dallin let out a breath. 'I didn't think it was that big a deal at the time. I'm sorry, but that's just – that's how I felt. I figured you'd only invited me out of politeness. It never occurred to me you might actually want me to be there.'

I couldn't stop myself from saying, 'It was Beth who invited you. It was important to her.'

'I know. That's what confused me.' He scrubbed his face

with both hands. 'She knew how I felt about her. It felt like – I don't know. Like she was trying to twist the knife or something.'

I looked at him for the first time since we'd got back to the house. 'You genuinely thought Beth would be like that?'

'I don't know. It was a lot clearer in my head at the time.' Dallin hesitated, then said, 'I was maybe in denial. You know I loved her, a lot. Right?'

I pressed my lips together. 'Yes. I know.'

'And you know we slept together one time.'

I closed my eyes. Yes, I'd known that too. Beth had admitted it to me in a fit of panic, right after we'd agreed we were definitely in a relationship and we didn't care who knew about it. At the time it'd felt meaningless to me. In my mind, it'd boiled down to a simple question – did I care about anything except the fact she was here now, with me? And if I *did* care, then how much? Enough to burn a whole relationship because I couldn't deal with sharing her affection with anyone, even from a time before we'd been together?

'I know that too, Dallin,' I said with a sigh. 'What's your point?'

'I'm just trying to explain. I wasn't thinking clearly at the time. I was confused. But I should've been able to put my stupid feelings aside. It wasn't fair to you. Or Beth.'

I suspected it was as close to a full apology as I was likely to get. So why did I still want to kick him in the shins? 'Okay,' I said. The backs of my eyes were prickling.

'I wish I'd come back to see her.' Dallin leaned against the kitchen counter. His gaze was distant. 'I genuinely didn't realise how ill she was. If she'd just come out and told me ...' He sighed. 'But, you're right, she shouldn't have had to. I should've known she wasn't the type to make stuff up.'

'Not like me, right?' I put on a smile that was wholly fake. 'Not like Cora.'

'Ah, Rosie, don't be like that.'

'Why not? It seems to be a recurring theme with you. I say I've found a body in the curraghs; you assume I'm making it up. Beth tells you she's ill; you think she's exaggerating. Cora finds her tent's been vandalised; you say she's done it herself. What'll it take to convince you we're telling the truth?'

Dallin grimaced. 'I just don't think you should take everything Cora says at face value. That's all. Being cautious isn't a character defect.'

I rolled up a response and let it sit on my tongue for a moment. Then I blew it out with a sigh. What was even the point of arguing with him?

'Here's your coffee,' I said instead.

There were tears and recriminations. I sat at the top of the stairs, invisible, and listened to you argue with Da. It wasn't the first time he'd tried to ground you; but it was the first time he'd locked the doors and refused to physically let you out of the house.

Your voice rose in anger but Da's remained weirdly unemotional. He sounded tired, like he'd been fighting this battle too long.

'You can't stop me seeing him,' you said.

'You should stop yourself,' Da said. 'I taught you to have more self-esteem than this.'

'He wants to be with me.'

'I don't doubt that.'

I pictured Da, weary, eyes exhausted, as he blocked your way to the front door. For once it was him being battered by the storm instead of us.

'He loves me,' you said.

'I don't doubt that either.'

'So let me leave.'

'No.' The word was a sigh. 'I know you think I'm wrong but you'll see it eventually. He's not good for you. I won't stand by and let him hurt you as well.'

You stormed upstairs and I didn't get out of your way fast enough. With sharp nails you pinched my arm, hard enough to bruise.

'Snitch,' you hissed.

Chapter 30

I phoned Mum when I got home. As soon as Dallin heard me say hello to her, he made himself conspicuously absent by going upstairs. That was fine by me.

'How's your friend getting on, pumpkin?' Mum asked.

'She's fine. No luck yet.'

'And how about your brother? Has he spoken to you about the house?'

My pulse stilled. What about the house? 'He's said a few things, yeah,' I said cautiously.

'What do you think about it?'

'I ... I need time to think.'

'Well, we both do, that's for certain. It's all well and good him making these grand plans, but it's my property and your home we're talking about. I sometimes think he doesn't take that into consideration.'

I closed my eyes. I felt a sick headache brewing. 'Mum, can I call you back? I forgot to do something. Ten minutes, okay?'

I barely let her say goodbye before I hung up.

In the kitchen, I snatched up the Filofax and flipped to the first bookmark. According to the date, last year Dallin had paid Lenny two thousand pounds for 'drainage'. Dallin hadn't even been on the island then. On another page, he'd again paid Lenny a significant sum, this time for 'access'. None of it made sense at a glance. But Cora had seen a pattern and, with sickening certainty, I thought I saw it too.

'Everything okay?' Dallin asked from the doorway.

I could barely make myself look at him. 'You want Mum to sell this house,' I said.

He grimaced. 'I asked her not to say anything till I'd had a chance to—'

'Don't, Dallin.' I lifted the book. 'You paid Lenny to do surveys on my house. Drainage, access rights ... you asked him to do it on the quiet.' How many times had Lenny popped round last year, apparently just to check how I was doing? How many times was it due to genuine concern, and how many for Dallin's agenda? 'You wanted to find out the state of the house so you could get it on the market.'

'That's not—'

'And then what happened? You ran out of money before you could pay him for his work? No wonder he's pissed off at you.'

Dallin glowered at me. 'You're making this sound like a conspiracy.'

'You're trying to sell my house!'

'Except it's not yours, is it? It's Mum's. She's letting you live here but it's not yours. Be realistic, Rosie. This place is too big for you. You could fit a whole family in here.' He spread his arms to demonstrate. 'If we sell, we can split the money between you, me, and Mum. She can get somewhere nicer, with an accessible garden. You can use your share of the money as a deposit on your own place.'

His words shocked me. *A whole family.* Didn't he know that was what we'd dreamed of?

'And what do you get?' I sounded breathless, like he'd kicked me in the stomach.

Dallin rubbed the back of his neck. 'What does that matter? What's important is—'

'No, if it didn't matter, you'd leave things well enough alone.' I steadied myself against the table. 'What do you need the money for?'

'It's not that I need it. I just – look, I see you here, in the house I grew up in, while I'm living in some horrendous flat above a vape shop, with no job, and I just—' He lifted his hands in exasperation. 'Is it really so bad of me to want to stabilise my life? Pay off my debts and start living like a proper person?'

I didn't answer. I couldn't find the words.

Apparently Dallin had run out of justifications as well. 'I'm going to the pub,' he said.

At the front door he glanced back, like maybe I would stop him. Like I didn't intend to lock the door and never let him back in again.

Chapter 31

I texted Cora a few times that afternoon. I suggested she might want to come for dinner at my house. I didn't tell her what'd happened with Dallin.

I was only as the sun started easing down towards the horizon that a niggle of worry wormed its way into my belly.

During the afternoon, I'd also tried contacting Eloise a few times, and Nicole twice. I still wanted to hear Eloise's side of the story. And I wanted to ask Nicole about the discrepancies between her story and Patrick's. It probably wasn't anything to draw attention to, given how long it'd been since Simone was potentially here, but I was interested to get them to compare notes. At the moment, I couldn't help but feel one or the other was lying.

With Dallin gone, I had the house to myself again. I wasn't sure how to deal with it. Before, I'd embraced the silent, empty nature of the house. The few sounds I made as I walked from one room to another were more than enough to make the place sound full. I was suddenly, acutely aware of every slight noise I made; and equally, I was aware how it didn't fill the rooms at all. I could've shouted and screamed the house down and the echoes would've still sounded hollow.

I opened my laptop. It automatically brought up the last search page, when I'd been looking for details of Nicole. Again I felt the sting of defeat. What exactly had I been hoping to find?

I tried Cora's phone twice more, without a response. Possibly it'd run out of charge again.

Don't these people ever think to charge their phones? The thought was a brief flare in my brain, there and then gone. I was a fine one to talk, since I'd left my own phone uncharged for the last several months.

To distract myself from my whirling thoughts, I tried to tidy the house. But everything was wrong. Cora and Dallin hadn't made a massive impact on the house, but still, a delicate balance had been disturbed. There were extra pairs of shoes at the bottom of the stairs. Extra towels in the bathroom. Cora had left a window open in the guest bedroom and a healthy breeze was ruffling the curtains.

None of this was particularly difficult or upsetting, but it was different enough to cause a knot of unease in my stomach. I didn't want to tidy the guest bedroom because that felt like I'd be invading Cora's privacy. I didn't want to go into the study, because Dallin's clothes were on the floor. All of a sudden, my house didn't feel like it belonged to me anymore.

It shouldn't have mattered. Yet somehow it did.

You could fit a whole family in here.

Faced with not knowing how or where to start tidying the house, I retreated to the kitchen. I glanced out of the window at the curraghs. The dullness of the late afternoon sun made the spindly trees look like they were etched in shades of grey onto the green background of the distant hills.

Are you out there? I thought automatically. This time I wasn't sure if I was thinking of Bogbean or Cora.

From where I stood, I could see down to the bottom of our garden. In the low shadows around the bench by the wall, I imagined Beth sitting there, just as she'd sat on her last evening.

I left the kitchen and went out into the garden.

I shivered as I made my way down the path to the end of the garden. The rain was taking a break, but the wind was rising, tussling the trees into constant, chattering motion. The chill of evening was already seeping in. Give it another hour, and it would be freezing out there. Despite that, I didn't go back for my coat.

The bench at the bottom of the garden was wet from the recent rain. I perched on the wooden slats and peered out over the curraghs. Somewhere out there, Cora was searching in vain for her sister's lost remains.

I've got to go, Beth had said to me.

It was at times like this when I heard her voice most clearly. Like, if I could just concentrate in the correct way, her voice would reach me again, not just as an echoing whisper in my mind.

I need you to help me, Beth had said.

I sat in the cold as the sun, behind its veil of clouds, sunk towards the horizon.

I'm not strong enough alone.

It wasn't something we'd discussed. Even when we'd realised how bad things would get. But that was how things were with us. Sometimes we didn't need to say anything out loud.

I'd left her there on the bench while I walked around the garden. From the lean-to at the side of the house, up on a shelf where no one would stumble on them, I took down a jar from the row I'd made. The label said Foxglove. If questioned, I could've said honestly it contained clippings and seeds, the same as the half-dozen other jars on that shelf. I'd risked asking Nicole's advice on the best seeds to save.

I brought the contents back to Beth, cupped in my hands. A last offering from the garden we'd cultivated together. She smiled at me.

In her weakened state, she didn't take long to go. I sat with her through the night, until long after she went cold, until I myself was half-gone from hypothermia. I'd hated the way my body shivered, trying to keep itself warm, when all I'd wanted to do was freeze solid.

At last, as the sun came up, I'd left Beth on the bench, her head slumped onto her shoulder as if she was drowsing, and gone back into the house. I washed the itchy stains of foxglove shoots off my hands. Even then, I'd wondered why I hadn't picked up enough for both of us.

There was no need for a post-mortem, the doctors told me. It was an expected death. No one thought to take a sample of her congealed blood to check for toxicity.

I'd never told anyone, not even Mum. But I couldn't help but think Beth's parents somehow intuited what'd happened. When they resumed sending me the printed pseudo-medical pages in the post, they started highlighting interesting factoids, such as the propensity for someone abnormal like me to become a murderer.

My mobile phone rang, startling me out of my thoughts. I so rarely carried it around that it took me a moment to remember which pocket it was in.

My chilled fingers tapped the screen. 'Hello?' I answered.

The reply was blown out by the wind. Distantly, I heard Cora's voice. 'Hello? Rosalie?'

I covered my other ear with my hand to hear her better. 'Cora? Are you okay?'

The words came through patchy. 'I think I ... turned around—'

'Cora? Hello?'

I hurried up the path back into the house. The warmth of the kitchen was like a balm after the chill outside. But I couldn't enjoy it because I was anxiously trying to hear Cora.

'Rosalie? Are you there?' Her voice was still distant but more audible.

'I'm here. What's wrong? Are you okay?'

'I think I've got myself turned around. I don't know where—' Another blast of wind drowned her out. It sounded like static from a broken TV. 'I'm trying to find the road.'

'What about your GPS?'

'The battery went. And I left my compass at your house. I think I've veered off course.' Her voice crackled and broke up. '—maps are wron—'

'Cora? Where are you? Wait, hang on.' I went back out into the garden and hurried to the rear wall. 'I'm going to shout for you.' Covering the phone with my hand, I yelled, 'Cora!' several times.

I listened but heard nothing in response.

Into the phone I said, 'Can you hear me? I'm shouting from my garden. If you can hear me, head towards me.'

'I can't hear you. Try again.'

I shouted until my throat ached, but the wind kept snatching up my words and bundling them away. Cora must've been too far off to hear.

By then the sun was touching the horizon. 'Stay where you are,' I told Cora over the phone. 'I'll drive round to the car park.'

'Okay. Thank you.' Cora's voice trembled. She was obviously exhausted from trudging through the curraghs, but I could also hear the undercurrent of fear in her voice. I understood all too well how unnerving it was to get lost out there.

I threw on my shoes and grabbed my coat. At the last instant I remembered Dallin was out, and might return before I got back, and he didn't have house keys. I dithered for a moment before leaving the door unlocked. It was the first time I'd deliberately done that in a year. Even though I was so concerned about Cora, I still found room to worry about leaving our house unsecured.

The first fat, heavy drops of rain spattered my windscreen as I drove the short distance to the car park in the curraghs. When I got there, Cora's car was parked in what I was already thinking of as her usual spot. No other cars could be seen.

The sun was below the horizon. It was going to get dark out here very quickly.

When I phoned Cora she answered right away.

'I'm in the car park,' I told her. 'I'm going to beep the horn. Let me know if you can hear it, alright?'

I bipped the horn. It was louder than I expected in the quietness of the forest. I drew up my courage and beeped louder. It felt wrong to be so noisy out there. I swore I saw the trees shiver in distaste.

'I can hear you!' Cora said through the phone. 'It's – hang on—'

I couldn't be sure if she was still there or if the line had broken up again. I beeped the horn three more times to be sure.

'I can definitely hear you,' Cora said. 'It's just – it's difficult to be sure which direction—' She broke off, swearing. 'Sorry, I tripped. The light isn't great out here.'

Added to that, the rain was starting in earnest. Fat drops bounced off the roof of my car; a few at first, then increasing to a fierce drumming. I turned on my headlights and flashed them on and off a few times.

'Can you see my headlights?' I asked Cora.

'Not yet. Can't see much of anything. Okay, I'm going to keep coming towards you. I'll call you back in five minutes, okay? I can't stay on the phone, I've not got much battery left. Keep beeping for me.'

I ended the call with a sense of foreboding. But Cora was right, it wouldn't do us any good to be on the phone while she walked. She needed her concentration to avoid tripping over. I turned the car engine off, although I left the headlights on. To give myself something to focus on, I waited a thirty-second interval then blew the horn three times. Another thirty seconds, another three blasts. It stopped my thoughts from spiralling.

After five minutes of this, I figured everyone within a mile radius must've known I was there, and would probably come to find out who was making such a godawful noise. I glanced in my rear-view mirror, half expecting to see an irate dog-walker bearing down on me. But for once, the area was deserted. The rain and wind had pushed everyone away.

Another five minutes passed with me marking the time with the car horn. Hadn't Cora said she would call back by now? Should I call her? I turned the engine back on so I could use the wipers and lights without running down the battery. The last thing I wanted was to get stuck out here as well.

It was dark enough now that my headlights reflected back to me from the wet trunks of the nearest trees. I waited another three minutes, then phoned Cora.

It took her a worryingly long time to answer, and when she did, she sounded more breathless than before. 'I've found a path of sorts,' she told me. 'I thought it was leading me towards you but it doubled back. So I'm going cross-country again now. I can still hear you though. It can't be much further.'

'Can you see my lights?' I flashed the headlights again.

'No ... wait, do that again.' I did. 'I think ... I think maybe I saw something. God, it's so difficult to tell.'

She sounded thoroughly wet and miserable. 'Keep going, you're almost there,' I urged her. I beeped the horn and flashed the lights like a demented person. Was it my imagination, or did I hear the echo of the horn through the phone?

'I definitely saw the lights that time!' Hope tightened Cora's voice. 'I'm coming right towards you. Don't move, okay?' She let out a breathless giggle.

'I'm not going anywhere,' I reassured her. 'I just wish I'd brought a towel. You're going to be soaked by the time you get here.'

'I was soaked an hour ago. I tripped over a root and went sprawling. You're not going to want me in your car.'

I giggled as well. Relief made me giddy. 'I'm not going to make you walk home just because you're a bit muddy, am I?'

'I don't know, people can be irrational about – oh my God, there's the road! I can see the road!'

I leaned forward to peer through the rain-dappled windscreen. 'Where are you? Can you see me?'

'I can see the lights of your car. Oh my God. Here I am. I'm on the road. I'm right in front of you.'

'Where?' The stretch of road in front of my car remained empty. I squinted at the trees on either side. 'I can't see you!'

'It's okay. I'm right here. I'm at the car.'

I got out. Rain pelted the top of my head. 'Cora? I can't see you. Where are you?'

'I'm right here!' Through the phone I heard the clunk of a car door opening. Not my car door. 'I—'

At that point, the line went dead.

Chapter 32

'Cora? Cora?'

Fear froze me stupidly to the spot. I clutched the phone to my ear as if the call might spontaneously reconnect. All around me, the trees whispered and chattered in the hissing rain.

I finally got my fingers working and dialled her number again. For three seconds there was nothing, then the recorded phone informed me, sorry, the mobile phone is switched off at present.

Where was she?

She'd gone to a car. Obviously not my car, so there must've been another on the road near here. I tried to listen. All I could hear was the rain, the putter of my idling car engine, the sweep of the wipers, the wind in the trees. I ducked down and turned off the engine. Still I couldn't hear anything. I held my breath.

Cora must've come out of the woods along either this road or the next one along, which ran down towards Ballaugh. If she'd found a car with its engine running and its lights on, it couldn't be far away. Unless it'd arrived after me and was on the road somewhere behind ...

I got in my car. I would drive to the end of this road then loop around. If I didn't find Cora, I would check the Ballaugh road. If I still couldn't see her or the car ...

Don't think about it. She's fine. She's no longer lost out in the woods. So, she's fine.

There was a weird squirmy sensation in my stomach that made me scared I was wrong.

In the dark and the rain, on that horrendous lumpy road, with the headlights bouncing off the grey-green tree trunks, I could barely get out of first gear. I was terrified of ripping the bottom out of my car. At each turn I expected to see red taillights in front of me or headlights coming towards me. Or maybe I would see Cora, sheltering at the side of the road, waving me down.

There was no one out on the road except me.

I got to the end of the road and turned right. I circled round and came back down the narrow road that went past the car park. Still nothing. I pulled in at the car park and tried Cora's phone again. It was still switched off.

At the end of the road, this time I turned left, and headed around the opposite edge of the curraghs. Still no one.

When I paused at the next give way sign I closed my eyes. *Alright, think.* If a car had stopped for Cora, she would've asked the driver to drop her at my house. When she got inside, she might've immediately gone to charge her phone, but even so it would've taken a few minutes until she could call me back ...

The smartest thing I could do, for her and me both, was to go home. Cora was probably already there waiting for me.

I took the main road home. It was longer in distance but definitely quicker than wiggling along the rutted back roads in the dark.

When I reached my house, it was in darkness. I ran inside.

'Hello? Cora, are you here?'

I knew as soon as I stepped through the door that she wasn't. The house felt empty. No, it felt normal, which was the same thing.

Cora, where the hell are you?

Her phone was still switched off. In desperation, I tried phoning Dallin, because I didn't know what else to do.

He answered on the eighth ring. 'Hi,' he said. 'What's up?' Behind him, I heard voices and laughter, the background life of the pub. It occurred to me I'd driven pretty close to Ballaugh and could've picked him up.

'I can't find Cora,' I blurted.

'Oh for—' There was a rustle of static, then the background noise dropped away, as Dallin stepped outside. 'She said she'd be back around seven. It's only eight now. Give the woman some space.'

'No, that's not it. I called her, and she said she was lost, but then she got back to the road. A car stopped for her. But now her phone's turned off and I don't know where she is.'

Dallin was silent for a moment. 'And you reckon that's reason to panic?'

'She got into someone's car, Dallin. That was—' I checked the clock on the kitchen wall. 'Fifteen minutes ago. Nowhere around here is fifteen minutes' drive from my house.'

He sighed. 'I'm still not convinced that's—'

'I don't know where she is. She's missing.'

'Okay, look.' I could almost picture him running an exasperated hand through his short hair. 'I'll come home, okay? You wait there in case she comes back. I'll be there soon.'

I wanted to correct him for using the word 'home' to describe my house. Was that even important right now? 'Alright,' I agreed. 'I don't want to sound like I'm overreacting. I'm just ...'

'You're worried, I know, I get it. Keep phoning her, okay? She's bound to turn her phone back on eventually.'

It wasn't much more of a plan than I'd had. After I hung up, I sat on the third step of the stairs and called Cora, over and over again. I kept one eye on the clock. Ten minutes passed, then twenty. I tried to come up with other reasons why she might not have found her way home from half a mile away.

Should I call the police? I had no idea what the appropriate response was right now. What would I tell the police if I called them? Would they tell me I was justified, or advise me to wait? What was I actually afraid of?

I'm afraid someone knows what happened to Simone. And they don't want anyone to find out about it.

I went out onto the driveway. From there, if I stood on my toes, I could see part of Eloise's house. The lights were on in her front room and it looked like her car was parked at the side of her house, rather than on the road in front where she usually left it.

Rain pelted my face. The wind lifted my hair. I hurried around to the side of the house and tried to see Nicole's house.

I could see a glow of light reflected off the road which suggested their lights were on as well.

I ran back inside to grab my coat and my keys. As I was searching for a hat, I heard a car pull up outside.

When I came out, Dallin was getting out of a taxi. 'Hey,' he called. 'I got really lucky. This guy was just clocking off for the night when I waved him down. Overwise I would've had to walk all the way back.'

'Cora still isn't here,' I told him.

Surprise smoothed out his expression. 'She's not?'

'No! I told you she wasn't. And you said you'd be five minutes. That was half an hour ago.'

'I had to get a lift.' Dallin gestured with a sweeping arm at the taxi, which was pulling away. I realised he was more than a little drunk. 'Do you have any idea how difficult it is to get a taxi in Ballaugh on a Sunday? You're lucky I got home at all.'

'I think we should call the police.'

'About—? Because Cora?'

'Because Cora has suffered two separate acts of vandalism in one weekend, and because she hasn't answered her phone in almost an hour, and because the last I heard, she was getting into a car with persons unknown and she hasn't been heard from since. So, yes, Dallin, I think we should call the police.'

He opened his mouth a couple of times. In the end, all he said was, 'Okay.'

I got him inside the house and put the landline phone in his hands. 'Here,' I said. 'You call them.'

'Why me?'

'Because I'm going to look for Cora. You call the police and tell them what's happened.'

It maybe would've been better if I made the call myself. But I figured the best place for Dallin was here, in the house, where he could wait for Cora. If she ever found her way back.

I left Dallin dialling the number, shoved my hat on, and took the car to Eloise's house.

As I'd thought, her car was parked at the side of her house. The lights were on in the front room. I parked up on the road.

When I banged on the door, Butterscotch immediately started barking. But no one came to the door.

'I know you're here, Eloise,' I called through the letterbox. 'Stop being ridiculous. It's Rosalie. Let me in.'

I stood on the doorstep, breathing heavily from all the running. How difficult would it be to kick down someone's door? Was that an overreaction? If I genuinely believed my friend was in danger, it'd be justified ... wouldn't it?

Before I had the chance to find out whether panic was enough to break down a sturdy uPVC door, the door unlocked with a clack. Eloise pulled it open a scant half-inch.

'What's wrong?' she asked. She had the same slur in her voice as Dallin.

'What do you think is wrong? Let me in.'

'Why?'

'Eloise.' I struggled to keep my voice level. For over a year I'd kept my anger squashed, at the cost of feeling anything at all. I couldn't let it spill out now. 'Where's Cora? Is she here?'

Eloise shook her head.

My anger swelled up. I drew back my foot and kicked out at the door. As it turned out, it didn't take nearly as much effort as I'd expected to boot a door open.

Apparently it surprised Eloise as well. She jumped backwards as the door burst open.

For a second we both stood there in amazement. *Did I do that?* The door swung on its hinges. I stepped forward and caught it before it could swing closed.

'Is she here?' I asked.

Eloise shook her head. Her eyes were a little wild, her curly hair standing out in crazy frizzes around her head.

I came into the hall and closed the front door. It wouldn't shut properly. It appeared I'd pushed it out of shape. The fact frightened some of my anger away.

'Is she here?' I asked, softer. 'Have you seen her?'

It took two attempts for Eloise to find her voice. 'I shouldn't have done it.'

Oh no. 'What? What did you do?'

'I shouldn't have cut her tyres like that. It was dis ... disproportionate. I shouldn't have done it.'

Eloise grabbed a handful of her hair in distress. I held out both hands to stop her. 'Eloise—'

'I know people would think it was petty,' she said. 'But it's important. You understand that, don't you? You can't just let people trample around in the curraghs. They had no respect. I told you about the damage they were doing and they – they – it was like they didn't even care. People are so entitled. They don't care about anything except their own selves.'

I stepped past her. The living room was empty. On the sofa

there was a large in-progress crochet project, and a half-empty bottle of wine.

At the end of the hallway was a kitchen. Also empty. I switched on all the lights as I went. No one was in the dining room either.

'You shouldn't leave lights on when you're not in the room,' Eloise said. 'Do you have any idea how much energy that wastes?'

'Is Cora here?' I asked.

'You know ...' Eloise lifted both hands in exasperation then let them fall. 'If you'd just listened to me ...'

I debated going upstairs, but honestly, I knew it'd be a waste of time. Cora wasn't here.

'Have you seen Cora today?' I tried instead.

Eloise shook her head. Her frizzy hair fluffed back and forth like a mane. 'I haven't been home. I went to stay with a friend last night.' She blinked. Belatedly, a flash of anger came into her eyes. 'I was *afraid*, you understand? Your friend *assaulted* me.'

'What? No she didn't.'

'She was coming right at me.'

'You kicked her in the knee!'

'She was going to assault me. It was self-defence. You saw it.'

I wanted to argue. I wanted to grab her by the shoulders and shake her. But I didn't have time. Cora was still missing.

I walked out of there with Eloise still attempting to apologise.

Chapter 33

'Rosie?' Dallin called as I came in through the front door.

'Is she here?' I called back, although I was sure she wasn't.

'No. Rosie, what's this?'

I went into the kitchen. Dallin was sat at the table with my laptop open. I felt a flash of irritation.

'Dallin, can't you leave my stuff alone?' I asked. 'What're you looking for now?'

'This.' He tapped the screen. 'What is it?'

I glanced over his shoulder. 'Is this important right now? What did the police say?'

'What is this, Rosalie?'

The use of my actual name stopped me. 'It's the pages I was looking at earlier.' I ran my eyes over the screen. 'Cora asked me to look into, y'know, our neighbours. I didn't get very far.'

'This is Nicole? From down the road?'

'That's her. You remember her, don't you?'

'Vaguely. I probably know her by sight. But I never knew her middle name.' He tapped the screen again. 'Vanaella?'

'That's her. Nicole Vanaella Willson. Like a strange kind of ice cream. Why?'

'Did Cora tell you about her Aunt Florrie who was carrying on with a married man and was so stupid about him she changed her surname to match his?'

'I – yeah? What the hell does it matter?'

'It's the same name. Vanaella. Cora's aunt has the same weird name as her surname.'

I frowned. 'Are you sure?'

'How many people do you reckon have that name? In the whole of the UK? Can't be many, can there? So, what're the chances of someone else with that exact same name living right here, right next to where Cora reckons her sister was last seen?'

My brain felt like it was struggling to catch up. I blinked several times. 'Cora said her sister was seeing that guy as well. The one who messed her aunt around so much. You think ...?'

Dallin hopped up from his chair. Together we ran to the car.

I drove faster than I'd ever gone on those awful roads. Even so, Dallin probably could've reached Nicole's house faster if he'd got out and run. I sped up as much as I dared, sending us bouncing and jolting over the potholes.

As we drove, Dallin called the police.

We slowed to a stop outside Nicole's house. I abandoned the car and ran to the front door.

'Nicole!' I shouted as I banged on the door. 'Cora! Are you there?'

The door wasn't locked. It swung open as soon as I thought to try the door handle.

'Cora?' I called.

'In here,' someone called from the kitchen. But it wasn't Cora.

When I came into the kitchen, I found Patrick hunched at the breakfast island, his head in his hands. He was still in the fleecy jacket he'd been wearing when I'd seen him in the field earlier. Next to him on the counter was his mobile phone and a half-eaten plate of curry.

To Dallin I said, 'Check the rest of the house.'

He nodded and took off up the stairs.

I approached Patrick. 'What's going on?' I asked.

Without looking up, Patrick made a loose gesture towards his phone. 'If you're looking for your friend,' he said, 'she's not here.'

'Then where the hell is she?'

Dallin came back down the stairs, breathless. 'No sign of her.' He stalked into the kitchen. 'I know who you are.'

At last Patrick looked up. His eyes were reddened but he had an amused look on his face. 'Of course you do,' he said. 'We've lived next door to each other for years. I watched you grow up.'

'Except for the time you were living in England, when Cora and her family knew you as Paddy.'

Patrick's expression was immovable. 'That was her Florence's daft nickname for me. No one's ever called me Paddy.'

'Why did you pretend you never heard of Simone?' I asked.

'Because that family is bad news.' Patrick straightened up

in his seat. He smelled musty from the fumes of the quadbike. 'I barely got away from Florrie with my balls intact. The last thing I wanted to do was stir up the past.'

'Cora told me about you,' Dallin said. 'You strung her Aunt Florence along for two years. You just kept telling her *of course* you would leave your wife. She changed her name for you.'

'Exactly. You see what I mean? Batshit crazy. What sort of woman does that? And for the record, I never promised her *anything*.'

'It wasn't even your real name! You lied to her about everything.'

'What about Simone?' I asked. 'What did you promise her?'

Patrick held his hands up briefly in annoyance. 'I never did anything with Simone. I didn't touch her, I didn't kiss her, I didn't lead her on. Everything she thought was going on was entirely in her head.'

'So why did she tell her family you were her boyfriend?'

'To wind them up, probably. Or to hurt me. She never liked me. She probably thought it was the quickest way to get rid of me, to get her dad to chase me off.' Patrick touched a finger to his forehead. 'You see that scar? That's where her dad glassed me. Bunch of psychos in that family.' He winced then, as if the vitriol had a physical effect on him.

'That's not the way Cora tells it,' I said.

'Look, I met Cora and Simone a few times at parties. All I did was a bit of flirting, before I realised who she was and how old she was.' Patrick's expression twisted in disgust. 'Soon as I realised, I walked away.' He winced again. 'Her family overreacted. There was never anything between me and

Simone. Do you have any idea what they threatened me with? You'd have thought I'd started World War Three.'

'Where's Cora now?' I asked.

Dallin said, 'We've already called the police. They're on their way.'

Patrick's expression paled. He held up a defensive hand. 'I don't know anything about Cora. I've not seen her since she got here.'

'Lucky for you,' Dallin said. 'She would've remembered you straight off.'

'I bet. Her family still curses my name, right?'

'With good reason, the way I hear it.'

Patrick washed a hand over his face. He looked more than a little green. 'I don't know how I could've been any clearer with Florrie,' he said. 'We told each other a hundred times it wasn't anything serious. We were just having fun. She said that's all she wanted. God knows I never lied to her. She knew from minute one that I was married. Then all of a sudden she started talking about how things would be different after I left Nicole.' He wiped his forehead was a shaky hand. 'I told her that would never happen. But it was like she was hearing something different. I honest to God never meant to hurt her. She started acting crazy.' He covered his eyes with his hand. 'That business with changing her surname. She sprung it on me as a surprise. Said it was an anniversary present.' He grimaced. 'I realised right then that I had to break things off.'

'Was that before or after you started seeing Simone?' Dallin asked.

Patrick glared at us. 'I told you, I spoke to her a few times, at her dad's house. She followed me round trying to cadge cigarettes off me. She was fun, but she was also fifteen. I'm not stupid.'

'Cora showed me the letter you sent to Simone,' Dallin said.

Patrick paled further. He pressed his lips together tightly.

I'd walked around the table to the shoe rack by the back door. Two pairs of upside down boots stood on the rack. The larger pair had mud on them. The tread pattern was the same wavy pattern I'd seen in the mud behind Cora's tent.

'Why did you ransack Cora's tent?' I asked.

Patrick slumped in his seat. He shoved aside the half-eaten plate of curry so he could put his head in his hands again. 'I didn't believe it was definitely her,' he said. 'I needed to make myself sure.'

'Did Simone come here?' I asked.

It looked for a moment like Patrick wouldn't answer. 'I've always wondered how she knew where to find me,' he said at length.

'So, it's true then? She came here?'

'She tracked me down,' he said. 'God knows how she managed it. I never told anyone where me and Nicole lived. Didn't even tell them my proper name. I was worried about what her aunt might do with the information.' He flicked another glare at Dallin. 'Turned out I was right to be worried. I had to block Florrie's number in the end.'

I said, 'Florrie was, presumably, a grown-ass woman who can make her own mistakes. Simone was a child. Do you expect us to believe she somehow tracked you down when no one else could?'

'I'm not saying I was hiding. I've kept the same name and the same address since I came back here. If it was that big a deal, anyone could've found me, if they'd cared that much.' Patrick lifted his shoulders in a shrug. His face was getting paler by the minute. 'Apparently, Simone cared enough. She turned up on my doorstep one night. Thank God Nicole was away.' His hands were shaking again. 'I told Simone to get lost. Slammed the door in her face. She was telling me she had no place to go, nowhere to sleep the night ... she stayed out there for an hour, crying and shouting. I thought I'd have to call the police.'

'Let me guess.' Dallin's lips twisted. 'You took pity on her and let her stay the night. Out of the goodness of your heart.'

Patrick glared at him. 'You don't have to tell me I was crazy. Of course I shouldn't have let her in the house. Obviously it was a sure-fire way to make a bad situation worse.'

'How long did it take you to figure that out?'

'Not long. In the morning she came downstairs wearing Nicole's dressing gown. Pretending it was her house, her life.' Patrick wiped his mouth with the back of his hand. 'I tried to throw her out. She threatened to call Nicole and tell her everything. She'd got hold of my phone and gone through my contacts. She found – a while ago, alright, when I'd gone through a bad patch, I started thinking I should split with Nicole. Not because of Simone or anyone else. Just because, because all marriages are a strain sometimes, and sometimes you think about leaving. That's just the way it goes. I got as far as writing a note for Nicole. I never finished it. I shoved it away in the bottom of a drawer and forgot about it. Simone must've stayed up all night to go through everything I owned, because she found the note. It was a nightmare.'

'I'm sure it must've been terrible for you,' I said.

'She kept shouting and screaming.' Patrick's gaze was unfocused as he relived the incident. A chill went down my back. 'All day. She'd play nice and talk sensible, then an hour later she'd be all teeth and nails again. I couldn't make her leave. I couldn't say anything to shut her up.'

'What did you do?' I asked quietly. I wasn't sure I wanted to hear the answer.

'I went for a walk.'

Dallin let out an incredulous laugh. 'You went for a walk,' he repeated.

'I wasn't gonna stand there and let her scream abuse at me. You can't deal with kids when they're like that. So, yeah, I walked out. Simone stayed in the house. I figured I could sit in the pub for a few hours until she calmed down.'

'And what if she'd called Nicole? What then?'

'Wasn't going to happen. Simone was all drama. If she'd called Nicole, she would've had nothing to bargain with. Nothing to stop me throwing her out.' Patrick struggled to refocus his eyes. 'I didn't get as far as the pub. Opal was having some kind of party in her back garden. She was friends with whats-her-name ... Eloise's mum. I think Eloise was there as well. She was a sweet girl when she was little.'

Had he been drinking? His concentration was wandering. When he lifted his gaze to look at me, his eyes were red.

'Opal used to have people round all the time. She would deck out the whole garden. Drinks, and lanterns sitting on the back wall, and Opal sitting there with a bunch of people, the lot of them laughing at God knows what. Couple of kids as well.' His baleful gaze went to Dallin. 'You were there. Doubt you remember. You were just a little squirt back then. Opal sent you off to bed after I arrived.'

'What about Simone?' I asked. I was certain we were getting off topic. 'What happened with her?'

'I stayed for a few drinks. Cheaper than the pub, isn't it?' Patrick attempted a grin, but it came out lopsided. 'Then Nicole showed up.'

'Nicole? I thought she—'

'Yeah. So did I. She wasn't supposed to be back for three weeks. But something fell through—' Patrick gestured with a weak hand. 'I forget. God, it was so long ago. But, there she was. She'd gone to the house. Planned to surprise me. Found Simone instead.'

I glanced at Dallin. Patrick looked more than just ill – he looked awful. 'Is he ...?' I started to ask, but Patrick wasn't done talking.

'Nicole came to Opal's house and found me. We – you can imagine how it went. I don't—' He shook his head. 'She picked up one of those decorative lamps. Full of oil, or kerosene, or something like that. Winged it straight at my head. Missed me, just. It hit the tree instead. I'd been telling Opal for a year that the tree was dead and needed to be chopped down. She wouldn't hear of it. Turned out I was right. When the lamp hit the tree, the oil went up like *whoosh*, and the whole tree was on fire. Twenty foot high. Flames all up the side of it.' He closed his eyes as he relieved the memory. 'The fire brigade ... I spent an hour talking to them with Opal. She was worried the whole house would burn down.'

I glanced at Dallin. He was frowning as he tried to reconcile his own memories of that night.

'When I got home, Nicole was gone,' Patrick said. 'Simone too. Nicole came back a week later. We patched things up. And I never saw Simone again. Thank God.' He covered his face with both hands. 'I thought I'd buried all this years ago.'

If Patrick's story was true, Nicole could've been the last person to see Simone alive. 'Where's Nicole now?' I asked.

'Now?' Patrick seemed surprised by the question. 'She's gone into Ramsey to visit Opal. Left me dinner.' He made a vague gesture at the curry. 'She'll be back soon.'

'Call her,' I said.

Patrick gave a slow blink. He didn't look capable of speaking, let along making a phone call. 'I just spoke to her,' he said. He nodded at the phone next to him. 'She's in Ramsey. Like I said.'

Dallin walked to the other side of the kitchen and snatched up the landline extension. A list of important numbers was written in sharpie on a sheet of paper pinned to the fridge. Dallin quickly found Nicole's number.

'I don't think she's answering,' he said as he listened to it ring.

I felt so helpless. Cora was out there somewhere, and if she was safe she would've definitely contacted us. Even if her phone was dead, she would've found a way to get a message to us ...

I used my own phone to try Cora. 'Cora's phone's still switched off.'

'Can't you trace a phone?' Dallin asked. 'Like ... triangulate it, or something?'

'I'm assuming from your tone that you have zero idea of the type of technology that involves. Wait.' He'd made me remember something. 'Cora's got a GPS. She said the battery had run out but – I don't know if there's a way to trace it?' I dug in my pocket for the note Cora had left me. 'Cora told me to call this number if I needed—'

'Oh Christ, is that her half-brother?' Dallin grimaced. 'Jason? I've spoken to that guy. He's a right knob. Here, give me the number, I'll call him.'

I gave it to him, then went into the hallway so I could hear myself think.

I took out my phone and called Mum. I put a finger in my other ear and stepped into the front room so I could hear the phone ringing on the end of the line.

I was almost ready to give up when Mum answered. 'Hello?'

'Hi, it's me. Rosalie.'

'Hello, pumpkin. Everything okay? You said you'd call back in ten minutes.'

I'd completely forgotten that. 'I just wanted to check, is Nicole there?'

'Nicole? No ... no, she's not here. Why would she be?'

'Was she there earlier? Have you seen her today?'

'No, no. I haven't seen her since ... oh, Tuesday last week, I think? She borrowed a couple of books from me.'

I closed my eyes. 'Mum, do you remember the night the tree burned down in your garden?'

'The tree? Yes, I remember. Terrible. I was so scared the whole house would catch light.'

'You told people it was struck by lightning.'

'Well.' Mum paused. 'It was a lot of years ago. I don't remember as well as I used to.'

'Were you having a party that night? Did you have friends in the garden?'

Mum let out a small sigh. 'Who's been telling you stories?'

'Patrick. He was at your house that night, wasn't he? There was a party in the garden, and Nicole showed up unexpectedly. She and Patrick argued. She threw a lamp and it set fire to the tree.'

'Well, it seems like you know all the relevant details already. I don't know what else you want from me.'

'Is it true? Why did you say the tree was hit by lightning?'

'Because that's what I've always told Dallin. He was frightened half out of his wits that night. I certainly wasn't about to make things worse by telling him the fire was started by one of my friends, by accident or not.'

I thought of Dallin as a child, when he'd stayed at my house, sheltering under the blankets every time there was a thunderstorm. Mum might've been trying to protect him from the knowledge that grownups sometimes did stupid, irresponsible things, but in return she'd given him a pretty healthy fear of lightning.

'What else happened?' I asked. 'Did you speak to Nicole after she set fire to our tree?'

'Oh ... not that night, no. But she came round the next day to apologise. It was a terrible thing that'd happened to her.'

'Did she tell you what it was? What Patrick did?'

'Not the details, no.' I could almost hear her lips pursed prissily. 'I wasn't going to pry if she didn't want to talk. I know she came home and found another woman in her house. A teenager. Her niece, she told me.'

'Simone,' I said. 'Cora's sister.' *Patrick's sort-of niece*, I realised. That was what Nicole had meant.

'I never saw her myself. Well, I was never introduced, shall we say. But I saw her at a distance, when I was driving past. She was sitting on the front doorstep of Nicole's house, smoking a cigarette. In fact, I thought she *was* Nicole at first, because she was wearing one of her dressing gowns.'

'What did Nicole do when she found Simone at her house?'

'Once she got past the initial shock, I think she felt quite sorry for the poor girl. Patrick had obviously been spinning the girl a tale, telling her he would leave Nicole for her.' Mum's voice was thin with disgust, and for the first time I realised the real reason why she'd never liked Patrick. 'Nicole told me the girl was upset, in tears, with a big ugly bruise on her cheek. Awful. Nicole gave the poor girl a torch and some money, and showed her the path that led to the main road. Given the circumstances, it was more than anyone would expect Nicole to do.'

The coldness I'd felt down my back spread out over my

middle and into my stomach. 'The path to the main road,' I repeated. 'The one that goes through the curraghs?'

'Well, I don't know, pumpkin. You'd have to ask Nicole, I suppose. She might remember.'

'Okay,' I said. 'Thank you. I'll call you tomorrow, okay?'

When I opened my eyes, I found myself looking at a folded piece of paper on the mantlepiece. It was wedged behind a small bronze ornament shaped like a hare. The mantlepiece was a lot emptier than mine, with only one ornament, one carriage clock, and a pair of matching narrow glass vases containing two carnations each. It didn't look like the sort of mantle where Nicole or Patrick would store random bits of paper. Whoever had left it there intended it to be seen as soon as someone walked into the front room.

I plucked the folded sheet of paper off the mantlepiece. The crease was sharp and crisp.

Inside, in handwriting that'd pushed so hard on the paper it'd left an imprint on the outside, it said, *'Nicole, I've tried to make things work out, but we both know it'll be easier if I go—'*

In the kitchen, Dallin called for me.

'It's Cora!' he yelled. 'He's done it. Her brother found her GPS.'

Chapter 34

I almost left without Dallin because he took so long coming out of the house. I turned around in the stupidly narrow road. By the time I was facing the right way, Dallin was jogging down the path from Nicole's house. I pulled away before he had his door all the way closed.

'Where are we going?' he asked. He had one of Cora's maps unfolded in his lap. 'How do we get to that place?'

It'd taken just a few seconds for an internet search to turn the string of GPS coordinates into a location. Smeale beach, less than ten minutes' drive to the north. I'd driven up there just the day before with Cora to visit Lenny's house.

'I know the way,' I said.

'I want to know where it is.'

'I don't need you to navigate.'

Angrily, Dallin shoved the map into the passenger footwell. 'What the hell point are these maps anyway?' he asked. 'Cora's been mooning over them for weeks, and what have they told her? Nothing.'

We drove north at speed, but there was no way to go directly from where we were to where we wanted to be. I had to wind my way through the narrow, twisting roads, with the headlights throwing glaring light up onto the hedgerows on each side. The rain was pelting down. Thick puddles had formed at the side of the roads. Several times I didn't see them in time and ploughed into the water, throwing up waves on either side.

'Are you alright?' Dallin asked.

I was breathing too hard. 'I don't usually drive at night.'

'Are you okay? Can you do this?'

I glanced at him. 'Do you want to take over?'

'I can't drive. I lost my licence, same time as I lost my job.'

'Oh for—' *He can't drive, he can't navigate – why the hell did Cora bring him along?* But I bit my tongue. 'Just hang on.'

'Where are we going?' Dallin asked as I took a corner too fast.

'North. You remember Smeale beach, don't you?'

'Of course I don't. I went to a bunch of beaches when I was a kid. Doesn't mean I know where any of them are.'

'Look, make yourself useful and call the police back. Tell them where we're going.'

If the police had done like they'd said, and sent a car up here to search for Cora, then they couldn't be far away. I hung onto that thought.

We barrelled up to a junction. I was hunched forwards, glaring through the windscreen, hands so tight on the steering wheel my knuckles stood out white against my skin.

A give way sign flashed past. I spun the wheel. For an instant the tyres aquaplaned. A squeal rose in my throat. I swallowed it down and yanked the wheel in the other direction. The tyres found purchase. We leapt forwards. I saw a hedgerow rear up in front of us. This time I did squeal.

Somehow I regained control of the car and kept us on the road. I accelerated, ignoring the shocking condition of the road surface. Each pothole that we hit jolted me almost out of my seat. The undercarriage bounced and scratched off the road. How many hours had I spent trying not to ding my car on the lanes around my house? What damage was being done to it right now?

But none of that mattered. All that mattered was finding Cora.

I glanced down at Cora's map balled up in the passenger footwell. I wished Dallin could've made sense of the tangle of blue and pink lines that crawled across the page. Did I absolutely know where we were going? I rarely came up this way. Despite the fact I'd lived in the area for so many years, I didn't often go out to the beach up here. Me and Beth had gone other places. Now and again we'd gone up to Point of Ayre, or down to Kirk Michael, but Smeale and Blue Point and the other beaches around there ... we hadn't often visited.

What if I got us lost?

I was worrying so much that I almost missed the signpost. 'There!' I shouted.

The beach was indicated by a single metal signpost that read '*Smeale (beach only)*'. A tiny sign, so easy to miss. We almost blasted past it.

I stomped on the brakes and brought us slewing to a near-stop. In the passenger seat, Dallin didn't brace himself in time and bounced his head off something. I cranked the wheel and stamped down on the accelerator again. The back end of the car stepped out. Again, I somehow kept control of the vehicle, more by luck than judgement.

The road was even narrower than the one we'd been on before. Hedgerows scratched our windows on both sides. I hung onto the steering wheel to stop from being jostled out of my seat. The engine was making some horrible noises whenever I touched the accelerator. It sounded like someone had tipped a bag of spanners into there.

A flash of lightning washed everything into sharp black-and-white shapes. Dallin swore loudly.

All of a sudden the hedgerows dropped away and the headlights speared off into the rainy dark with nothing in front of them. I instinctively stomped on the brakes. The car bounced over another hidden pothole. Dallin whacked his head and swore again.

'It's a dead end,' he said. 'Where are we?'

I pulled the car forwards so the headlights illuminated the flat, empty car park. It was barely twenty feet wide. Beyond its edge, the ground fell away into darkness. The heavy rain and the darkness prevented us seeing the rocky beach which I knew was there.

'There's nothing here,' Dallin said. 'We're in the wrong place.'

I drove right up to the far edge of the car park. 'There!' I caught a flash of something pale and angular, way down near the sea. 'Look!'

I tried to pull forwards again but my foot slipped off the clutch and the engine stalled with a lurch. I yanked open my door and was outside before Dallin could even finish swearing.

The rain immediately flattened my hair. Outside the protective bubble of the car, the thunder of the sea overwhelmed everything. The tide was coming in. I saw a wave burst against the rocks at the edge of the car park. Some of the water hitting the car was from the surf.

I ran forwards until I was standing at the rocky slope that led down to the sea.

At the sea-line, listing at a bad angle and with its nose already underwater, was a white van. I recognised it perfectly well, because usually it was parked outside Nicole and Patrick's house.

Its lights were off. It looked like it'd been abandoned, maybe, at the edge of the car park, with the handbrake off, and had bumped and rolled down until the sea caught it. Even as I watched, a wave broke over its bonnet, hard enough to jostle the vehicle. Within minutes it would be swamped by the sea.

I started climbing down the rocks. They were slick with rain and salt. Several times I almost fell.

Another wave lifted the van onto two wheels. I heard the creak and groan of stressed metal.

The driver's door stood open. I angled towards it. A small amount of illumination from the interior dome light of the van showed me that the driver's seat was empty. But there was a shadow in the passenger seat that looked like a person.

I had to wade through a foot of water to reach the door. The tide was so cold it shocked the breath out of me. If I hadn't grabbed hold of the door I would've fallen. Water swirled up around my knees and tried to haul me off my feet.

I made a grab for the steering wheel. The van was moving continuously, buffeted by the waves. I felt the thrum of the ocean through the wheel.

My heart stuttered as I saw Cora in the passenger seat. She was slumped against the door, eyes closed, with a splash of red across her forehead that looked almost too bright and garish to be real.

I hauled myself into the cab of the white van. My grip on the steering wheel made the axle turn. The front right tyre slipped off its rock and plunged downwards. The whole vehicle lurched. I screamed.

With a squeal of metal we ground to a halt again.

'Cora!' I yelled. She didn't respond.

I threw myself across the driver's seat and grabbed her arm.

A wave hit the driver's door behind me and tried to slam the door shut on my legs. I cried out in pain. I felt another lurch as another tyre slipped. It would only take a few more waves before the whole vehicle was lifted and tumbled and sent crashing into the water.

I got up onto the driver's seat. Leaning across Cora, I grabbed for the door release. The door swung open, helped by the backwash of a wave.

The front end dipped suddenly. Part of the undercarriage sheared away in a protracted squeal.

A wave came in. Lifted us. Retreated.

As it pulled the passenger door wide open, I wrapped my arms around Cora and shoved her out of the van.

We fell. We landed in the water. I came up spluttering, blinded, with the freezing water fastened around me so tight I couldn't breathe.

Someone grabbed my arm and hauled me up. I tore my knees on the barnacled rocks. The tide washed up and around me. Then somehow I was out of the frozen current. There was solid ground beneath me.

'Cora!' I yelled, with what breath I had left.

'I've got her!' Dallin's voice came from shockingly close. 'Help me carry her.'

I couldn't see him at all. I grabbed onto what felt like Cora's limp arm. Together, we pulled her up over the rocks and onto the hard tarmac of the car park.

I stayed on my hands and knees as I retched up the seawater I'd swallowed.

'Rosalie,' Dallin said. 'Rosalie, are you okay?'

'I'm here.' I didn't have any breath to put behind the words. 'I'm here.'

I stumbled to my feet. The car park was lit up in two stark beams from the headlights of my stalled car. They illuminated little more than a waterlogged stretch of ground, pockmarked by rain. In its backwash, I saw Dallin hunched over Cora.

'Is she okay?' I asked. 'Is she—?'

'I've got her.' Dallin was cradling Cora's head in her arms. 'I don't – I think she's okay, but—'

Cora was breathing. I could see her eyelids fluttering as she tried to come awake.

Lightning split the sky again. Again it froze us in place.

Dallin let out a noise that could've been a sob. As the light faded, thunder rolled and boomed above us.

I searched my pocket for my phone. When I found it, it was dead, fried by the water.

'Phone,' I said to Dallin. 'Your phone. Where is it?'

'What?'

'Call the police. Tell them to send an ambulance.'

I knelt in the wet grass next to Cora. Dallin was attempting to wipe the blood off her forehead with his thumb.

'Lie her on her side,' I said. 'Don't keep moving her like that. She might have other injuries we can't see.' It probably wasn't necessary to give Dallin all those instructions, but it got him moving. He dug his phone out of his pocket. I was relieved to see it light up to his touch.

I wished I had a torch. Out there in the dark, I couldn't begin to guess what'd happened to Cora.

Except ... except I probably *could* guess.

Someone had driven the van out here, let it roll down the rocks, then left it there for the tide to take. It could've happened anytime in the last hour and a half since I'd lost contact with Cora. Whoever had done it could've left in another car, long before we arrived.

I had a feeling that wasn't the case.

I straightened up. My eyes had adjusted a little but it was still too dark to make out anything except ill-defined shapes.

There was a sudden, blinding flash of lightning. This time I saw it in the sky, a jagged fork that broke the clouds right above the curraghs.

In that frozen moment of light, I saw Nicole. She was no

more than fifty feet away from us, sheltering next to a hedgerow. It looked like she'd been trying to find the footpath that looped around back to the main road. In the dark she'd been as blind as us.

She met my eyes. Before the lightning faded, while the rest of the world was still immobile, Nicole took to her heels and darted off towards the road.

I tripped and stumbled over the tussocks of grass as I tried to follow. My legs felt like lead in my wet jeans. As soon as the lightning faded I could see nothing but darting after-images. I kept running.

Ahead of me, Nicole reached the edge of the grass and jumped down onto the road. She'd started at a sprint but now dropped to a hitching jog, punctuated by awkward bursts of speed. She was not used to running.

Then again, neither was I. It'd been a very long time since I'd run so far or so fast. But I wasn't about to stop now. I ignored the pain in my ankles and hip, ignored my wet jeans dragging at my legs, ignored everything except closing the distance between me and Nicole.

'The police are on their way,' I yelled at her. It came out one word at a time as I gasped for breath. 'You can't – you – where do you think you're going?'

Perhaps my exasperated tone got through to her. Or perhaps she realised there genuinely was no way to escape. She slowed, then stopped, then whirled to face me. Rain dripped from the flattened curls of her hair. It couldn't dampen the anger that flared in her eyes.

'Why're you here?' she demanded.

The question was so unexpected it stumped me for a moment. 'You were going to kill Cora,' I said.

Nicole rubbed the centre of her forehead with two fingers. 'It should've never happened this way,' she told me. 'I planned it better than this.'

I stared at her. 'You planned this?'

She flapped an irritated hand at me. '*Twenty years ago,* I planned how this would go. When I found that stupid girl at my house, I knew it wasn't enough just to get rid of her. I had to make sure my own back was covered.'

I glanced behind me. Dallin hadn't followed me from the car park. I could only assume he'd stayed with Cora. Likewise, in the other direction, the road was still dark and empty, with no sign of the police.

'You led Simone out into the curraghs,' I said. 'You killed her.'

'There's literally no proof of that.' Was it my imagination, or did a smug smile touch her lips? 'But if you look hard enough, there's plenty of proof my *husband* killed her.'

'What? Why?'

'It was a precaution. I expected someone would find the girl, sooner or later. I made sure that, if and when they came knocking at my door, there was nothing to link me to the girl, but plenty to link her to Patrick.'

'Why would you do that?'

'Because he deserved it.' Simone's eyes flashed in the darkness. 'You know exactly what he put me through. I knew he'd been carrying on with other women. But to come home, and find a *fifteen-year-old girl* in our house,' she drew a shaky breath. 'What would you expect me to do? I wanted him out of my life. I wanted the police to find the girl and link it all to Patrick. But—' She lifted her hands in annoyance. 'They never did. Weeks, then months, then years, and no one missed that stupid girl at all. It was like she'd dropped into our lives like a bomb then disappeared without a trace. I came *this* close to phoning all the police stations in England to ask if anyone was missing her. But I suppose ... that sums her up, doesn't it? No one cared. Not even enough to raise an alert when she didn't come home.' Nicole laughed then, a brittle sound that was swallowed by the rain. 'The closest anyone came to finding her was when you came out of the curraghs that day, crying about seeing a body. I thought, at last, *here we go,* and I was *relieved*.'

I remembered her hugging me on that long ago day. She'd given me biscuits.

'After twenty years,' Nicole said, 'I'd genuinely given up hope of anyone coming for her. And Patrick never strayed again. Everything would've been fine, if your friend hadn't stirred it all up.'

I felt like someone had kicked me in the stomach. Was this genuinely my friend, Nicole, who'd always been there with a cup of tea and a kind word when I needed it? The woman who'd responded with gentle, unspoken understanding when I'd asked her about foxglove shoots. I couldn't reconcile that with the woman standing in front of me.

'Cora wasn't going to find anything,' I found myself saying. 'Why hurt her?'

'There was always a chance she'd find something. I started

pulling together the evidence I'd accumulated – evidence that pointed to my wandering husband – in preparation for the day some police officer would turn up demanding to hear our side of the story. I was *prepared.*' Nicole wiped rain from her face. 'But as soon as Patrick caught wind of Cora being here ... he maybe wasn't as stupid as I assumed. He knew what I'd done to his underage girlfriend. I never realised he'd seen me coming out of the curraghs that night. He's been getting shirty. He had to go.'

I was already soaked through and shivering from the rain, but her words made me cold right to the core. 'What do you mean?'

'Why do you think I brought his van here instead of my own car? The police were supposed to find it in the sea and trace it back to Patrick. Not too quickly, of course.' The faintest smile touched her lips. 'Not in time to save him.'

I edged towards her. 'Save him from what?'

'He was considerate enough to write a note for me.' Nicole shook her wet hair out of her face. 'He wrote it twenty years ago, granted, when all he meant to do was walk out. But it serves its purpose.'

I remembered the note on the mantlepiece in her house. What had I done with it? I had a vague memory of dropping it onto the side table when Dallin had shouted to me from the kitchen. 'What did you do?' I asked.

'I poisoned his dinner.' She gave a shrug. 'Simple, effective. Don't bother,' she added as I reached instinctively for my non-functioning phone. 'It's too late for him now. You of all people know how effective a few things from the garden can be.'

In the distance, over the noise of wind and rain, I heard the wail of a siren in the distance. 'The police are on their way,' I said.

'I know.' The smile reappeared. 'I'll be gone before they get here.'

'Gone?' I didn't like the way she said that.

Nicole pointed to the side of the road. I hadn't realised she'd stopped right near a stile that went over the hedgerow and linked up to the footpath back to the main road. 'I'm going that way,' she said. 'You'll let me go.'

'What? No, you should stay here. The police will be here any minute.'

'If I say here, I'll tell them what happened to Beth.'

I closed my eyes. Rain pelted my shoulders. 'Beth died. It was no one's fault.' My voice didn't sound like my own.

'That's as may be, but she had a little bit of help, didn't she? I know perfectly well why you came to me that week, asking about foxgloves and nightshade. I know what you did. And I'm more than willing to tell everyone.'

She turned away from me and walked towards the stile.

Without stopping to think, I threw myself at her, grabbed her around the waist, and dragged her to the ground.

We both landed badly. I hit my elbow on a sharp stone and my arm went numb all the way up to my shoulder. Nicole cried out in pain. I'd landed half on top of her, so she'd partially cushioned my fall; at the same time I'd squashed the air out of her.

For a second we both lay there, winded and bruised, then Nicole tried to struggle out from underneath me. She drove her elbow into my shoulder. I clung to her, unable to do much more than prevent her getting up.

But it was enough. Light suddenly washed over us – headlights, but also blue flashes, as the police car came bumping up the lane. It slewed to a halt ten feet in front of us.

As soon as Nicole saw the car, she redoubled her efforts to get away. She slapped at my head with her free hand. At that point I let go of her. There was no point getting hurt. I protected my head with my arms as Nicole aimed a last elbow at me. Then she scrambled to her feet and ran.

I heard car doors opening and a police officer shouting at Nicole to stop, and feet splashing through the puddles towards us. I stayed on the ground. I was soaked through, and pain sung in my arms and knees. I wasn't completely sure that I could get up even if I'd wanted to.

Someone approached me. 'Are you hurt?' they asked.

I managed to nod. With assistance, I got back to my feet. Off in the distance, I could hear more shouting, but beyond the wash of the lights I could see nothing, so I had no idea whether Nicole had got away or not.

'We need another ambulance,' I found myself saying to the police officer. 'For Patrick.'

The night you left, you said to me, 'It's not your fault. Okay? I never should've blamed you.'

'I didn't tell them,' I said.

'I know you didn't.' You brushed a curl of hair back from your face. 'Those stupid letters he sent me. I didn't hide them well enough.'

It wasn't like you to be so careless. Not like you at all.

'I gotta go,' you said. 'You understand, right?'

I studied your hands. You were good at hiding secrets. Spinning stories. Inventing truths.

I wondered if you'd finally got what you wanted.

'I understand,' I said. 'You've gotta follow your heart.'

Chapter 35

Cora rode in the first ambulance to Nobles Hospital in Douglas. The paramedics said she was likely fine, no permanent damage, but she'd had a nasty scare and a blow to the head, so they wanted to take her to the hospital for proper investigations.

The second ambulance took Patrick.

I drove down to Douglas with Dallin. Both of us were subdued. The weather was so dreadful I took the long way round, via Kirk Michael and Ballacraine, rather than drive the mountain route in the darkness and rain. It took us nearly an hour to get to the hospital.

When we arrived, we had another wait before we could see Cora. She'd been taken into a treatment room. It took us a while to find out which room, and another while to know whether we could go into said room to see her.

When we finally found her, she was sitting on the end of a bed in the small treatment room. The rest of the bed was covered with the maps she'd taken out of her backpack.

I was so grateful to see her, alive and unhurt, albeit very pale. A dressing covered the cut on her forehead.

'Hey.' Cora smiled at me. 'There you are.' She hopped down off the bed and came to hug me.

I clung to her. I had to squeeze my eyes shut to keep from crying with relief. 'Are you okay?' I asked.

'More or less. No lasting damage, they tell me.' Cora pulled away from the hug. Her eyes were shiny with unshed tears. 'Thank you.'

My gaze when back to the maps on the bed. 'What're you up to?'

'Planning.'

My heart sank. 'Cora, I don't think you should—'

'I'm not going back out there straight away, don't worry. But I *am* going back. And I'm not doing it on my own.' She eased herself back onto the edge of the bed. 'I'm going to talk to the police. They're coming back to get our full story.'

'Is that why you've got the maps out?' I asked.

'They'll have to believe us this time,' Cora said. 'They'll do a proper search of the curraghs. Top to bottom.'

I wondered what that would involve. How much disruption or damage would it cause to the wetlands? Perhaps Eloise was right to worry.

Dallin asked, 'Do you think Nicole will tell the police where Simone's body is?'

'Hopefully. If not,' Cora shrugged, 'we'll still find Simone. It'll just take longer. I know for certain she's there to find, which is more than I did last week. And we can narrow down the area a bit.' She tapped her pencil on the map. 'We can guesstimate where Nicole entered the curraghs. From there, we can plot possible routes she might've taken. It won't pinpoint the exact spot but it'll certainly narrow it down more than before.'

I chewed my lower lip. I wondered what else Nicole would tell the police.

'Are you sure you're okay?' Dallin asked. 'It must be horrible, to know your sister's definitely dead.'

'I cried all the way here in the ambulance,' Cora admitted. 'I'll probably have another cry later.' She gave me a wobbly smile. 'I always knew she was dead. It's hard, having it confirmed, but it feels like ... progress. Does that sound weird? I've spent so long chasing ghosts. Now I feel almost like ... like I can stop. I can restart my own life instead of having to puzzle out Simone's.'

I smiled to show I understood. Cora reached out and took my hand and gave it a squeeze. For that one moment, I didn't want to think about what had happened in the past, or the lies we'd all told. I didn't want to consider what I would have to do in the future. For one moment, I was happy just to be there with Cora.

She didn't let go. Neither did I.

THE END

If you enjoyed Little Girls Tell Tales, be sure to follow Rachel Bennett on Twitter @rakie and check out their website at rakiekeig.blogspot.com for all the updates on their latest work.

You can also find us at @OneMoreChapter_, where we'll be shouting about all our new releases.

Acknowledgements

Thank you to everyone who has helped and inspired me with this book. Y'all are awesome, don't you know.

In particular:

To (the possibly-imaginary) Simon Smart, who took a bunch of us out for a guided stroll around the Curraghs on a lovely summer day, showed us some wildflowers and, quite offhand, mentioned how he had once got lost out there while trying to follow a wallaby trail ...

To my wonderful agent Leslie Gardner and everyone at Artellus, for always being on hand to help, reassure, talk me down from a ledge, or shout *corraggio!* when it's most needed.

To Hannah Todd, Claire Fenby, and the whole team at One More Chapter, who put in so much hard work. It's always a joy to work with you.

To everyone at our various writer groups for the support, encouragement, and coffee.

To Manx Litfest (currently sashaying towards their ninth festival), Bridge Bookshop, Henry Bloom Noble Library, and the Family Library for their continual and tireless support of books and authors. You guys are the best.

To everyone who has read, reviewed, spellchecked, complained about, and/or beta-read my work over the years ... I wouldn't be here now if it wasn't for you, seriously.

A non-zero number of the anecdotes in this book are based on true events, although names have been changed to protect the guilty. I will tell you the full story of the KFC incident if you ask me about it in the pub. The wallaby colony in the curraghs is also real (and if this book had been written a few months later, it could've included a cameo from Kush, the escape-artist red panda), as are most of the places mentioned. I've taken some minor liberties with geography, for which I apologise.

Finally, obviously, thank you to my parents, my sisters, my in-laws, my extensive network of cousins, and everyone else in my family. And to John, Jacob, and Elliott, for being my best cheerleaders. Heart emoji to you all.